35.99

LARGE
PRINT

Danger in Numbers

Danger in Numbers

Heather Graham

THORNDIKE PRESS
A part of Gale, a Cengage Company

GALE
A Cengage Company

LIBRARY OF CONGRESS CIP DATA ON FILE.
CATALOGUING IN PUBLICATION FOR THIS BOOK
IS AVAILABLE FROM THE LIBRARY OF CONGRESS.

ISBN-13: 978-1-4328-8567-0 (hardcover alk. paper)

Published in 2021 by arrangement with Harlequin Books, S. A.

Printed in Mexico
Print Number: 01   Print Year: 2021

For Ali Kareem with thanks and love
from the "White Rabbit."

PROLOGUE

Fall 1993
Sam

Sam Gallagher stood in the forest, deep within the trees, holding his wife and son to him as closely as he could, barely daring to breathe.

They would know by now. He and Jessie would be missed. He could imagine the scene: Jessie wouldn't have appeared bright and early to help prepare the day's meal with the other women. He wouldn't be there to consume the porridge and water that was considered the ultimate meal for the work-day — the porridge because it was a hearty meal, the water because it was ordained as the gift of life.

Their absence would be reported to Brother William, sitting in his office — his throne room, Sam thought — where he would be guarded by his closest associates, the deacons of his church.

The family had been in the woods for only a few minutes, but it seemed like an eternity. Jessie was so still Sam couldn't hear her breathing, could just feel the tremor of her heart.

Cameron was just six. And yet he knew the severity and danger of his situation. He stood as still and silent as any man could hope a child might be.

Panic seized Sam briefly.

What if Special Agent Dawson didn't come? What if there had been a mix-up and he hadn't been able to arrange for the Marshals Service to help?

What if they were found?

Stupid question. He knew the *what if.*

He gritted his teeth and fought against the fear that had washed over him like a tidal wave. Dawson was a good man; Sam knew he would keep his word. He'd arrived at the commune undercover, having the intuition to realize Sam's feelings, his doubt, and his fear for his wife and his son. Together, Dawson had told him, they would bring down the Keepers of the Earth. His actions would free others. No, *their* actions would free others.

Today was the day. Just in time. Sam had known the danger of remaining, felt the way he was being watched by the Divine Lead-

8

er's henchmen.

They had to leave. Leave? No, there was no leaving the compound. There was only escaping.

Alana Fisk had wanted to leave, and they knew what had happened to her.

It had been Cameron who had found his beloved "aunt" Alana's body at the bottom of the gorge, broken, lying beneath just inches of dry dust and rock, decomposing in her shallow grave. It had been Cameron, so young, who had become wary and suspicious first. He'd seen a few of the older boys in the area when he'd last seen Alana there, and he didn't trust them. They were scary, Cameron said.

Sam tightened his hold on Cameron. Seconds ticked by like an eternity.

Sam closed his eyes and wondered how they had come to this, but he knew.

He and his wife had wanted something different. A life where riches didn't make a man cruel.

Jessie hadn't hated her father; she had hated what he stood for. And Sam knew the day when her mind had been made up. Downtown Los Angeles. They had seen a veteran of the Vietnam War, homeless, slunk against a wall. Only one of his legs remained; he had been struggling with his prosthetic, his cup for donations at his side. The homeless veteran had looked at Jessie's father and said, "Please, sir, help if you can."

Peter Wilson had walked right by. When Jessie had caught her father's arm, he had turned on her angrily. "I didn't get where I am by giving away my hard-earned money. He's probably lying about being a vet. He can get himself a damned job doing something!"

Sam had been walking behind them. Embarrassed, he tried to offer Jessie a weak smile. He hadn't come from money, and he had lost his folks right after his twentieth birthday, but he was working in a coffee shop, dreaming he'd get to where he could work, go to college and have time left over to be with the woman he loved.

He had given the man a dollar and wished him well.

Jessie had turned away from her father.

It was the last time Jessie saw her father. Despite the man's efforts to break her and Sam up — or because of them — Jessie and Sam had eloped. The plan was to both get jobs and finish college through night school. Her father had suspected her pregnancy; he'd wanted her to get over Sam and terminate the baby.

Jessie quickly made friends at a park near

their cheap apartment. They were old flower children, she had told Sam. Old hippies, he'd liked to tease in return. But those friends had been happy, and they'd talked to Jessie about the beauty of their commune, far from the crazy greed and speed of the city.

In the beginning, Brother William's commune did seem to offer it all: happiness, unity, love and light.

But now they knew the truth.

Brother William — with his "deacons," his demands on his "flock" and the cache of arms he kept stowed away as he created his empire — was demanding absolute power for himself, complete obedience among his followers. And it became clear Brother William's will was enforced; he had those deacons — Brothers Colin, Anthony and Darryl, and the squad beneath them. They received special treatment.

Sam clutched his family as he strained to hear any unfamiliar sound in the woods. Were those footsteps? Was the rustling of branches just the breeze?

He had to stop dwelling on fear.

He had to stay strong. Maybe not ruminate on what they'd been through.

But there was nothing else to do while

they waited, barely breathing.
Think back, remember it all.

1

Now
Late summer
The woman had been strung up on a cross, her wrists and ankles tied in that position.

And a spear had been run through her, right in the region of the heart. The weapon appeared to look something like a medieval javelin.

Blood dripped from the body and the stake, only half-congealed in the damp heat of the day.

Her head hung low in death and a wealth of dark brown hair fell around her face, tangled and matted with blood. Slashes had been cut through her cheeks, and an eerie mask had been painted on the woman's face, creating a jester's oversize smile and giant, red-rimmed eyes.

A cloud of insects made a strange, buzzing halo around her head.

Special Agent Amy Larson absently swatted at one of the flies that had deserted the corpse and was humming near her ear. She was aware somewhere in the back of her mind that she was going to be bitten to pieces by the time she left the crime scene. Amy had been called to several murders during her time with the Florida Department of Law Enforcement, but none so grisly, so gruesome a display.

They were almost in the Everglades but not quite. This stretch of old road had once been the main connection between the extreme south of the state of Florida, Central Florida and all the way on up to the north and connecting with east-west highways stretching out to either coast.

People enjoying the beaches on those coasts probably had little knowledge — nor would they care to have any — regarding the whole of the state. Here was this no-man's-land that was at the edge of the Everglades, dotted with sugarcane fields, churches and cows.

She drew out the small sketch pad she kept in her pocket; she also kept notes, but Amy liked to sketch out what she saw, always wondering if there was something that would particularly catch her mind's eye.

"Hey, Picasso, you know there will be —"

"Photographs, yes," she told her partner,

14

Special Agent John Schultz of the Florida Department of Law Enforcement.

They'd been partnered for two years and worked well together. He was fifty and had been with FDLE for most of his adult life.

She'd been with the FDLE two and a half years, after a stint with Metro-Miami-Dade. She was thirty-one, and John had been admittedly annoyed and amused when they'd first been paired on major state crimes, but he was quick to tell others now that they were an odd couple who worked.

Amy sketched every crime scene.

John mentioned it — every crime scene. Even though her sketches had proved valuable in the past, and she knew he liked that she did them.

He gave her an odd, grim smile. He was a tall, rugged man with a sweep of snow-white hair that gave him no end of happiness since most of his male friends and coworkers his age were already bald. But it was hot out here, and he had to swipe back a wavy lock from his forehead; the sweat was causing it to plaster to his face. His smile faded as he took in the scene again.

While no one entered law enforcement without knowing they'd have to face brutality and death, what they saw here was especially grotesque. Despite what he had

15

seen in life — or maybe because of it — John Schultz was a kind man, a good man, and knew the scene was causing an effect on her, as it was on him.

Amy arched a brow to him, and John nodded. They walked over to Dr. Richard Carver. The ME was from this county, which stretched from the beaches to this no-man's-land. They knew him well and had worked together before, though he looked like he should still be honing up for final exams. His looks were deceiving; Carver was in his late thirties.

Carver was just moving up his portable stepladder, asking one of his assistants to check that he didn't pitch forward to the road and bracken, dry in some places, wet in others.

Amy noted the area offered a fine cropping of sharp sawgrass, as well.

"Anything to tell us yet?" Amy asked.

"She's been in rigor and out of rigor . . . I'm going to say she's been here about a day. The insects are doing a number on her."

"Method and cause of death?" John asked hopefully.

"Well, the method could have been this sharp pole sticking into her. With the amount of blood, I'm thinking the cause of death just might have been exsanguination.

They were pretty damned accurate in slamming that thing right through her chest and into the wooden pole here. Don't think they got this wood from around here, but I do bodies, not trees. So, sorry — right now, I'm thinking she's been here somewhere between twenty to thirty hours, and she was killed here."

He hesitated; even the doctor seemed bothered by this one. His voice was hard when he spoke again. "She struggled," he said. "I think they cut her face while she was alive. Her wrists are ragged, which shows she tried to escape these ties. And when they came at her with this spear, she knew they were coming."

John turned to Detective Victor Mulberry, from the county's sheriff's office, who had been standing, silent and greenish, behind them. He'd been routed by the hysterical call from a tourist about the body and had been first on the scene. "Do we know of any active cults in this area?" John asked him.

Mulberry shook his head. "Small communities out here, minuscule next to the coast. But we got Lutherans, Catholics, Baptists . . . and two Temples. I know two of the rabbis and several of the pastors and priests. The people are churchgoing, but in truth, we're a little haven of diversity — all kinds of backgrounds, religions, colors. All the leaders of the local houses of worship get together once a month to make sure there's friendship between everyone. Heck, they put on charity sales and the like together. We have no fanatics, no Satanists, no . . . no cultists. I guess those church guys made it so it's just . . . cool. Good, I mean. Good. Folks get along. They like each other. They help each other."

Amy smiled grimly at him and nodded. "Nice," she told him.

But someone, somewhere, wasn't so nice.

She realized Dr. Carver and his assistants had started their work while she and John had silently stared at the scene.

Well, that was work, too, trying to take in every small detail of the scene; it was impossible to know what might become important in the end.

She'd barely been through this area before — and only because both the turnpike and I-95 had been plagued with accidents, and the old road had been just about the only chance of getting up to the middle of the state.

She glanced John's way, shaking her head. "There are a lot of churches, but as far as I know, they're pretty traditional. The population in this area is sparse. Most of the land was owned by the big sugar companies for years, and we're not far from Seminole tribal lands," she said.

She was close enough to one of their best crime scene investigators and forensics team leaders, Aidan Cypress, and she winced when he looked at her with a question that was almost accusation in his eyes.

"This is nothing Seminole, I assure you," he said.

"No, Aidan, I wasn't implying that. This is different than anything . . . from most anything else in the state," Amy said.

He nodded; he knew her better than that.

"No, nothing traditional, for sure," John said. "Ritual overtones. Both cheeks have been slashed identically. The weapon . . . half-makeshift, as if a poor cosplayer was trying to recreate a medieval halberd. She's naked, but that could be the work of a run-of-the-mill sicko."

"The cross she's on — I *think* it looks like Dade County pine," Amy said. That wood was almost impossible to acquire these days. But the CSI team would know more on that; she was hardly an expert on wood or trees herself.

"I think you're right," John agreed. "And it wasn't recently chopped down — more like crude carpentry. I think the wood might have been taken from various demolition sites, a house or some other building. Though you'd think we'd be preserving our older homes. It was abundant here once, used in most of the Victorian-era houses down in Key West. I'm going to say reclaimed from somewhere."

"We're looking at something planned, yes, with religious overtones," Amy said. "Something extremist . . ." She looked around at their group. "As we all know well, any extremist is dangerous . . ."

Dr. Carver twisted on the ladder to look at her. "And you're afraid this is a harbinger of more?"

"Dear God, let's hope not," she breathed.

Aidan Cypress walked over to them. "We're trying to pull tire tracks, but as you can see, the ground is mostly muck. And it's rained, so even the paved area is giving us just about nothing. One thing about being on an old road almost no one uses anymore — not a lot of trash. But we're doing our best to get everything, the tiniest scrap. And some of this is sawgrass — long sawgrass, but we're doing our best."

"Thank you, Aidan. You guys are the best," Amy assured him.

"Sketching again, eh?" Cypress asked.

"You never know."

"Okay, Picasso!" Dr. Carver called out. "I'm going to get my crew busy taking her down so I can get her to the morgue. From what I'm seeing, and what I believe, she was killed just as darkness was falling last night, and she was between twenty and thirty years old."

Amy stood just to the side of the corpse, swallowing hard as she saw the blood had covered the body in such quantities and had dried so it was almost as if she were dressed.

"Like Fantasy Fest down in Key West," John murmured.

She turned to stare at him.

"All the blood . . . it's almost as if she'd been body painted."

Somewhere inside, Amy trembled at the horror of what they saw. Death had taken the woman in such a way she was almost surreal, like a Halloween prop set out for a wickedly scary party.

"That's what happens," Carver said, "when you pierce the heart and rip up veins and arteries. Anyway, we're good to go, team. We're going to need to get her off the cross — carefully, carefully, my friends," he said to his assistants.

"And we need to get the cross to the crime lab, as much as is possible," Cypress said.

Detective Mulberry had been watching and listening. He spoke up. "Yes, please, get everything. This had to have been wackos from somewhere else in the state — or the country. This sure as hell didn't come from anyone local! And my citizens are going to be terrified. And there aren't a lot of homes with fancy alarm systems out here."

Amy hoped he was right: that the murderer — or murderers — had come from somewhere else, and that they would not strike again. She looked down at her sketch of the scene; it was one that would probably give her nightmares.

She swatted another mosquito buzzing around her face. It was going to be a long morning.

The body was removed from the stake with painstaking care.

Dr. Carver wanted the murder weapon left in the body until he reached the lab; his assistants argued over fitting the stake into their vehicle, but it was done. Then Aidan Cypress's crew began working on the crude cross to which she had been tied.

Amy was watching them work, sketching their efforts, when she thought she saw something tiny fall off the top of the cross as they lowered it.

No one else had seen anything, it seemed,

and she wondered if it was a trick of the light, or maybe a small leaf blowing in something that resembled a breeze that had come up as the day had worn on.

Rain was coming.

Floridians liked to joke among themselves about their seasons: they came in hot, hotter, blazing hot and then hotter than hell. The atmosphere didn't always acknowledge the changing of the seasons, and while winter caused an ease in the rain that tended to come daily in summer, early fall was still part of their hurricane season.

They'd been lucky so far that day. It had rained the night before, a weak rain, ruining much of the crime scene, but not enough to wash away the pints of blood that had half-congealed on the body. Some of the blood had run again; some had stayed hard and crusted.

The forensics crew finally had the cross down.

She walked over to the great hole that had been dug to set the cross. Now it was an area of mucky darkness against the rich saw-grass and foliage that grew around. Her heart sank.

Whatever it had been — *if* it had been anything — had sunk deep.

Amy went down on her knees, wishing her

hands were covered by something a bit tougher than crime scene nitrile gloves.

"What are you doing?" John asked her.

"I think I saw something . . . something falling off the cross," she said.

Dr. Carver shouted out to them, "I'm heading out. She'll be set for autopsy tomorrow. My crew will get her cleaned up and prepped by about nine."

"Thanks!" John called to him. He turned to her. "Amy, come on, we have a fantastic forensics team —"

"They were busy finagling that cross, John. I saw something."

"You're going to cut yourself on all that sawgrass."

She kept her eyes on the ground, scanning. "It will drive me insane if I don't look, John."

He sighed. "All right, I guess I'll get down in the dirt, too. When I'm itching like crazy from all the brush scratches tonight, just know I'm going to be cursing you out in my sleep."

Amy continued diligently pawing through the sawgrass when she vaguely heard the arrival of another car.

Cypress called out in greeting to someone, and Amy finally looked up.

Another man had arrived at the scene. He

was tall, dark-haired, midthirties. Wearing a suit, he must have been sweltering in the heat. Then again, both she and John were clad in their daily business suits — blue, light cotton blends, but the kind of outfit that meant work clothing.

The man seemed impatient, pushing back the hair from his forehead, looking around at the scene with keen eyes that were light against the bronze of his face.

She watched him, and John rose, frowning, then smiling in recognition.

"Hey, Hunter! What the hell are you doing down here?" John greeted the newcomer.

"Who is that?" Amy asked.

John hadn't heard her; he'd gone to meet the man.

Apparently, Aidan Cypress knew him, too. After calling out his own greeting, Aidan left his work for a minute to go over and shake hands with the man. "Sent out already, eh?" she overheard.

She shook her head; she'd know soon enough. If she was going to find something, she had to keep looking.

She carefully delved her way through the cutting grass.

But then she had the sense that John had come to stand near her, on the pavement off the mucky embankment.

"Amy, look up for a minute?"

She raised her eyes.

He'd brought the man with him. She waited, watching the stranger. He had the perfect face for law enforcement — which she figured he must be of some kind. His expression gave away nothing. His eyes, she saw then, were a rich, piercing blue that could certainly quell many a suspect. Hard jaw, lean face, high cheeks — the old classic-sculpted bone structure. He stood a few inches over John, which made him at least six-foot-three.

But she didn't get up; if she did, she'd lose the grid she'd created in her mind.

"Amy, Hunter. Hunter, Amy," John said.

"Mr. Hunter," Amy acknowledged.

His mouth moved in something that might have been a dry smile. A severe one.

"Hunter is my first name," he said.

"Oh, I'm sorry —"

"No, I'm sorry," John said. "I know you both so well that I forget myself. I'll start over. Special Agent Amy Larson, meet Special Agent Hunter Forrest."

"Hunter . . . Forrest?" she murmured, immediately regretting the words that had slipped out. She quickly added, "You're FDLE? I'm surprised we haven't met."

26

"No, no, Hunter is a G-man, a fed," John said. "He thinks he had something like this — not as elaborate, but when the info went out . . ."

"I might have had a practice run for this event," Hunter said.

"Oh?" John asked.

"A practice?" Amy heard the surprise in her own voice.

"North in the state, little town near Micanopy. I'll be joining you at the autopsy tomorrow. Joining the investigation," he said.

She tried to be as expressionless as he was; she wasn't sure what this meant. The FBI had to be invited in, and she wasn't sure how and when he could have been invited, since they'd just started with the crime scene.

And what had he been doing north in a small town near Micanopy?

Maybe he was so confident that he thought he could just make decisions on his own.

"He'd like to see us tonight, go through the cases. You didn't have plans, did you?"

"Not after this," she said.

"Drove here as fast as I could," Hunter Forrest said.

Special Agent Hunter Forrest.

"And I'm sorry I missed the scene in situ," he continued. He looked at John. "But I'm assuming — and I know your guys are good — that we'll have plenty of photographs."

"And sketches," John offered. "Want to see them now?"

"Sketches? You had a photographer and a forensic artist working?" Hunter asked.

"Nope, my partner," John said. "Amy, can he see your book?"

"Really, I'm not trained in forensic art in any way — they're just something I do for myself," Amy protested.

"Amy, come on," John said.

She reached into her pocket, digging out her little pad, and handed it over.

Hunter leaned down and accepted it with a quick, "Thank you."

He fell silent, studying her work. Amy went back to her search.

She was startled when he spoke, hunching down beside her, the book still in his hand.

"These are really good."

"Uh, thank you."

"Mind if I ask what you're doing now?"

He was studying her carefully, and she had to wonder if he was thinking she was probably in way over her head, incompetent to handle such a crime and crawling around in the sawgrass just to prove she could do something.

There was nothing to do but explain — evenly and articulately.

"I thought I saw something. A tiny object, but something flew from the body or the cross. I saw it when they were taking the cross down."

"You *thought* you saw something?" he asked.

She smiled through gritted teeth before speaking with assurance. "No, I did see something. I don't know what. We may never find it, but my eyes are good, and I know I saw something."

"Leaf. I think we're looking through grass and leaves — for a leaf," John said, grinning. Of course he was joking with her. He never minded when she had an idea, or when she was convinced she needed to explore in a certain direction.

But his joke didn't sit well there and then — when she was certain she was being looked on as too young and possibly too fragile or maybe even too *female* to handle this kind of job.

"And that's sawgrass," John said. "Careful, it can cut you badly."

Hunter Forrest grimaced. "Only if you let it," he said lightly. "Special Agent Amy Larson has said she saw something. I believe

29

her. We'll search. Let's do it."

Grudgingly, she liked him a little better than her first impression of him.

Special Agent Forrest pulled gloves from a pocket and knelt in a cleared area by the hole in the ground, careful not to press any tiny little thing deeper into the grass or ground.

He didn't seem to give a damn about his suit, or his own physical welfare.

John sighed and got back down.

Aidan walked over. The vans had been packed up.

"What's up?" Aidan asked.

"Amy thought she saw something," John explained.

"Some tiny thing that fell off the cross or the body," she explained.

"Okay, then. I should get down there with you. Amy, can you tell me, what exactly did you see?" Aidan asked, concerned. He took his work seriously. He was never afraid to admit he might have missed something, but if he had, he wanted to get on it.

"Something tiny that, yes, that flew . . . no, fell, I guess, sorry . . . when you all moved the cross."

"A piece of flesh? Hair . . . ? Can you help any with a description?" Aidan asked.

"Something like this?" Hunter asked

before Amy could reply.

She looked at what he was holding.

It was a small plastic figure.

A horse.

It might have gone with a child's farm or ranch set. It wasn't quite two inches high and the same width. The little creature had a flowing mane and tail.

It was white.

But it looked as if the eyes had been given a touch of paint. Red paint.

Blood, she thought sickly at first.

But it wasn't blood. The paint was too precise. The tiny eyes had been specifically painted a crimson shade of red.

"Maybe it's just some kid's toy, dropped out a car window," John said.

Hunter Forrest was staring at the object, shaking his head. "No, it's not. It was part of the ritual." He looked at Amy.

Aidan grimaced. "It must have been on the body, or attached to the cross, and . . . I don't know how the hell we missed it. Amy, you're sure it fell off when we moved the cross?"

"There's nothing else I've been able to find," Amy said. "Maybe it got caught in the ties binding her up there or was even behind the body in one way or another."

"Maybe . . . Let's not jump to any conclu-

31

sions," John suggested. "We don't know where that came from for sure, or if it has anything to do with our crime scene."

Hunter Forrest was still staring at the small toy.

He looked up at them, shaking his head. "No," he said firmly.

"What is it?" Amy asked him.

"Death rides a pale horse," Hunter said quietly. "And I'm afraid this is just the beginning."

2

Hunter heard Amy Larson speaking in hushed, indiscernible tones as he headed down the hallway of the Central Florida offices of the FDLE toward the conference room that had been assigned for their joint investigation. FDLE was still the lead on this case, and since the murder had taken place just about an hour and a half south of Orlando, they'd all decided to come here and make use of what the central office had to offer with support staff and facilities.

Tomorrow morning they'd head back south — the autopsy would take place in the county where the murder had occurred.

While Detective Mulberry would join them at the autopsy, he had been only too happy to hand over the investigation; he didn't see many murders, much less one that had been gruesome in the extreme, possibly the work of cultists, and might relate to other crimes in the state or elsewhere.

At this moment, the investigation had yet to be taken over by the FBI.

It would be.

But Hunter didn't really give a damn who had the lead on the investigation; he knew that something deep and dark was behind this murder, just as it had been in Maclamara. A place, he thought, where there were still lots of old houses that had been built with Dade County pine.

Others would die. How many depended on how quickly they could root out what was happening?

He'd reported in to his superior, Assistant Special Director Charles Garza, and Garza had told him that, hell yes, he was to follow through.

"You feel we need to be concerned and involved, right?" Garza had asked him.

"Beyond a doubt."

"You'll get all the help you need on this. Just call, ask," Garza had told him. "FDLE has been in touch. Stay right on top."

"John Schultz is on it for FDLE. We're good — I've worked with him before."

"Fine. Keep me in the loop."

Mulberry had been absolutely convinced the murder had not been committed by anyone local. Such a thing could only have been done by a crazy person from a large city, probably a northern city — someone who had come down, from the areas of massive population to the boondocks, to use the complexity of his county to commit the atrocity. Therefore, the state or the federal government should take over. He'd be there ready to assist in any way. He was distancing himself from the horror.

Eventually, the FBI would take the lead. For now, Hunter had to hope his old friend John Schultz would make it a dual investigation. He could only assume John would have the final say, since he had so much more experience than his young partner. And John knew Hunter, too.

They'd work together easily.

As he neared their assigned conference room, Hunter could hear John's new partner more clearly.

And he could hear quite clearly that she was talking about him.

"I'm so lost. He was here — I mean, in the state — because of a murder near Micanopy that had shades of a ritual, but why is he *here*? Micanopy is a long drive. And exactly why was he in Micanopy? He's federal. Shouldn't it have been the local police or the county or us, as it proved to be? We don't know the two murders are related. They took place far enough apart."

35

"He's a specialist in ritualistic killings and extremists and the occult," Hunter could hear John explain. "Hunter came down here because the governor asked him to. Our governor called the FBI's main offices. You remember our governor, right? The guy who is at the top of our food chain?"

"Ha ha, yes, I remember our governor," Amy replied. "I just . . . Look, we are competent here. Our department is good."

"Good enough to know when to accept help."

"John, we've barely had a chance to begin," Amy protested.

"You just don't like him."

"That's ridiculous. I'm just . . . Come on. Our state has problems, but we're good at what we do, John. How does one just assume these murders are part of a major plot of some kind?"

"But if they are?"

"Okay, but —"

"You don't like him."

"I can't dislike him. I don't know him."

He heard John's booming laugh.

"That doesn't mean a thing. You didn't like me, remember?"

"No, I had nothing against you. You felt you were saddled with me."

"Guilty as charged, but don't go thinking

everyone is an old chauvinist like me."

"I'm just lost as to why the feds are in. He made it from the Micanopy area almost as fast as we did from Orlando."

"Not much difference. And you know Florida, it can be thirty minutes, or two and a half hours, from place to place in certain areas —"

"Depending on traffic. Yes, I know."

Hunter knew he was standing in the hallway eavesdropping.

He pushed open the door to the conference room.

He'd known John a long time — almost a decade, since he'd come into the bureau. They'd met under similar circumstances when the head of a land-grabbing company had created their own form of a twisted Voodoo-Santeria cult, terrifying the downtrodden into murdering their neighbors.

John was a good investigator.

About this new young partner of his . . .

Hunter forced a grim smile. She'd just have to live with the chain of power that was going to come down. Live with it — or leave.

Standing, she was about five-ten. He'd thought at first she might have been wearing heels; but no, sensible shoes for wherever one might find themselves walking for the day — or for crawling around in the muck on the edge of the Everglades.

Her hair was a deep glossy brown, held back in a sleek low ponytail.

She couldn't have been more than twenty-eight or so, but he thought at least that, because agents with the state department had to have four years of other police work beneath their belts. But she had the look of a college kid — not that looks meant anything, which he damned well knew.

She also seemed severe. Hair so tightly tied back, straitlaced suit — of course, they almost all wore them. She had fine features, but bold, striking green eyes with just a touch of gold at the center.

And she was looking at him as if he might be the Antichrist himself.

She and John had already set up a board to work with. Crime scene photos were displayed, along with what initial observations Dr. Carver had been able to give them.

Questions were written in marker on the erasable surface.

Identity?
From where?
Next of kin?
Groups/cults with which she might have been involved?

Previous murder — associated? Same killer/killing duo or group?

"Hunter, hey, thanks for getting here so quickly," John said, rising to shake his hand again. "We've gotten called out on some weird-ass stuff. Hell, you know, this is Florida. When we don't breed our own wild ones, they find us the same way the tourists do."

Hunter walked to the board, setting the folder he carried, with facts and figures from what he considered to be the initial case in the investigation, on the table.

He studied the photographs on the board, and then turned to Amy Larson, who had yet to speak and hadn't risen when he'd entered.

He smiled inwardly, thinking he could make up a few labels for a board regarding her.

Young. Suspicious. Ambitious? Resentful of the FBI coming in on what she might see as a Florida case?

She was silent, but watching him — waiting?

He was trying to play well with others. Her turn to lower her guard.

"May I see your sketchbook again?" he asked Amy.

She pointed. It lay on the table by a folder.

"Thank you," he said.

She spoke at last. "What were you talking about, regarding the little horse? 'Death rides a pale horse'? I do realize you're talking biblical, and about the Apocalypse, but I'm not sure how you're so convinced so quickly."

"The slashes on the face of the victim."

She arched a brow, waiting.

"About fourteen years ago, there was a cult leader named Thorne Logan. He started up in the northwest, then brought his family down to farm country on the border between Florida and Alabama."

"You think he did this?" John asked.

Hunter shook his head. "Logan is dead. He fired on one of our agents, who fired back. It was one of my first field experiences. Logan was down on any of his 'harem' straying in the least. To be fitting sacrifices, their faces were slashed. Physical beauty needed to be blotted out because the soul needed to shine in death. And in his teaching, only death cleaned a dirty soul. His principles were . . . long and involved."

"I remember the case. The media had him billed as Father Killer," John said.

"I do remember something in the papers," Amy said.

"You would have been about ten," John said.

"Seventeen," Amy said, "and I was horrified, but . . . sounded like they got him. And at the time, it brought up stories of so many other bad cult situations, so it became one for the books."

"Right. It was a big case, but there were others," Hunter agreed. "Many more that didn't end with so much death and weren't as well-known."

Amy's brows were knit. "But if this man is dead," she said, "it can't be him. You think it was someone who was part of his family or congregation, or whatever you call followers like that?"

Hunter nodded. "You know there are many people — and many religions — that believe in the Apocalypse, right?"

"Of course," Amy said. "There's all kinds of speculation about the Apocalypse, the End of Days, all that. Different religions, sects, ethnic groups. Some people thought the world was supposed to end in 2012, according to the Mayan calendar. I've heard it could have meant the end of one era, the beginning of another. And you get groups who believe comets are omens, or that a certain politician in power means the end is coming. People who have dosed themselves with poison to die ahead of the bloodshed and violence. That's the kind of thing you're talking about?"

"More or less." He indicated the folder that lay on the table. "I was called down to Maclamara to work a murder. It's a little township outside of Micanopy. They're so small up there that any murder is handled by FDLE. I've worked with the detective there before, and when he saw his victim, he called me immediately. And then the FDLE called the FBI and asked for me specifically because I have had some experience with this type of thing. We don't believe the victim was local — no missing person reports from anywhere near the area match up with what we know."

"We?" she asked pleasantly. "As in you and the local authorities?"

"Yes — we — as in me and other authorities on the case."

Amy looked at John, clearly oblivious to the fact Hunter had heard her speaking just moments ago. There was a query in her eyes. He could almost hear her question to her partner.

One murder — and a fed is called in?

He waited for her to speak.

"You said that murder was similar . . . or a practice for this?" Amy asked. Her fingers were moving around the paper coffee cup in front of her. She seemed to remember she had the coffee, and she took a long sip of it while she awaited his answer.

He opened the folder, pushing it toward her.

The first photo was of the Maclamara crime scene.

The victim had been stripped and her face had been slashed. But nothing protruded from her chest, though it was a bloody mess.

Amy Larson was appropriately grim and ashen, he thought, even after the day they'd endured.

There was a fine line to tread when working with violent crime. You couldn't let it get under your skin too deeply. You'd be worthless at work from the nightmares that plagued your sleep and kept you up.

But to forget humanity was just as bad. You forgot why you were doing what you did, trying to stop the worst monsters before they did more damage. And every life was sacred, from that of a top scientist or scholar to that of a homeless person on the street.

Hunter knew it was likely that the first victim — the woman in the photograph he was showing John and Amy now — had been a prostitute. Dr. Levy — one of the state's most experienced medical examiners

43

up in the northern counties — had informed him she'd been a drug user and showed signs of habitual sexual abuse.

He'd believed her to have been about twenty-one years old.

"Practice?" John muttered. He looked at Hunter. "The slashes . . . yeah, they're almost the same."

"More than just the same," Hunter told him.

"How so?"

He gave John a grim smile and looked back at Amy. "You can't see it as much in the photos . . . Well, I saw the first girl in situ. I didn't see the victim today, but Amy's sketch shows something that the flatness of the photos didn't."

Both John and Amy studied him.

"You caught it clearly with your pencil," he told Amy. "The slashes are enhanced — they weren't just wild. Yes, quick slashes down the cheeks with a sharp blade. Dr. Levy suggested a scalpel might have been used for such clean, deep cuts. But see . . . on your sketch. That wasn't done with one swipe. There are little hooks curved into the upper end, by the cheeks."

They all studied Amy's sketch. Even Amy, who had done it.

"Yes," she said slowly. "They almost resemble . . ."

Her voice trailed; she was lost in a memory.

"What?" John pressed.

"I'm not sure if it's relevant or not. I had a cousin who was rammed by a bull on the expressway," she said. "West Broward ranch and farm country, at the time. Anyway, his description to me was he thought a demon was coming after him. All he saw at first were two red eyes and horns and . . ."

"The little curves look like they could be 'horns' sketched in, and if you look at your drawing, it's almost like a dot on the eye in the center of the hook."

"The eyes . . . the horns and eyes of a demon?" John asked.

"Possibly. It's all *possibly* right now. We think the first victim was a street kid, engaging in sex work for survival — the kind of young down-and-outer who might easily do so for the leader or recruiters from a commune, or a cult. I believe the young woman today might have been basically seduced the same way."

"Why not a single fanatical killer?" Amy asked.

He shrugged and grimaced. "The way the killing was done and with what was done to the body . . . It was as if she was killed as part of a rite. To me, it has the markings of a cult."

"But . . . the white horse?" Amy asked.

They were all seated at the conference table, and he leaned back, looking at them, studying them.

"The white horse — the first horse. I think we're looking at someone who is playing on the fears of others, fashioning his own religion. And now he's getting people to kill with great ritualistic savagery. He'll be convincing them they'll be saved, because the blood they reap is a sacrifice, and their victims will be cleansed by their actions. And because of it, they'll be welcomed by God and heaven, and all must be prepared for the coming of the Four Horsemen and the coming of the Apocalypse. The first horse — pestilence and conquest. The pestilence might not be something as literal as locusts, but rather what lies in the mind or the body." He hesitated. "Bear in mind that, sadly, there are people who believe themselves better than others, and anyone who infringes on them or their world might be considered no better than an insect or a pest. And there might be a leader who can convince others that sacrificing such inter-lopers can give them souls or raise them from the dirt to the clouds."

"Yeah," John said dryly. "They are out there — people who would squash others just as if they were bugs."

John's phone started buzzing and he answered it quickly. After listening a moment, he said, "Cool, thanks — can you bring it all on in?"

Whoever he was speaking with agreed. John ended the call.

"Can we put the pictures away while we keep discussing this?" he asked. "I've ordered a couple of pizzas. Sorry, I haven't had a meal all day. This one here —" he nodded toward Amy "— seems to go on youth and adrenaline, but I need more. I have been at this a long, long time — still don't like pictures out while we're trying to enjoy Orlando's finest pizza."

John swept the pictures into his folder just as one of the office workers came to the door, lugging bags and two boxes of pizza.

Amy leaped to her feet to help, grabbing the bag that contained their drinks while John handled the boxes, bringing them to the conference table.

"Pizza!" Amy chastised. "John, you know that —"

"Yeah, yeah, I'm supposed to be on a more healthful diet. I'm watching it, kid, I promise. Usually. This is just for today."

47

Amy groaned, shaking her head as she looked at him.

"Just today!" he promised.

She dug into another bag, finding a cardboard box of coffee, cups, water bottles and paper plates and napkins. With his pictures carefully secured, Hunter set out a few of the plates.

Amy poured coffee, and they each took a healthy slice of pizza. Hunter noted that Amy watched John, worried, it appeared, over his healthy appetite for the greasy slices.

But John was undaunted. "Special Agent Forrest, please, fill us in on everything. Start with this Logan guy — now dead — who had followers who killed in the same way."

"From the beginning. We were on the Alabama border — one of the bodies discovered had a limb across a state line, so both states wound up involved, along with the federal government. We'd already been in contact with Alabama. They'd found three women, all garroted, set against trees, bound by rope available at thousands of stores. The killing mechanism had been created from hangers, also available at thousands of stores and possibly found in just as many hotels. But the slashes on the face were like those found at the site just across the border in Florida. Naturally, we looked at all possible suspects, but Logan's cult had been intriguing the DEA and the FBI for quite some time. One woman had managed to disengage herself from the cult before complete indoctrination. She didn't know about killings, but she knew the man believed himself to be a great father. All children in the 'most holy family' must be his. He therefore had several wives. Men were welcome in the family, but if they had wives or girlfriends, they could only keep them if Logan granted them that right. Our witness only went to three meetings. She was due for her 'baptism' when she found out Logan had chosen her to be one of his brides, and she must have realized she wanted something else out of life." He shrugged with an odd grimace. "Not that I'm judging, but she was young, and Logan, at the time of his death, was in his late fifties."

"Did he have children? Could it be one of his actual family who might be doing this?"

"I doubt it. His children were young, all under five years old, and the five of them wound up being taken by child welfare services."

"Crazy," John said, the word muffled around his pizza. "Two murders, at least two hundred miles apart. In, what — three days total?"

Hunter nodded grimly. He looked at Amy. "Do you see why we all need to be on this?"

"Yes. He had five children, by five mothers?"

"Three — two of them each had two children."

"Where are the mothers? Have they been released?" Amy asked.

"No."

"Then?"

"They drank the juice. Although it wasn't juice — they had cyanide capsules. And no, I don't know how they got them."

"And other members? I mean . . . men in this group. It was okay with them if their wives were taken away? The men stayed?"

"Four men were arrested and tried. They, too, were doing prison sentences."

"Were?"

"They took their poison and left notes as to how they'd be with Logan and sit among the angels."

Amy looked over at John, obviously somewhat incredulous, and then at Hunter.

"How?" she murmured. "How does one person manage to brainwash so many others?"

"I'm sure you know the basics," Hunter

50

said. "Cult leaders look for the down and out or the disenfranchised, those who are miserable with their lives. Those who have no family. They give them a family, a reason for being and probably, most importantly, faith. I have several books and tapes I can give you. I'm not a psychiatrist, but I have studied cults and I've been on any number of cases that revolved around them. I can give you plenty of reading material."

"That would be good," Amy agreed.

John stood, rolled up his paper plate and said, "We'll get on this fresh in the morning. I'm guessing you two haven't noticed, but it's getting late and we need to be back down south for autopsy in the morning. We should be on the road by seven. We'll compare notes and make a plan of action tomorrow — if that's all right. Do we concentrate in Maclamara, or to the south? Both victims were found in areas not heavily traversed, so God alone knows where the killer — or killers — will strike again."

"The Everglades stretch miles and miles," Amy said. "And we have forests and wildlife preserves all around the state — from the Keys to the Georgia line, and out into the panhandle." She looked at Hunter. "A pale horse."

"A pale horse," he repeated.

"I know there are Four Horsemen, but I'm not well versed in the Apocalypse."

He nodded. "Try Bible verses," he said. "Revelation 6:1 to 6:8 — good place to get a handle on what the prophecy was. But remember, most likely there's an agenda. Someone with the ability to charm and manipulate others and make them do his bidding — no matter how cruel or irrational — most probably has a very personal agenda for power. Or maybe just murder," Hunter said.

He stood, as well. John was politely waiting, but he looked worn out.

And Hunter had plenty to go through on his own when he reached a motel room: files, maps, profiles . . .

"Um, I'm not going to get a lot of sleep," Amy said.

"You have to sleep," John told her.

"I know. I'll try. Who is picking up who, where and when?" she asked.

"I'll get John at six-thirty. Then we'll come for you," Hunter said.

"Good — you do the driving," John agreed.

They started out; Amy paused, seeing that Hunter was looking at the table.

"I'd like to take your sketchbook," he told her. "Any objection?"

She shook her head and then turned, following John out.

Hunter looked after the two of them, studied their board one more time and then followed.

They were going to have to move fast. If he was right, the pale horse had been honored, but there were three more to come.

Amy was ready, outside the small house she rented about a mile and a half east of one of the city's massive theme parks, when the car pulled up for her.

It was precisely 6:50 a.m.

John was in the passenger's seat, so she was happy enough to crawl into the back.

"Get any sleep?" John asked her.

"Some," she said, buckling up, and then quoted from the reading she had done the night before. " 'I looked, and there before me was a pale horse! Its rider was named Death, and Hades was following close behind him. They were given power over a fourth of the earth to kill by sword, famine and plague, and by the wild beasts of the earth.' "

Hunter glanced at her through the rearview mirror. "Good memory. I can only paraphrase."

"Johnny Cash just gave us a taste of it," she said. " 'The Man Comes Around.' "

She thought Hunter offered her either a grim smile, or a grimace.

"But she wasn't killed by famine or plague," Amy continued.

"She was killed by something like a sword. A spike. Okay, spikes and swords are different, but she was struck through the heart with metal," Hunter said. "I'm not saying they're going to follow the Bible exactly, but I do believe they're planning on something happening."

She leaned forward.

"Sad and tragic and horrible as these killings are, they haven't unleashed the plague."

"No, they haven't," Hunter agreed. "You know, there are dozens of interpretations of the book of Revelation," he said. "Some saw the white horse as Christ, coming to save the souls of the righteous. Some see that white horse as Satan himself."

Amy watched the landscape roll by out the window.

"How about some music while we're on the way down?" John asked. "I might be able to get another few winks. And then let's hope the forensic teams and medical examiners have something useful for us."

"Identities would help," Hunter said, but

he turned the music on.

They arrived at the morgue by a quarter of nine, and Dr. Carver was in reception speaking to the receptionist about another case.

Carver told them he was ready to get started. The victim had been bathed and prepped.

They suited up, ready to stand for the hours the autopsy would take.

Carver adjusted the microphone that would record his every observation. He began with the obvious — the victim was in her early twenties.

She had not been sexually assaulted. There were traces of sedative in her system, but that sedation had mostly worn off. She had fought desperately against the ties binding her, rubbing the skin at her wrists raw.

Death had indeed come from the metal spike that had been thrust through her — with considerable force.

Amy watched in silence, breathing through her paper mask, and trying to remain completely still to listen.

Observing an autopsy was always painful but could be crucial. Or not. She did believe the medical examiner spoke for the dead as no one else could. But sometimes, the dead had little to say that wasn't already known.

Suddenly, John grabbed his chest; his eyes caught Amy's as he keeled over, slamming into the autopsy table. Before he could crash to the floor, Hunter was at his side, lowering him down carefully, saying something to Carver about his heart.

Amy cried out, ready to run to him.

"Larson, I need room!" Carver said.

She stopped, standing still as a rock, barely breathing.

Dr. Carver left the dead to help the living, ripping off his gloves as he bent over John. He began shouting orders to his assistants in the room.

Before she could dig her own phone from her pocket, one of the assistants had dialed for an ambulance.

"His medicine!" Amy called out to Dr. Carver. He searched John's pockets, then slipped a tiny pill beneath his tongue.

Sirens could be heard. An ambulance, coming to the morgue. It seemed like an oxymoron.

Carver explained to the EMTs that John had suffered a heart attack.

And all she could think was that they shouldn't have had that pizza. And she couldn't let her partner go off to the hospital alone; she had to be with him.

He was the best partner.

He had become the best friend.

She stared at Hunter Forrest, who had quickly and efficiently seen to John, and to every command Dr. Carver had given.

His face was hard, but knit with grave concern.

Then his eyes touched hers as she wavered. "Amy, go." Hunter told her. "Go with John. He'll need you. I can be our eyes and ears for this." He seemed to hesitate. "Go," he repeated. And then he added, "Trust me."

She was aware then that he must know she was skeptical about him, not at all sure she wanted to work with him. But she knew something else at that moment, too.

She did trust him.

She turned and ran out of the autopsy room.

3

Hunter stripped off his paper gown. The autopsy, at last, had come to an end. Dr. Carver left his assistant to close up the body, and he and Hunter headed for Carver's office for a recap of the results.

"It didn't appear that she was sexually assaulted before the murder," Carver said, sitting behind his desk, "but she led a very active sexual life."

"You think she was engaging in sex work," Hunter said.

"I think it likely," Carver said. "Again, her age was somewhere between twenty and twenty-four, tops. She must have been on the streets for a while as she was showing signs of malnutrition. As to the murder, yes, she was tied to that stake. She struggled fiercely. And it took more than one person to drive that spear into her heart. She was on the cross when it was done — that was obvious from the blood flow." He hesitated and shrugged. "The slashes were done to her face before she was raised on the cross. That murder was carried out with great cruelty. She didn't just die. She was tortured before she was killed." He leaned back, shaking his head. "South Florida, especially the big cities on the east coast, has their share of violence. It's mostly drug-related, domestic or even accidental when people become the victims of gunfire when they happen to be in the wrong place at the wrong time — mostly stray bullets. I've been at this job for almost ten years now. Started in the lower ranks, of course. I've seen bodies in barrels, half-consumed by fire, stabbed, strangled and shot. But I've never seen anything so brutally carried out as this. Hunter, you've got to catch this guy." He was silent a minute. "These people . . . As I said, the force needed took two people."

"Two strong people, right?" Hunter asked.

"Yes — to lift and wield that spear. But that's not just my knowledge as an ME. I'm going to say that it's simple logic. It isn't easy to pierce through bone and the human body like that. But that doesn't mean both killers had to be male, though it's likely."

Hunter's phone was buzzing in his pocket. Carver checked his, as well.

Amy had them both on her list for sending out messages from the hospital; they were receiving the same information at the same time.

And it was another text from Amy. Dr. just came out again; John remains stable. They'll be moving him to intensive care. He doesn't believe, at this point, that irreparable damage has been done. Still in the waiting room; hope to be let in soon.

He saw Carver was busy texting back even as he texted back himself.

Thank God. Keep us posted.

He saw Carver's reply. Thank God. Keep us posted.

They looked at each other and grinned.

"Medically, we should be optimistic, right?" Hunter asked.

Carver nodded. "He had the good sense to have that heart attack with a medical doctor near. Yes, I'm a medical examiner but I went to med school to get that job, you know."

"Right," Hunter said, and smiled. "I'm glad you were there."

"You don't need to go over there yet," Carver said. "They'll let in one visitor at a time, when they do. Give it until tonight."

"John was divorced, and his ex-wife passed

away in a traffic accident around six years ago," Hunter said. "But he has a son and a daughter. I'm sure Amy is contacting them now. Might take a bit for them to get here. His daughter is in Virginia and his son is up in Jacksonville. I know Amy isn't going to want to leave until someone else has arrived to be with John."

"He's going to need to be in that hospital a few days, though — and then he's going to need to get some rest and change some of his habits."

Hunter shook his head. "Amy was just scolding him for eating pizza last night. He's a good man, and we're going to need him around a long time to come. I've known John to down a twenty-two-ounce steak. Yes, he will have to change a few of his ways." Hunter stood. While he wanted to see John and assure himself that his friend and sometime coworker was hanging in, he knew there was nothing he could do at the hospital.

"All right, I'm going to head back out to the murder site and interview a few of the locals."

"Have a nice conversation with the cows," Carver said.

"Yep, lots of cows. And a big enough population to support several different churches and a synagogue."

"But the population just isn't that big. You don't think the murderers were looking for isolated places to carry out their barbarity?"

"I don't have a theory yet. I have a body in Maclamara, which is a tiny place. And a body on a road through the beaten edge of the Everglades, although it's hard to tell what natural topography is in many places now. Thing is, that road is barely used these days with the highways. Locals use it — easier access to point A and point B when they're close enough to each other. But that's the point — someone knew there was a good likelihood they could spend hours out there without being seen, and yet, eventually someone would come by. A display like that is meant to be seen."

"You don't mean the killers intend to be caught?"

"No," Hunter said. "But they do mean for their murders to be a message."

"And you think there will be more."

He nodded grimly.

Carver rose to shake his hand. "I'm happy to help in any way at any time."

"Great, and thanks again."

Hunter left the morgue behind. Carver had spoken for the dead.

Now he needed information from the living.

Amy had held John's hand in the ambulance, but since he'd been rushed into Emergency, she'd been relegated to sitting. And waiting.

A few other members of the FDLE had dropped in. They'd checked with her and moved on. It didn't make sense for too many people to just sit.

She'd kept up with Dr. Carver and Hunter Forrest, had tons of coffee, paced and wasted a great deal of time with her head in a whirl. She'd contacted John's children, though she had waited to be able to give them the good news that he was stable before she had done so.

She was still waiting.

Her phone rang. They would be taken off the case, she thought, seeing the number for Mickey Hampton, her immediate supervisor, on her caller ID.

John had been the experienced agent in their duo; Hampton was probably going to hand it over to another agent.

Hampton asked her first about John. She told him what she could.

"I have a feeling John will pull through fine," Mickey told her. "When you're comfortable, get back out to the murder site. I have orders from above that we're to stay on this. When the kids get there to be with John — and you can think and act rationally, of course."

"I'm . . . lead?" she asked.

"For a few hours at least," he said dryly. "The same great voice that wants you on it has warned that the lead investigation is going to be FBI. But this is still Florida, and he'll be working with us. We had a recent meeting here in the office. Their tech and our tech will follow any digital leads, and you can call either with questions — or for help. Apparently, ownership of the swath of land she was found on is debatable — state or federal. Anyway, this is Florida. You'll partner with that specialist fed."

"Yes, sir. Do you . . . know this man? The FBI agent?"

"Only by reputation, but he has a great reputation and he's worked with FDLE before. They say he's a team player, so you should be fine. Stick with him."

"Like glue."

"You'll make a fine team."

"Yes, sir," she said again. There was nothing else to say.

When she finished the call, she found she was still waiting.

She wished she had files; she wished she had a laptop or a tablet with her. She did, however, have her phone. And finally, she settled down enough to pull it out and explore what she could on the internet. She thought she'd read up on cults.

And it was terrifying.

Ugandan police had reported more than nine hundred people had recently committed suicide. Equal to or above the number dead from the People's Temple, the followers of the charismatic Jim Jones in Jonestown. There had also been those who had died over several years related to the Solar Temple, those who had died following David Koresh of the Branch Davidians, and notable cults in Korea and Mexico that had brought about suicides — and possible murders.

Charles Manson's followers, his "family," had perpetrated horrendous murders.

She began reading about the horrors of Jonestown — how some had escaped before the end had begun. When Congressman Leo Ryan had visited, members had tried to leave with him. His truck was attacked, but he survived that attack and made it to the airport. He was then attacked by other members of the cult at the airport and shot and killed. Four others died and eleven were wounded.

Soon after, the murder/suicide began, with three hundred of those dead being under the age of seventeen.

Jones had gained his followers in several ways; he had convinced them he was a mind reader and a faith healer. He convinced people of color that if they weren't under his protection, the government would round them up and put them in a concentration camp. He used blackmail and beatings to keep control. And he brought his "family" to Guyana, hoping to better leverage his position there.

"Special Agent Larson?"

Amy looked up. For a moment, she felt as if her heart stopped. At the very least, it skipped a beat. John's doctor, looking weary, stood by her.

She almost dropped her phone as she stood to face him.

"I'm so sorry. I didn't mean to frighten you. You may see John now. He's resting, but conscious, and he's doing well. We have him in the ICU, and we ask that you keep him restful and calm." He directed her toward the correct room.

She walked quickly, stopping to use the intercom to gain entry, and then hurrying to the door. Large windows were open to the nursing station; if John was in distress, he would be seen.

That was assuring.

When she entered the room, she did so as quietly as possible. His color remained pale, but he appeared to be breathing easily.

Sleeping, she thought.

But as she paused by the door, he spoke to her.

"Get in here, kid."

A swell of relief washed through her; his voice sounded surprisingly strong.

She strode to his bedside; he was ready to take her hand.

"How do you feel?" she asked him.

"Like I was hit by a triple-decker bus. But I'm lucky. I'm going to be good. And no more pizza. They have a dietitian coming tomorrow, and by then my kids will be here, and with them being as obnoxious as you are . . . well, I'll eat better in self-defense!"

She smiled and sat on the chair by his side, still holding his hand.

"What are you doing, sitting?" he asked her.

"I'm staying here."

"You have a murder to solve. But I suppose Hunter is out there, and you wanted to come with me, and he insisted you did."

"Maybe he was just trying to get rid of

me," Amy said.

John laughed at that, then stopped. Laughter seemed to cause him pain.

"Guess we can't joke around for a while," he said.

"Don't laugh, but I'm not sure I was joking."

John didn't laugh; he did smile. "He's a good man, kid. You're going to do all right with him. And you're going to have to do all right for the two of us."

"We'll be fine," she assured him quickly.

"They're going to have me on sick leave for some time, I imagine. That doesn't mean I stop being an officer of the law. You make sure you keep me up on what's going on."

"Definitely. I'll be in —"

"Don't say you'll be in here every day," John said firmly. "You just keep me updated every few days. I'll get a tablet in here —"

"Your kids are not going to want you working. The department is not going to want you working. John, you had a heart attack —"

"Right. Not a brain attack. I can still use my eyes and deductive reasoning."

"But you need to rest and be calm."

He lowered his voice, though it was just the two of them in the room, as he said, "I can lie here and think while you two do the

68

grunt and footwork. Amy, promise me —
yes, I know, the department, everyone else,
will want me just sleeping. I can't do that,
Amy. I'll go nuts. Please, you want me to
rest and relax? Then promise me that you'll
keep me in the loop."

She nodded slowly. She knew John.

"All right," she said softly.

"And give Hunter a chance."

"I will, of course, just —"

"Good. You two will do all right together."

"John . . ."

"That's it. Now, I'm tired," he said. He
closed his eyes, then slipped one open.
"You're still here? Get going — get out of
here. Go to work."

Amy sat stubbornly still.

He looked at her again.

She smiled. "Not to worry. My industri-
ous FBI partner is out there doing his thing.
He'll report to me, and I'll join him for our
next step." She leaned toward him. "Just as
soon as one of your kids gets here."

Detective Victor Mulberry met Hunter at a
local coffee shop between several stretches
of sugarcane, ranch land, cows, a small
neighborhood and several houses of worship.

"How is Agent Schultz doing?" Mulberry

asked him anxiously. Hunter was happy he could tell him John was stable, doing as well as could be expected, talking already, and the doctors believed he'd make a full recovery, along with lifestyle changes.

Mulberry was glad to hear it.

"I have Rabbi Goldstein — the mainstay of our Jewish community — on his way. Along with Father Brennan, of the Catholic church, Father Westin, Episcopalian, and Pastor Colby, Unitarian. Naturally they're all horrified, and they've assured me their congregations couldn't have had anything to do with the murder. So . . ."

He looked at Hunter warily, as if afraid Hunter would rip the men apart, determined they had to be involved.

Hunter smiled and shook his head. "They are holy men in their various houses of worship. People come to them. They know what's going on with people, especially in a small community like this."

"I'll tell you, a Catholic priest will not break a vow regarding words he hears in the confessional," Mulberry told him.

"I don't want him to. Trust me, please," Hunter said.

Mulberry nodded, then he turned slightly, looking toward the door.

Hunter had taken the seat facing the door;

by habit, he never chose a chair from which he could not see the entrance of any establishment.

He didn't need Victor Mulberry to tell him it was Rabbi Goldstein who had arrived first; the rabbi was wearing a prayer shawl and a yarmulke. He appeared to be in his forties, and he was quick to smile as he greeted a few of the other diners in the small coffee shop.

Hunter stood and Victor Mulberry did the same. They had the only large table in the little place, toward the back to the left, behind the counter.

But Rabbi Goldstein saw them and hurried to them, offering his hand as Victor introduced him to Hunter and Hunter said, "Thank you for your help, Rabbi Goldstein."

"Call me Rabbi David. I always felt more comfortable with my given name."

Hunter inclined his head.

"I'll cut to the chase," the rabbi said, taking a seat. "I love many of my colleagues. I'm sure Victor will tell you we all get together now and then and discuss ways to help the town so that it helps everyone. We're a small community, very neighborly — strange when you think of the size of the cities and counties near us. But few people think of the middle of the state or cows when they think of Florida."

"You're right, sir," Hunter said. "But I'm hoping you might have heard something. Had a stranger drop in, or maybe even lost a member of your synagogue to a different type of lifestyle."

"No, I haven't lost anyone. But while I haven't heard or seen anything unusual, Pastor Colby thinks he might have something to tell you. I'll let him explain. I only know his story secondhand."

"Would you like coffee? Something to eat?" Hunter suggested.

"I would."

Rabbi David Goldstein called to their waitress, a young woman he obviously knew.

But then it seemed everyone here knew everyone else here.

While she brought coffee — a carafe and more cups, the others might want coffee, too — the rabbi asked her about her family.

"Mom is doing better. The Parkinson's medication is kicking in," she said.

"I'm so happy to hear that," he told her.

When she was gone, Hunter asked, "One of yours?"

"No. I just know the family. We are the epitome of a small town."

Hunter smiled and then quickly stood.

The other three men they were expecting were arriving.

Fathers Brennan and Westin, and Pastor Colby.

Brennan was an older man with neatly clipped graying hair and a handsome face, somewhat worn, and bright blue eyes. Westin was perhaps just about fifty, lean and balding, and Colby was the youngest of the group, forty or so, a man with a quick smile who moved with energy.

"Coffee on the table! Leave that to a cop," Colby said, happily pouring a cup.

But Rabbi David corrected him. "No, sir. Leave that to a rabbi!"

There was laughter.

"Thank you, Lord, for the rabbi," Father Brennan said. But then he looked at Hunter and said, "I'm here, Special Agent Forrest, because we're all ready and willing to help with this horrible situation. I've weighed my thoughts, as have the others. But I honestly can't think of anyone in my congregation who could even conceive of such a brutal and vicious thing to do to anyone."

"Nor can I," Father Westin said, "but again, we're here if you need to ask any questions, if we can think of anything."

"I may have something," Colby said gravely. "It wasn't a situation that occurred with me, specifically, but with one of our younger ministers, a young woman named Karyl Vine. She was at the back of the church a few Sundays ago singing — we do a lot of singing, have a great group up at the altar — and she noted a girl in one of the rows who was singing her heart out, but who looked as if she was a bit down and out. She had a strange conversation with Pastor Vine about sin and redemption. I thought she had to be someone's cousin, a relative . . . new to the area? But even though she stayed for coffee and donuts, talking, and Karyl invited her back and to groups, assuring her we were there to help at any time, she didn't make another appearance."

He hesitated and glanced at Father Westin.

Westin said, "He's afraid she might have been the victim. Karyl got the feeling the young woman was running from something — or someone."

"Can I speak with Pastor Karyl Vine?" Hunter asked.

"She went a few days ago to see her family in South Carolina, but I think she might be coming into church this afternoon. She was due back last night, and she always comes to choir practice, which starts at seven. I can find out if she's there now, or when she will be there. I know Karyl is going to want to help as she's our liaison for troubled youth — a very sweet and wonderful young lady."

The others at the table nodded. "Very caring," Rabbi David said.

"Can you call her?" Hunter asked.

He glanced at his own phone while Pastor Colby called Karyl to make sure she was back and find out if she was going to be at the church ahead of the choir practice. He had another text from Amy.

John is doing well. His daughter is arriving soon.

He hesitated. He could handle the rest alone. But he wasn't the lead investigator on the case yet; John Schultz had been, officially, which now meant it was Amy Larson's case.

He assured himself he was a team player.

She might be young, but she was intriguing. A determined agent, she seemed able to handle herself well. And then there were her sketches. He remembered watching her at the autopsy, thinking she was just right for law enforcement. The grotesque nature of the crime demanded empathy with the victim, without falling prey to an emotional reaction that could cause problems while questioning those who might help with the case.

He did need to give her a chance. He wondered what made him wary of her.

There was something about her — maybe the fact she seemed to like him just as much as she might like Florida mosquitos. Or because she thought this was her state — and he didn't belong.

She didn't know how much it was his state, as well.

He needed to pull her in. He put through a few calls to the field office, arranging for transportation for his "partner."

Pastor Colby looked at him and gave him a thumbs-up sign, ending his call.

"Karyl is home. She heard about the woman who was found . . . murdered," Colby said. "She's afraid it's the young lady she met, too, just because the girl was so distraught. She's happy to do anything at all that will help."

"We can meet her at your church?" Hunter asked.

Pastor Colby nodded. "An hour or so okay for you? The café here has good food."

"I could eat," Father Brennan said.

"It is dinnertime. Early dinner. But neither

Father Brennan nor I are spring chickens anymore. Early is supposed to be dinnertime for the aged," Father Westin said.

"Dinner, it is," Hunter said. "And you can tell me about your churches. And what you know, if anything, about ritual murders."

The men looked at one another and then back at Hunter.

Brennan cleared his throat. "None of our religions condone ritualistic murders."

"No, of course not," Hunter said. "But, Rabbi David, the punishments for certain sins are pretty harsh in the Old Testament, right?"

"Stoning to death for adultery," Rabbi David said, "and various other infractions. But your victim was strung up on a cross. I didn't get that from the news, and none of us intends to share specifics — Detective Mulberry told us she was up on a cross."

Hunter glanced at Mulberry.

"I was asking for help," Mulberry said.

"We would never share things like that," Rabbi David assured him.

"We have to answer to a pretty high power, so we're careful that way," Father Westin said.

"I didn't say a word," Hunter muttered. "Still, in this case, I'm all ears when it comes to anything at all you can tell me about the various books of the Bible."

"Old Testament," Rabbi David said.

"New Testament," Father Westin said, grimacing slightly at Father Brennan and Pastor Colby.

"What interests you?" Colby asked.

"The Apocalypse," Hunter said.

"Well, you need to read —" Father Brennan began.

"I have read," Hunter interrupted quietly. "What I'd love to hear is your interpretations. I mean, what do you think? Revelation 6:8. Is the rider of the pale horse Satan himself? Or, as some say, do you believe it might be Christ, and He has come to take us all home?"

For a moment, the rabbi, two priests and the pastor were silent.

Then the discussion began — lively and passionate, with even the rabbi putting in his opinion.

Hunter sat back and listened.

Brenda Schultz Nelson arrived about a half hour or so after Amy at last convinced John she wasn't leaving until his daughter arrived.

Amy saw her moving through the ICU with such an anxious look on her face that she hopped up to meet her outside the door.

John was attached to all kinds of medical tubes and lines, and she wanted to assure Brenda her father was stable and coming along well.

She made it out and closed the door just in time, catching Brenda just feet away.

Brenda, an attractive young woman with short-cropped dark hair and her father's gray eyes, had obviously been crying as she'd anxiously made her way there.

She threw her arms around Amy, sobbing, "Oh, my God! He's alive, right, he's . . . he's okay?"

"He was helped right away, Brenda, and yes, they say he's going to be fine. He'll need rest, here, and then at home. But —"

"He has to retire!"

"Brenda, I'm just going to suggest you'll give him a second attack if you say that to him. You know how your dad loves his job," Amy warned, and then hoped she hadn't been offensive.

"I know, I know, but —"

"We'll all look out for him. And don't worry, the department is going to keep him behaving while he recuperates from all this."

"Of course, of course. And I guess it's not just his work. Dad hasn't ever seen a hunk of fatty meat that didn't have his name on it."

"We'll watch him, I promise, Brenda."

Brenda seemed to stand a little straighter. She wiped her face and tried for a smile. "Right, I know. I know he loves you and you care for him. I mean, I think my dad believes he's just about working with one of his own kids." She managed a laugh. "That has to be hard at times." She sighed softly. "So, he wasn't running after anyone or anything?"

"We were in autopsy," Amy told her.

"Well, that's ironic."

"It was lucky. Dr. Carver was there and knew what to do."

"And you stayed with him. Thank you, Amy. I'm . . . I'm fine. My husband has the kids for the next few days. He took the time off. He wanted to be with me here, but I didn't want the kids seeing their beloved grandpa like this, so . . ."

"I'm here if you need me. Your dad is on the mend."

"I'll take over. You go and do what you need to do." She hesitated. "The media is all over it. I know about the case you're working on."

"Of course. Sensationalism. I hope we've kept most of the details out of the press."

"All I got from the media was she was found dead, and it appeared to have been a ritualistic killing. No other details."

"Good. So, your dad is in and out of sleep. I know how happy he will be to see you and your brother, too."

"Johnny Jr. is driving, and he will be here soon." She stood very straight. "I don't forget I'm a lawman's daughter. I've got this. Go!"

Amy smiled. "All right."

Brenda hugged her fiercely again, and Amy headed out of the ICU and down the stairs, only then remembering she didn't have her car. She'd come with the ambulance after Hunter Forrest had driven them to autopsy.

As she debated the issue, her phone rang.

It was Hunter, right on cue.

"I've sent a car for you. John just called me on his daughter's phone and said he kicked you out. An agent from our satellite office is picking you up and bringing you out here. Sending you a picture of the car and license plate. Special Agent Ryan Anders will be there any minute, outside the main door."

Amy was startled and silent for a minute.

"You do want to come out on the investigation, right?" Hunter asked.

"Yes, of course, thank you. I'm outside the main door."

"Good. This is an interesting little town. Nice people."

"Oh."

Apparently, nice people could prove to be vicious killers. They both knew that.

And they both knew how to play the game.

"Where is he bringing me?"

"The Church of the People," he said.

"The Church of the People?" she said suspiciously. "A sect? Are they a cult?"

He laughed softly. "No, not a cult — we'd have been all over that like fleas on an old dog. Unitarian."

"But you think that —"

"No. I don't believe any legitimate pastor, priest, rabbi, imam or leader of any recognized religion would sanction such a thing. But we may have found what I'm looking for — someone who passed through such a church, searching for redemption. Anyway, I'm heading there in a bit myself. I've just enjoyed a lovely meal with several men of various creeds, and I've met a pastor who may lead us somewhere. See you soon."

4

"I'll show you around," Pastor Colby said. "I'm not taking anything away from the others, but I think we allow a bit more free thought and bring in a younger crowd. That means we have great music — not just organ music. We have guitars, drums, violins and keyboards, not all together all the time, but upbeat and conducive to camaraderie. We are careful to respect one another around here. But I was bragging about my church! So here we go — we're traditional in the layout of the main church, vestibule, the nave and the sanctuary. Oh, and we have a balcony for the choir, when not just down in the sanctuary. We have great woodwork, touches of Gothic here and there in our arches, and a very open feeling." He paused, grinning at Hunter. "My colleagues and I are big believers that God is where we are — the beauty of the sky and the earth are

His temple, just as any man-made structure."

"A very handsome place," Hunter agreed as they entered the vestibule. The other clergymen had returned to their own business, and Detective Mulberry had been called away on an urgent matter.

Hunter surveyed the church.

As Pastor Colby had said, there were fine arches and woodwork that managed to give the church both a bit of Gothic beauty along with spaciousness. The seats in the church resembled rows of carved chairs more than typical pews he had seen in other churches.

"The kitchen is over in our function building. We have childcare there, Sunday school and meeting rooms, too. I just wanted to give you the lay of the land. Karyl is in her office. That's out in the function building."

"Thanks, Pastor Colby."

The man grinned. "I'm Jared, by the way. I'm not even Pastor Colby all the time to my parishioners. Given names create an atmosphere in which people can be more relaxed."

"Jared," Hunter said.

The man smiled and then his smile faded to a worried frown. "Do you think that . . . that we might have had that poor young

84

woman in here? Karyl will be devastated, of course. She'll feel she didn't do enough. She'll feel she should have brought her into the flock, and kept her safe."

"Hopefully, we'll discover the young woman's identity soon," Hunter said. He glanced at his watch. "My partner on this from the FDLE should be here any minute. You know, I've noted this is a large church. And it has a spectacular stained-glass window."

"Some of the wealthier members of the congregation like to donate."

"For a small town, you have several houses of worship. Are they all this big?"

"Sure. People come from the north, south, east and west," Jared Colby said. "Think of where we are — the next big thing you've got to the north is the Greater Orlando area. You'd have to go through the Everglades and state, tribal and federal land to the west. Big stuff to the east, but it's a long drive. We collect from all this not-quite-Everglades, not-coast, not-theme-park town here. And I know this sounds too much like cotton candy and bull, but we practice what we preach — respect. So . . ."

"Sounds good," Hunter said. "Let's step back outside. Special Agent Amy Larson should be arriving any minute."

One of the field office sedans was just pulling up. Special Agent Ryan Anders, fresh out of the academy, was driving. Hunter could see Amy next to him, studying the church as they arrived.

"John?" he asked as soon as she got out of the car.

"Considering the circumstances, he's doing very well," she said, looking past him to Jared Colby.

"Hello," Colby said.

Hunter performed the necessary introductions.

"Need me to stick around, sir?" Anders asked.

Hunter had his own car, but he thought it might be a good thing if he and Amy took their time; he wanted Amy to make a sketch of the woman Karyl Vine had talked with, and he wanted to send it back to the morgue as soon as possible. Before putting it out on any media, he wanted Carver's opinion to determine if it was the murdered woman, *if* it appeared that it might be her. Amy's sketches could put life into a rendering, and since he wasn't sure he wanted to release a crime-scene photo, he was hoping Amy's drawing would be accurate.

"Yeah, thanks. I'm going to have Amy do a sketch, and I'll have you run it to Dr.

Carver."

"Understood, but . . ."

"Yes?"

"Well, sir, you do realize it's nearly seven at night, and by the time I get back . . . I'm assuming Dr. Carver goes home at some time."

"Right. We could shoot him an image via the phone."

"But I don't care about the hour. I'll be happy to stay, do anything, go anywhere."

Anders was fresh, new, and the weight of his responsibilities appeared to be something he took seriously. Hunter liked that in him. He wondered if Anders thought it would get easier; he didn't want to douse the young man's vision and tell him he hadn't signed on for a job but for a vocation.

Nothing got easier, especially seeing the cruelty man could inflict on his fellows.

"Sure, stick around. We'll see if there is anything that comes up."

Anders started to get back into his car. "She's great, huh?"

"Pardon?"

"Amy. Oh, no disrespect meant. She told me to call her that."

"Sure."

"She studied the whole way over here —

talking, too, and listening to my opinion. She's so attractive . . . I guess I wasn't expecting such a sharp mind. Sorry again! No disrespect meant."

"We're all human," he said. "But you're an FBI agent. Best to make sure you're showing respect to everybody."

He turned and headed back. Amy and Jared Colby were waiting for him at the front of the church.

"Ready?" Hunter asked. Pastor Colby led the way.

A door behind the sanctuary led out to a covered walkway with a barrel-tile roof and slight overhang. The walkway was about fifty feet and led to another hall with doors, the first labeled Office.

Colby opened the door for them, and Hunter followed Amy in.

The office held two desks, both facing the door, and the woman in question — Pastor Karyl Vine — was seated behind the second.

She jumped up when she saw them, and Hunter could see the concern on her face. She was young — early thirties, tops — with sandy hair cut in a bob. She was wearing jeans and a T-shirt, comfortable for her work.

She had been waiting for them.

Colby made introductions.

When they'd grabbed chairs and were seated, Hunter smiled. "So, please, tell us about this young woman you met, Karyl."

"I do so hope your dead woman isn't her!" Karyl said passionately. "I don't know where to start."

"From the beginning," Amy said, reaching across the desk to squeeze the young pastor's hand. "How did you meet her? Your congregation is a decent size, though I understand many people around here know each other."

Karyl nodded, clinging to Amy's hand. "Jared was leading the service. I was in the back. We had a few of my favorite music people up there that Sunday, and I was . . . well, I love our music. I was rocking out in the back — you can rock out to God, you know."

"Of course. Sounds great," Amy said.

"She was in the back. I just . . . well, I saw her face. She turned to look toward the back doors. Almost as if . . ."

"As if?" Hunter encouraged.

"She was expecting someone, or even as if she was afraid someone might come. First, I thought she might be a teenager, trying out our church for the first time, the kid of someone who worshipped at another place. Except we're not like that around here —

religious-wise. We attend and help with fundraisers, no matter which church — or temple — is on it. Then I realized she wasn't as young as I thought at first. She had to be in her twenties. Not that parents can't still scare us when we're grown up. But . . . anyway, when the service ended, I made a point of meeting her. She never gave me a last name. But she told me her name was Billie — short for Wilhelmina. She laughed about it and we both agreed that Wilhelmina was a heck of a name for a baby."

"Did you just chat in the church?" Hunter asked.

"No, she, uh, looked hungry. And she was. Our coffee and donuts are served just down the hall. The last area serves as a conference room, and we have a little coffee shop opened after our services and during our groups." She gave them an awkward look. "Our childcare workers are volunteer, so I make sure there's plenty of coffee for them."

"You brought her in for coffee and donuts," Amy said. "And to talk."

Karyl nodded. "She didn't have a donut. She had a turnover."

"And you thought she seemed hungry? She ate it quickly?" Amy asked.

"Every bit. I offered her something else, but she refused. By the time she'd finished, she seemed to be growing nervous."

"But you did talk," Hunter said.

"For the length of time it took her to eat that turnover," Karyl said. "I couldn't help but feel she was nervous the whole time, afraid someone was going to come. She kept looking around. I asked her if she was afraid of someone and she just shrugged and said something like, 'We all have to be careful, right?' And I thought she might have muttered, 'They could be anyone.' "

"And you haven't seen her again?" Amy asked.

Karyl shook her head unhappily. "Everyone knows a young woman was murdered out here in a 'ritualistic' style, which has put incredible pressure on all of us. Then again, the fact she was found on a cross is something only shared with the various heads of religious houses, but I can't help but be afraid now. For her. When I look back, the more I'm convinced she was afraid someone was going to find her."

"Can you describe her?" Hunter asked. He saw Amy had leaned forward, slightly but intently. She was ready to listen. And he was sure she understood; a sketch was a kinder thing to show a friend or loved one or even an acquaintance. Autopsy and crime-scene photos could be heart-

wrenching. And they could even be mislead-
ing, if the death had been cruel enough.

"Amy, can you draw from her words?"

She looked at him, startled.

"I'm not a police artist . . ." she murmured.

"You're as good as any of them," he said
simply. "We can move your chair around
the desk — if Pastor Karyl doesn't mind —
and she can watch and correct you. You have
a pencil and a sketch pad, right?"

She nodded, reaching into the pocket of
her navy-blue jacket. It was a new sketchbook, he noted, about the size of a trade
paperback.

She brought her own chair around and sat
next to Karyl.

"Okay, I, uh . . ." Karyl began. "She was
about five-six or -seven, I think. That doesn't
matter here, right? You're sketching her
face?" she asked Amy.

"But it matters. Noted," Amy said.

Karyl was thoughtful. "She had an oval
face, very classical, I think. Large eyes, a
soft brown. Her nose was straight, and she
had an expressive mouth. Nice lips, large
and well formed. Her hair was a light
brown, just a few highlights in it." She
paused, watching Amy sketch. "Cheeks a
little thinner. Lips more defined. Her brows

92

had a perfect arch, and she had really light, feathery bangs."

Amy kept sketching; everyone watched in silence. When she finished, she picked up her drawing.

It seemed she had caught more than just an image. There was anxiety in the young woman's eyes in the sketch, a softness and a vulnerability about her.

Notes about her height and coloring were beneath the sketch.

Hunter wasn't sure if he was relieved or more worried. Their victim on the cross had been a blonde.

Then again, hair dye was cheap. And if she'd been trying to hide, it was an easy way to change her appearance.

He couldn't tell. The face of their victim had been too badly slashed. But Dr. Carver just might have a better idea.

"Is it her?" Karyl asked anxiously.

Hunter decided to be honest. He stared at Amy, meeting her gaze, noting the very slight shake of her head.

"No, I don't think so," Hunter said.

"Oh, thank God! I mean, I'm so sorry for whoever was killed, but . . . well, I had this terrible feeling I had failed, that I could have done more . . ."

Her voice trailed.

"We would like to find this young lady," Hunter said.

"We sure would," Jared Colby declared. "We help people. That's our mission, to help all our brothers and sisters."

"We'll need you to keep in touch," Hunter said, producing a card and his phone at the same time. He handed a card to Pastor Karyl and one to Pastor Jared at the same time, then angled his phone to take a picture of Amy's sketch.

Jared and Karyl were staring at him.

"We're going to ask the medical examiner to take a look, too," he said. "Make sure we're not mistaken. You do think the sketch is a strong likeness?" he asked Karyl.

"An uncanny likeness," Karyl said.

"Thank you so much. If you see her again, please contact us immediately. Or Detective Mulberry as he may be closer. She may be in danger. She might have been running from someone."

"But if she sees police —"

"She really may need to be in protective custody," Amy said.

Karyl looked at Jared, and he gave her a firm nod. Hunter rose and Amy followed suit, pocketing her notebook. They both thanked the two of them for their time and headed out.

"I'll have Ryan get you home," Hunter told her. "By the way, thank you. I didn't mean to spring it on you, but you are one hell of an artist. I'm surprised you didn't go in that direction."

She shrugged. "Thanks," she said, giving him no further explanation. Instead, she asked, "Where are you heading now? What do you see as our next step?"

"I'm going exploring," he told her.

"Pardon?"

"I want to hang around here awhile."

"It's night."

"I am that observant," he said lightly.

"Right. So —"

"I'm going back to the little coffee shop where I met up with everyone earlier. I'm going to check out the back when it closes, see if there's any suggestion someone came or went that way, and I'll try to chat with any locals. Maybe meet a few of the farmers."

"All this . . . tonight?"

"There's an old motel about a mile south. It's been there since 27 was one of the main ways north, I think. I'm going to stay over tonight."

She stared at him.

"What?"

"If you're staying, I'm staying."

95

"Look, Amy, there might be nothing to pursue here. You don't have to bunk out here just because I am. You're going to want to check on John —"

"His kids are there. I'm good. If you're staying, I am, too."

Ryan was out of the car, awaiting his orders from Hunter.

Amy was stubborn; that was clear. She wasn't moving, and he didn't have the right to move her.

"All right," he said simply. "May I have the sketch? I sent a picture, but I'd like the drawing to get to Carver so he can really study and compare it."

"I may need the notebook," she said. She tore out the sketch and handed it to Ryan. Hunter explained to the other agent that they had more to do, and Ryan could go home — but get the sketch to Carver first thing in the morning. Amy thanked him again for the ride.

"Special Agent Larson, my pleasure," he told her. He looked around. "I'm a born Floridian — Broward County. And I've never been out here before. It's an eye-opener."

"Glad to bring you something new. We may be calling you out again," Hunter told him.

"I've been told to obey your every command, so you just say when," Ryan told them. Then he keyed the ignition, waved to them and backed out of the parking space.

"Do you think it matters? A phone pic or the real thing?" Amy asked Hunter as they watched Ryan leave.

"I don't know. But Ryan is available and wants to work. And I'm starting to think we need to get that image around to all local law enforcement."

"Just because a woman is shy and nervous doesn't mean she's part of a cult."

He looked at her. "And it might well mean she's trying to get out of a cult. I know that you go on your gut feelings sometimes — all cops do. And on this . . . well, the behavior pattern fits. Go with me on this, will you?"

Amy nodded. "Okay. We don't have anything else."

"I just thought of something," Hunter said. "You probably haven't eaten all day."

She laughed softly. "Not true. Microwave sandwich for breakfast."

"I think you need to see the diner. After we get rooms."

"It's a plan."

Amy knew Hunter hadn't thought the little

motel could be full, and it wasn't. And it was much as he had thought it would be — established in 1930, probably enjoyed a heyday in the 1950s and, now, clean but very outdated.

The man at the counter was pleasant.

"One room?" he asked.

"Two," Hunter told him. The man arched a brow. "I'm traveling with my sister," Hunter said lightly.

Amy tried not to frown. The man gave them two old-fashioned keys with plastic tags bearing the motel logo dangling from them.

"Sister, eh?"

He shook his head and told the man, "We're both law enforcement."

"You'll be about that murder," the man at the check-in desk said sagely. He was middle-aged, with a pleasant face and mostly gray hair that fell nearly to his shoulders.

"Yes," Hunter told him.

"Damnedest thing! Can't believe it. Why, I think we had one murder out here years and years ago — in the 1970s. Some guy got mad at his wife's driving, pulled a gun from his glove compartment and shot her. They careened into a canal — and he quickly paid the price. If he thought her

98

driving was bad when she was living . . . well, he should have figured shooting her wasn't going to help it any!"

Amy smiled. "Have you had any strangers through here lately?" she asked.

He smiled back, a fatherly smile. But his words were dry when he told her, "Honey, this is a motel. Everyone who stays the night is usually a stranger. Have I seen any stranger than normal strangers? Well, I don't think so. Folks just check in here when there's been a few bad accidents on the highway. When the turnpike and I-95 get bottled up, this road still goes north and south. Oh, and some like the back roads and might be heading for the dude ranch on up before you get to Orlando. Families, usually, with kids who still like things you do outside and not just video games."

Hunter drew out his phone and showed the man the picture of Amy's sketch he had taken earlier.

"Have you possibly seen this young woman? Did she check in here?"

"I . . . No . . . Wait! Yes, she did start to check in here . . . maybe a week ago?"

"She started to check in?" Amy asked.

"She was really nervous-like. And I know we may look like something dredged out of the Dark Ages — my grandfather built and started this place — but I must have a credit card for a deposit. Some biker-musicians checked in here once with cash only, trashed a room and took off. Funny world we live in, huh, when plastic beats cash. But it does."

"She didn't want to give you a credit card?" Hunter asked him.

He shook his head. "She said she didn't have one. I felt sorry for her — she was so nervous, like a lost little waif. I was going to let it go, but she ran out of here too fast. Is there a reason you're looking for her? Do you think she did something wrong?"

"No, we're just worried about her," Amy said.

"Now, after what's happened . . . Well, I'll keep a lookout for her, and next time I see her, I'll just make sure that she's in and safe," the man said.

"And call us," Amy said.

He nodded. "And call you."

"Thank you," Hunter said, lifting his key. "I think we'll just need the night. But —"

"Go day by day, and stay as long as you like," the clerk told them.

They headed out of the office.

Hunter took in the building. "Remind you of anything?"

"The Bates Motel, right out of *Psycho*?"

100

she guessed.

He grinned. "Yep. Except there's no two-story Victorian mansion looming on a hill. That fellow —" he paused, looking at his key "— Mr. Martin Sanders of the Sanders Inn, must live in the ranch house just in back of the motel."

"It's hard to have a house on a hill in Florida," Amy said lightly.

They looked down the line of the outdoor path that led to the ten connecting rooms. "Well, we're next to each other if there is . . . anything." He turned to look at her. "I don't have any luggage to bring in, and neither do you. Do you want a minute in the room, or are you ready to just head to the diner?"

"I'm hungry as hell. Ready to go to the diner."

They stepped back into the car, and then they were on the road.

"He said the young woman was here about a week ago," Amy said thoughtfully as they drove. "A week. But it was only days ago Karyl saw her at the church. Do you think she could still be around? She wouldn't have a room, a shower or any facilities."

"I don't know why, but I think she might be. And her behavior is that of someone who wants help, but is terrified of trying to get it." He glanced her way. "Once you're in a cult, it's damned hard to get out."

"But . . ." She paused, frowning.

"Yes?"

"How could people — a cult — be here and no one know it?"

"I don't know. But it certainly isn't impossible."

"And it's possible someone here is involved." She glanced his way. "Maybe even something like a sleeper cell, people involved with something for years that is only now coming to light?"

"That's possible, too."

Amy was tired. It had been one hell of a long day — and it had followed another long day. But she found herself watching him, trying to fathom her own feelings. Her first impression of him had not been favorable. Arrogant. Know-it-all. Or, perhaps, despite the department always wanting to play well with others and accept federal help when needed, she might have simply read these things into the man because of the way he'd just shown up in the middle of her crime scene. Maybe he'd been asked to a murder scene in the north of the state, but he'd presumed to be involved here.

She glanced his way, trying not to be obvious. It occurred to her that he was a striking man, tall and fit, though lots of law enforcement officers were. He had a good face. Eyes that were intent; when he was listening to someone, it appeared that he was really listening. He had a heart — he cared about John, certainly. He had the ability to command space when he walked into a room. There was something almost electrical about him — he entered, and things seemed to snap and sizzle.

She looked back at the road. She wanted to find him palatable, not attractive.

"There it is — ahead," he said.

There were scattered cars in the lot, but it was easy to park. Hunter opened the door and she went ahead of him into the diner.

"New staff on," he said softly from behind her.

A sign said Seat Yourself, Please!

They chose a booth along the front; the windows looked out to the night.

"Pot roast is good," he told her. "Down-home cooking."

An older waitress, softly bleached platinum hair pulled back in a French knot, came to their table, a pad in her hand. She'd obviously heard the last.

"Absolutely," she said. "Hello, and welcome. I'm Ida Peterson. My husband Frank and I own this place. He's a meat master,

and I swear, I make the best mashed potatoes this side of the Atlantic. And if I do say
so myself, my grits are to die for!"

Amy laughed softly. "Well, whatever I
have, it must come with mashed potatoes."

"The pot roast, dear. It's my husband's
specialty."

"Then I will have the pot roast and
mashed potatoes. And an iced tea, please,"
Amy told her.

"And you, sir?" she asked Hunter.

"I had the pot roast earlier, and it was
delicious," he told Ida. "So were the mashed
potatoes — best I've ever had," he acknowledged.

"You were in here earlier with our holy
foursome," she said. "I was back in the
kitchen. You're law enforcement, right?
Working that horrible murder with Victor
Mulberry."

"Right. I'm Hunter Forrest and this is
Amy Larson. She's with the state of Florida
and I'm with the federal government."

"They've brought in the big guns. As it
should be. We just don't have things like
that happen around here," Ida said. "Well,
welcome. I'll get this order in for you. How
about some key lime pie, Mr., um, Hunter
Forrest? I'm sorry. How do I address you?"

Amy looked down, trying not to smirk.

"Hunter is my given name, and you're welcome to call me by that. Officially, I'm Special Agent Forrest. Nice to meet you, Mrs. Peterson. Key lime pie would be lovely. And a cup of coffee, please."

She laughed. "You just call me Ida, hon. We're all like family around this place." Her smile disappeared and she frowned. "You all catch that monster who came here, do you hear me? You have to catch him and catch him fast. This is a good place. We — we're not used to being afraid out here. Miles of dark highway and tons of cows and folks often far from each other — and we're still not used to being afraid out here."

"I promise you we'll do our best," Hunter said.

She nodded and hurried behind the counter and to the window that led to the kitchen. She handed the ticket with the order to a man Amy thought must be her husband, Frank. She spoke to him; he looked out at Amy and Hunter.

He didn't pretend not to study them; he waved as he did so.

They waved back.

"You do think someone here is involved with this murder in one way or another. Did you feel that way in Micanopy?" Amy asked him.

"My opinion? The head of the cult isn't in either location. Perhaps somewhere in between — maybe even enjoying all the rides and attractions in Orlando while his apostles carry out his dirty deeds in other locations. Do I think someone long-established in the community — or the head of any church — is secretly a cult member? Not impossible, but I don't think so. What we found out is that there's a nervous stranger around. We don't think she was the victim. And I do think she's around here somewhere. She'd be too afraid — especially since the murder — to move very far."

"If she finds out we're here, and we're able to keep her safe, she may just appear."

"Right," he replied. "But if she's involved, she could also be afraid of law enforcement."

Amy shook her head. "I don't understand. She should just head toward . . . the city. Any big city. They can be found in all directions. Of course, if she's walking . . ."

"She couldn't use the main road. They could be looking for her. She can't travel much to the west — she'd come across alligators for certain."

"You know, you can find them sometimes on the golf courses in Miami and Naples and on up."

"We've built into their terrain for years," Hunter acknowledged. "I'm not all warm and cuddly on alligators, but this is their domain. Along with cottonmouth snakes, rattlers, pygmy rattlers, coral snakes —"

"Not to mention an onslaught of pythons and boa constrictors."

He nodded. "You have farms, you have cows. Horses. Ranch animals. And there are miles and miles of sugarcane. You've still got tons of predators. They don't acknowledge the difference between nature preserves and farmland."

"So, you think she's smart enough to stay around here."

"I think she's still here somewhere. Afraid to move."

Amy leaned back, studying his eyes. "I think you're right," she said at last.

He reached into his pocket; she saw he was going for his phone.

He looked at the message he had received.

"Carver. Guess he never stops working, either. He says your sketch is not of our dead girl. Federal, state and local agencies are still searching for her ID." He paused, pursing his lips and shaking his head. "We still have nothing on our Maclamara victim."

"Should you have . . . . stayed up there?"

107

she asked.

"Probably. But now I'm here. The trail is fresher."

"So, we could be here a few days."

"Yes."

"I'm glad I always have a toothbrush in my bag."

He grinned. "You do? Good."

"And you?"

"Always."

"Well, of course," she said.

Her pot roast and tea arrived, along with Hunter's pie and coffee. Ida waited for them to taste her offerings, smiling.

"Delicious," Amy assured her.

"Best ever," Hunter said. "You have to try this, Amy."

Why not? She reached across the table and tasted a forkful of his pie. "Wow," she told Ida.

Ida was pleased. "You two must come back in while you're out here investigating this awful business. The least I can do is keep you well-fed!"

They thanked her.

"You — you really are law enforcement?" Ida asked.

Hunter produced his credentials; Amy did the same.

Ida sighed. "Can't say as I'd know if they

were fake. But Frank has a nose for bad things. He says you're all right."

Amy smiled. "Frank is — well, he's got good senses. I swear we're the real deal."

Hunter handed Ida a business card. "We're staying up at the motel. Here's my phone number. Easy to reach us if you need to."

Ida took the card and slid it into the pocket of her uniform. "Frank and I close up at ten — or as soon as we get the last customer out of here. But we live in a little house out back. You come see us any time you need to, okay?"

She smiled and left the table, sweeping up a coffeepot to refill the cup of a trucker sitting a booth or two down.

Amy looked after her, and then she looked at Hunter.

"She knows something," she said softly.

"Yes," he agreed.

"We need to question her, we need to —"

"No."

"No?"

"Let her come to us," he said softly. She was surprised when he didn't suppress a yawn.

"The company you're keeping?" she asked dryly.

He grinned. "The day. Eat up. Let's go.

You never do know when it might prove to be a long night, too."

His phone buzzed again. He glanced at it, mouthing to her, "John Schultz."

"I'm going to throttle him! He had a heart attack and he's calling us now?" she said incredulously.

Worry struck her first; then she wondered why he had called Hunter and not her.

Hunter answered the phone, his eyes telling her he had no idea why John was calling, either.

Hunter quietly repeated what John was telling him.

"He says to keep an eye on the Unitarian church. Apparently, our charming friend Pastor Colby is close friends with multi-millionaire Ethan Morrison. I'd talked to John about running a search on the donor who had supplied the money for that fantastic stained-glass window at Colby's church. A forensic accountant who didn't know John had had a serious health incident called him with the info — Ethan Morrison was the donor. And he's never trusted Ethan Morrison. Especially not with all the things in the news about him."

"It's not illegal to be friends with a millionaire," Amy said. "Except that . . ."

She let her voice trail. Ethan Morrison

had faced a lot of allegations in his life — accusations of abuse from two of his ex-wives, and there had been an attempt to link him to another millionaire friend who had been known to secure the services of under-age prostitutes.

He was known to have invested in private detention centers at the border. And there had been accusations that young women had disappeared from those centers.

"Not to worry," Hunter told John. "We'll be out there again in the morning. We'll do everything we can. We will find out what happened."

He ended the call.

"I don't know why John has possession of his cell phone, but that's interesting that Ethan Morrison is involved with Colby's church."

"I see," Amy said.

"Right," Hunter murmured. "But," he added, "what you don't see is why John called me instead of you."

She shrugged. Right. She didn't understand why John would bypass her so easily.

"He was just informed the FBI was asked in officially to take over the investigation."

"Oh."

"I know that doesn't sit well with you."

She shrugged. "Florida murders, Florida cases."

He nodded. "I'm sorry."

"You don't have to be. I mean, honestly, if we can just find out who did this — and stop more horrible murders — that's fine with me."

"Is that sincere?" he asked her.

She laughed. "Yes, actually, it is."

"Okay, then." He looked at her empty plate. "You all set?"

She smiled. "Hey. You told me to finish up. I did."

"Nice to have an agreeable partner," he said.

"An obedient partner?"

"An agreeable partner," he repeated.

She shook her head. "Okay, let's go, partner."

5

Amy liked to think she had never been a fool.

She didn't mind another agent being in the room next to hers. They were out in what many might consider a no-man's-land, where a woman had been savagely murdered.

The best and toughest agent needed someone at their back at times.

But she had just thrown her jacket on a chair and was pulling the elastic and pins out of her hair when she heard a rap at the room's connecting door.

She moved over to open it, looking cautiously at Hunter.

"I think we should keep these open — easy proximity and within earshot."

"Do you snore?" she asked him.

"Only when I have a really bad cold. Do you?" he asked.

"Not often."

113

"Then we should be good. And it's just in case. I won't bother you in the least," Hunter said.

She just nodded and turned away, leaving the door ajar.

She brushed her teeth and washed her face, but then she hesitated when she came out of the bathroom. She'd figured she would strip down to her underwear to sleep.

It had been a long day, and airing out her clothing overnight might help a little.

"Screw it," she muttered to herself, and she stripped down and crawled beneath the sheets. She was sure he was in his boxers or briefs or whatever he wore.

Checking her Glock on the nightstand and glancing at the door one more time, she rolled to her side.

She was exhausted.

But she was pretty sure she wasn't going to sleep well.

She'd drift off, then awaken again.

She realized she was completely doubting Pastor Jared Colby.

How could a man of any kind of legitimate house of worship count someone like Ethan Morrison as a friend? The multimillionaire had escaped prosecution because of missing evidence and because of the death of a witness — while that witness was in jail, awaiting trial. It had been a Florida case, but it had been in the news everywhere.

Personally, Amy never believed the man had died by suicide. He had been ready to testify that the disappearance of young women from his detention center had nothing to do with them being transferred to another place. There were no records of the girls arriving at their transfer. But no one had been able to prove he had been murdered while incarcerated.

There had to be a connection — or there didn't. Ethan Morrison might be involved in many criminal schemes, but that didn't mean he had anything to do with ritualistic murders. She knew she couldn't jump to conclusions just because she hated so many things the man had likely done, and gotten away with because of his position of privilege.

She drifted off, but awoke again, as if her thoughts had continued even into her sleep.

She kept thinking of the words in Revelation.

I looked, and there before me was a pale horse! Its rider was named Death, and Hades was following close behind him. They were given power over a fourth of the earth to kill by sword, famine and plague, and by the wild beasts of the earth.

Sword, famine, plague and wild beasts.

Its rider was named Death, and Hades was following close behind him.

There were so many theories on what the words meant. None of the riders were real — they were all parts of the way life would come to be on earth. The white horse was the devil, the white horse was Christ; Christ and Satan were riding together, because the End of Days was nigh upon everyone. A seal had been broken.

Her eyes flew open.

Two.

There were two of them, she thought. Two main leaders in the cult, or the murder company, whatever it might really be.

And they were going to seek out four victims. One, the girl they had found on the cross. The crude spear had cut through her, like a sword.

They would kill by . . . starvation? And then disease, and then . . .

Someone might meet his or her death through a brutal animal attack.

She lay staring at the ceiling, anxious for morning to come, wanting to share her theory with Hunter.

She heard something. A scratching sound.

She jerked up, listening.

The sound was coming from behind her

room, behind the motel. She crawled up and paused, listening. The noise continued.

She set her Glock at the foot of the bed and slid quickly back into her suit pants and shirt, not bothering to button it. Then she moved toward the rear of the room to hear better, the Glock in her hand again.

She heard a little clatter.

The sound, perhaps, of a garbage can falling?

She glanced to her side, to the connecting door.

Hunter, in his suit pants, was standing there, listening, as well.

"Is someone . . . spying on us?" she whispered.

He shook his head. "I don't think so. I think . . ."

"Wilhelmina — Billie?"

"Maybe. If she is in town, she must be surviving by hiding off the road. That might well mean she goes through garbage cans."

"It could be her, or raccoons," Amy said practically.

"Do you think it's raccoons?"

"No."

"You go around the office side. I'll head out around the last room."

"I should approach her," Amy said. "If it's her."

117

"Because . . . you're a woman?"

"Because I'm less intimidating."

He nodded. "You get the raccoons, too."

She smiled and nodded, and they headed out together, leaving by her door, then splitting to go in opposite directions.

The motel was quiet. Amy hadn't glanced at the time, but she reasoned it had to be somewhere around three in the morning.

She moved around the front of the motel, sliding quickly by the front door, and then around to the back.

A concrete slab there held several bins — several for recycling and several for trash.

One lay on its side, contents spilling from it.

But there was no one there, human or otherwise.

She saw Hunter at the far end hurrying toward her. He reached her and noted the downed bin, hunching to study the ground.

There had been no rain. The earth was dry. There were no footprints that might be followed.

"It was probably a person," he said softly, looking into the dense growth of trees and bracken behind the motel.

"Not raccoons?"

"There would be little scratch marks — the earth is dry, but those would have

118

shown. And there's some garbage in here that I think a raccoon would have gone for, but a person wouldn't think was still edible."

"Do you think she's living in the brush back there? That's dangerous."

He looked up at her from his hunched position. "Right. And a sad statement on whatever is going on. She'd rather face insects, snakes and more than whoever she's afraid of."

"We should go after her."

"Run around in the snake-infested wilderness to try to find someone who knows the lay of the land and will be even more terrified if she sees us coming after her?" he asked.

"We really need to find her."

"We do. But we won't manage it tonight. Let's hope she found something good, and try for a few more hours of sleep. We'll need to get back in to talk to Pastor Colby tomorrow."

"All right," Amy said, looking into the darkness of the night beyond the motel.

"We'd need an army — and by the time we could get a troop of FDLE, cops and FBI out here, she would be long, long gone."

"Right."

"Trust me. Sometimes, people figure out how to come to us. We'll have to make ourselves as visible as possible."

"Okay."

He stood. He was shirtless. Amy noted his chest was lean but extremely well-muscled, bronzed — nice. He should model for a denim company. For one frightening moment, she thought about just how attractive a man he was.

In the physical sense. She was still weighing in on his character.

"Great. Sleep. Let's go for it," she said, turning. As she headed back around the front of the old-fashioned motor inn, she remembered she hadn't bothered with the buttons on her shirt, and started surreptitiously doing them up.

The lights in the office were dim. She noted a sign on the office door she hadn't read before. Office Closes at 10:00 p.m.

"Wait," she told Hunter, running back around the edge of the building.

The owner's ranch-style home was a couple hundred feet to the right and rear of the motel itself.

The house was dark; a single light was on at the front, over a small, tiled porch.

Hunter came up behind her.

"I think we need to find out more about

our host, as well," he said.

"Billie could be in there."

"If so, I think he's helping her."

"Why wouldn't he have said something to us? And if she was being helped, why root through the trash?"

"Maybe Billie needed more than what was given — proud people, even desperate, don't take more than they need to. And just because we're FBI doesn't mean someone might trust us. If money like the kind Ethan Morrison has is behind any of this, we could be suspect — we could be on the take."

"I would never be on the take!" Amy said passionately.

He grinned. "*You* know that. *I* believe that. But our witness may not. We'll get someone on our motel owner tomorrow. I have access to records you wouldn't believe. For now —"

"Right. Be patient. Let people or things come to us," she said. "Or we could just march up to that door."

"And do what? Demand entrance? We'd need a warrant. And again, by the time we could do anything, our 'Billie' could be long gone. And if you're thinking about pounding a door in, give it up. I'm not losing a murderer in court because we made mistakes."

Amy sighed. "I know, I know."

He turned and headed around the motel again. She followed him. They reentered by her door and he headed straight for the connecting door to his room.

He paused there and turned back.

"The next time we hear raccoons, we have to move a hell of a lot faster. Good night."

The connecting door remained open. But he was gone.

Amy sighed and threw herself on the bed, frustrated.

And exhausted. While she was ruing the events of the night, she drifted to sleep.

When she woke again, the sun was shining through the drapes. She leaped up, glancing at the old clock on the bedside table.

It was just after 8:00 a.m. — time to get moving, certainly.

She started to make a mad dash for the shower, but when she reached the bathroom door, there was a tap at the connecting doors.

She called out, "Ready in ten!"

"Hey, no worries. I wanted to let you know I'm leaving a bag on your bed. Special Agent Ryan Anders drove all the way back here after agents from the Miami office gathered some things for us. Clean clothing

122

is in the bag."

"Oh — thanks!" she called.

She wondered how in hell agents in Miami knew what size she wore. But that wouldn't have been a mystery for the tech department of an FBI field office, she supposed. Photographs, maybe? Or an educated guess.

She closed the bathroom door. Time to get ready for work.

Hunter was impressed by Ryan Anders's dedication to his new job. While Hunter worked out of the DC offices — and had spent time giving and receiving information from the Behavioral Sciences Unit at Quantico — Anders had drawn an assignment to the Miami field unit.

Ryan had considered that to be icing on the cake — he was from a rural, north-central part of the state, far north of Disney and Universal Studios — and the concept of working by a beach was, to him, definite icing.

That Ryan had made the drive down to Miami and back again and still had the appearance of having slept through the night was impressive. That he'd gotten a skeletal night crew to arrange for a change of clothing for Hunter and Amy, something Hunter hadn't even thought to ask for, was excellent.

Amy rapped on the connecting door, showered and dressed. Ryan was seated at the foot of Hunter's bed, waiting on orders.

"Ryan, thank you!" she told him. "This is great."

"Hey, I had one of those moms who thought that cleanliness was next to godliness," Ryan said. "It was no problem." He looked at Hunter. "What's next?"

"Sometime during the day, I'll have you get to my hotel room and then —" he paused, then looked over at Amy "— if it's agreeable to Amy, you can head to her place in Orlando to pick up some things. Amy, do you have a friend or someone who could put things together for you?"

"Yes, yes, of course. A friend of mine is cat-sitting. She won't mind," Amy said.

"Give her a call sometime during the day," Hunter said.

Amy hadn't had a chance to wrap her hair up again yet. Her hair was long and shimmering, softly framing her face. Hunter caught himself staring. "Well, all right. We're going to head straight back to the Unitarian church and find Pastor Colby. Ryan, head to breakfast at the diner. Linger and listen. I'll be in touch as soon as we're out."

"Okay. Am I dressed right for this?" Ryan asked.

He was wearing jeans, a T-shirt and a tan bomber jacket.

"You're fine," Hunter told him. "We don't plan on denying you're an agent. Just don't mention it unless you find it necessary. We need to get eyes on this community."

"I'm Roman Catholic," he said. "I can check out afternoon Mass if you want."

"Not a bad idea."

"I checked the times — six, eight and then six in the evening," Ryan said.

"Times for the working man and woman," Hunter said. "Fine. Okay, so . . . let's move. Amy, you set?"

She nodded. When she'd said ten minutes, she meant ten minutes.

"Ryan, get going to the diner. Amy, let's stop by the office before we leave."

They headed out together, but Ryan headed for his car.

Hunter noted that Ryan was driving a typical dark agency sedan; he was glad his was an SUV, blue instead of black. Not that it meant anything — he and Amy had clearly identified themselves as law enforcement officers, and it was likely Ryan would wind up doing so, too.

But sometimes, when they were in a position where they weren't ready to state who they were, there was something about agency cars — besides the tags — that gave them away.

They headed for the motel office. Martin Sanders was behind the counter, as he had been the day before. There was a stool back there he was sitting on, busy on a computer while also petting the large gray cat lying at the computer's side.

"Beautiful cat," Amy said.

Sanders beamed. "She's Kitty — just wandered in one day and stayed. Probably because we fed her and fell in love with her."

"She looks like a Maine coon," Amy said.

"I think so, too. Of course, we don't know anything other than she wandered into the right place," Sanders said.

Amy stroked the cat. Good move, Hunter thought. Sanders seemed to like her.

He looked over at Hunter. "Was everything all right?" he asked.

"Oh, yes, thank you, very comfortable," Hunter said.

"Good, good!" Sanders beamed, but then he frowned. "Oh, okay — so you're staying on?"

"Is that all right?" Hunter asked him.

"Of course. I figure you'll have your rooms another few days?"

"That would be great," Hunter told him.

"Was anything wrong?" Sanders asked.

"Actually," Amy said, "we were just hoping you didn't have any problems around here."

"Problems?" Sanders appeared honestly confused.

"We thought we heard someone or something out at the trash last night," Hunter told him.

"Oh, well, we do have raccoons." He laughed. "At least I've only had raccoons! The ranch about five miles south of here, they came out one morning to find a big old gator in their swimming pool. Now, we've never had anything like that. Of course, we don't even have a pool, so couldn't have a gator in one. Not to worry — we keep our eyes on the trash, and yes, we do get critters in it now and then. Sorry if they woke you."

"No, no, not to worry," Hunter assured him. "We just figured if you did have trouble, you've been great to us and we're here — well, we wanted to help out."

"That's good of you, folks. But no, not unless you want to arrest a few raccoons."

"Not on the list today," Amy said lightly. "Hunter, this is the most gorgeous cat."

"Is Kitty a boy or girl?" Hunter asked,

stroking the animal, as well. He was standing so close to Amy that he felt her warmth.

She smiled as they shared the silky touch of the animal — even if it was an act, in a way.

And he noted how much he liked it when she smiled, that her eyes glimmered. He'd thought her severe. He realized now she was just dressing for the job.

"Kitty here is a girl, but she won't be having any kittens. I hate to think of all the animals that don't have families. Pet owners need to be responsible, right?"

"I absolutely agree," Hunter assured him. "Well, we'd better get going for the day. Thank you, and again, we're here, you know, if you need help with anything."

"Sure — and thank you!" Sanders said.

Amy sighed softly, leaving the cat. When they were in the car, she asked, "Well?"

"Something."

"Something evil — or something good?"

"I don't know yet. What did you think?"

"Hard to hate a guy who wants to be a responsible pet owner."

"True. But we did put away a serial killer once who donated huge sums to his local shelters. He went out of town to murder people."

"Don't go blowing all my faith in humanity," Amy said lightly. "The jury is out on Sanders. Maybe he saw us running around the motel last night and was prepared for the questions."

"Maybe he's protecting someone — as in our Billie."

"That is possible. But why not let her come to us?"

"He could still not be sure about us. Some people don't trust cops, agents or law enforcement in general."

Amy nodded and then said thoughtfully, "We're near the church. Back to Pastor Colby. I had the impression that Detective Mulberry was familiar with this area. But I don't think that he knew anything about Morrison having given the church money."

"I agree. I've known Mulberry a few years, but not that well. And remember, he's been called out here before, but he's working a big county. You might ask if he knows more about that church when we meet with him next."

"You don't care if I do ask?"

"Not in the least. I'd like any info we can get."

"I'm going to call John's daughter — although John seems to have his phone! Still, if he's sleeping, I don't want to wake him."

He nodded as he drove, and then listened to Amy's side of the conversation.

John was sleeping. He was doing very well; it had been a "minor" attack and he had been lucky.

When she finished the call, he was parking at the church.

There were several cars in the lot. Hunter wondered if they had one of their group sessions going on.

The church door was locked; they walked around the side where the long building stretched out. The office door was open.

Karyl was at her desk. She looked up with a welcoming smile.

Hunter thought it faded a bit when she saw who was there, but she rallied quickly.

"Hey!"

"Hi, Karyl," he said. "Is Pastor Colby in?"

"I'm afraid not. He's not due in today until lunchtime." She stood. "I have my youth group gathering. That's the way our structure works. I'm new at this, and I get the youth groups. I'm not complaining — I love the youth groups. But I'm afraid I have to get to it now." She walked toward them, making it clear she needed to leave, and so did they.

She stopped halfway, though.

"Did you find her, by any chance? Did

130

you find Billie?"

"No, I'm afraid not," Amy said. "She hasn't come back here, right? Do you think she might be part of your youth group?"

"Oh, no, Billie is twentysomething. Maybe just twenty-one, but . . . well, she wouldn't be in this group. I have older teens in this."

"Mind if we peek in?" Hunter asked her.

"Peek in?"

"I'd love to see your youth group. It's so inspiring to see young people in church," Amy told her.

"Well, just —"

"Actually, I'd like to ask them to be on the lookout for Billie. Would that be okay?" Hunter asked her.

"I, uh, I don't know. I mean, if Billie is hiding . . ." Karyl let her voice trail and looked at them a little weakly.

"We need to find her. Before someone else does," Hunter said flatly.

"Well, still, I'm not sure what Pastor Colby would say."

Amy smiled at her sweetly. "Pastor Colby has made it clear he wants to help us in any way."

"Yes, of course, yes, sure. Uh, we're down in Classroom B."

She made her way past them and then waited until they were out to lock the office door behind her.

"I'm surprised you have to lock up around here," Hunter said pleasantly.

"You never know who might drive by," she said, and then she winced, looking down. "Driving by or stopping just north of here to kill a woman. You — you don't know who she is . . . was . . . yet, do you?"

"I'm afraid not," Hunter said. "If anyone is missing from this area, it hasn't been reported. Police are out canvassing, doing door-to-door questioning, Detective Mulberry assured me."

"On the one hand, we've always been so easy around here . . . It's a friendly place. On the other hand, so many people do just drive through. I have always locked the doors," Karyl said.

"Locking up is always a smart thing to do," Amy told her.

Karyl looked down and her sandy bob wagged along with the shake of her head. "I still can't believe that this . . . that this happened! Our biggest crimes are usually bar fights." She shuddered and started down the hallway toward her class again.

Amy suddenly paused, reaching into her pocket for her phone. Hunter hung back, waiting. Karyl did the same.

She gave her attention to the call quickly,

thanked someone and ended the call.

"Be right there!" she told the other two.

Hunter nodded; Amy had to be getting good information. He smiled at Karyl. "Shall we?"

6

It was John's daughter on the phone again. John had asked Brenda to call her.

"Dad says he'll behave and lie in his hospital bed and let me help him at home — staying low and calm and healing — as long as we let him use his friends and resources to help the investigation. I guess it's better than him getting anxious," Brenda said wearily.

"Yes, I know your dad."

"I know you do — you're like his third child," Brenda said. "Anyway, he talked to some friends in Miami. Jared Colby's daughter, Casey, has been down in the Greater Miami area several Sundays in the last few months, attending a church down there. The pastors at the Miami church know Pastor Colby — the churches are all different but have a loose association because they are Unitarian. Anyway, Dad found out that a Pastor Marino down there was worried about Casey, so, Dad thought you might want to find out what you could about her, or about what might be bothering her."

"Thanks — and tell your dad thanks for us, too, okay? Tell him it's a deal — he can talk on the phone and do research, as long as he behaves."

Brenda laughed softly. "Will do."

Amy ended the call quickly. The door to the classroom was slowly falling closed, so she hurried down and entered the room just in time to see Karyl setting a folder on a chair at the front and center of the group.

The young pastor's youth group seemed to be composed of older teens in their last years of high school or first years of college.

They were chattering and whispering as she entered, and fell silent as they saw not just Karyl but Hunter and Amy enter behind her.

"Good morning, all!" Karyl said, nodding toward Amy, as if pleased Amy had managed to join them before they began. "We're going to get back to our Bible study and how it can affect the way we choose to live our lives in just a minute. But first, I wanted to introduce you all to Special Agent Amy Larson of the FDLE and Special Agent Hunter Forrest of the FBI."

"FBI!" an older boy with a thatch of dark hair over one eye echoed. "Oh, yeah, the murder."

"Right," Amy said. "But we're here because we need your help. You know about the murder that occurred just north of here. Police were out to most of your homes, I know, looking for anyone who might have seen anything unusual."

"Yeah," another boy, eighteen or so, wearing a band T-shirt said. "My dad was talking about it. He said whoever did it was smart. They made sure they were north enough so there were no houses near — just state forest and sugarcane fields. We're close to that area, but we didn't hear anything or see anything."

"No one did," a girl with shaggy blond hair said.

Hunter pulled out his phone to show them all the picture of the sketch that Amy had done of "Billie."

"We're looking for this young woman," he said.

"She was in church — here!" the blonde girl said. "She was in one of the back rows."

"Have you seen her since?" Hunter asked.

"Oh, my God — do you think she killed someone?" another teen asked.

"No. We think she might be in danger, and

136

we'd like to help her," Amy assured him.

They were met with blank faces.

"If anyone does see her, please make sure you get ahold of us right away," Hunter said. He pulled a stack of cards from his pocket and set them on the chair he assumed Karyl would be taking to begin her class.

"Please," Amy said. "Any help is welcome."

"Should we be afraid?" the blonde girl asked.

"Should you be afraid?" Hunter repeated, weighing his answer. "We don't believe the victim was from near here, so I don't believe any of you would be targeted by this . . . killer or these killers. But there's being afraid, and there's being smart. No one should ever have to walk through life being afraid. But everyone, anywhere, needs to be smart. Think about what you're doing. Pay attention to your surroundings. Especially out here where we have miles of brush and trees, and night can bring the deepest darkness, so don't be out alone right now. Remember to lock doors, and again — be alert to things happening around you. That's the way to be smart — not just here and now, but everywhere and always."

Amy noted the group had grown silent. A

few of the young women were watching him with starry-eyed wonder.

But the boys in the group also seemed to pay attention. Even with his impromptu words, Hunter was a powerful speaker.

"And be wise," Hunter added. "One of our biggest dangers is not believing with our rational minds what our instinct tells us is true. Then again," he added with a softening grin, "that goes with being smart! Thank you. Thank you all for your time and your attention. And don't forget, you can reach us if you need to — my cards are up there."

The group broke into applause and Hunter lifted his hand. "Thank you. Please, just be careful and wary and observant, okay?"

He turned and gravely thanked Karyl again and headed out of the room with long strides. Amy quickly followed him.

"That was excellent," she told him.

He let out a sigh. "I didn't mean to turn into a teacher. We do go out — you must know. I'm sure FDLE does it to, talking to high schools, even younger kids sometimes."

"We do. But for a two-minute off-the-cuff, that was good."

He glanced her way. "Thanks."

"Pastor Colby still isn't due for several hours. I say we need to know more about him and his family — and Ethan Morrison."

"What was the phone call?"

"Brenda Nelson. I guess we've made a deal with John. He'll be a good patient as long as we let him use his mind and his research abilities, and his relationships. Colby has three kids, two boys, Jayden and Chase, and a girl, Casey. The daughter, Casey, has been showing up at a church in Miami. The pastor there was worried that she might be upset. Then again, maybe she was just visiting friends in Miami."

"We need to know so much more about these people."

"Yes, we do need to know more. When this happened, Detective Mulberry sent men out, searching for witnesses. The story was always the same — no one saw anything, and everyone was horrified this could happen here. Thing is, I still don't believe this could have happened with no one knowing anything."

"We can't bring everyone in the area in for questioning. We haven't the time or the resources." Hunter shook his head. "But for now, I know where we can go to find out more, or at least try to get in on some gossip."

"True — gossip is an amazing help. But where is that we're going?"

He laughed. "I say we stop in at the diner. Ryan will be happy. I'm sure he needs some company by now."

"People do talk, and a local café is great for gossip. But I'd like some hard facts on this, too. And more on all the groups out here." She hesitated. "You know, when I was a kid, my parents encouraged me to find out about different religions. My dad believed good people just took different paths to the same place. I can't believe any legitimate rabbi, pastor, priest, imam or other leader of a legitimate church is doing this."

"Ah, but on that side, you do have fanatics. And any fanatic is terrifying," Hunter said. "I'm going to agree Pastor Colby looks suspicious — if this friendship with a man like Ethan Morrison is real. But it doesn't brand him a murderer. Nor does it mean the man is anything other than what we see — a good man who is the head of a church. Sects can happen, though. And it's terrifying and mind-boggling how one man can seize control of the minds of others. Thing is, a leader like that has an agenda. Sometimes money, sometimes power. We can all be fooled, but I don't see Jared Colby as that kind of a man."

Both of their phones buzzed simultaneously.

"Probably John or Brenda — with John having figured out he should just give us both anything he comes up with," Hunter said.

She looked at her phone; yes, John had sent a message.

"Okay," Hunter said. "So, the two priests and the rabbi check out as lily-white. But so does Jared Colby. We can't condemn him just because of his associates," he warned. "So far, no one has been able to prove anything against Morrison."

"Innocent until proven guilty. Too bad it's difficult to prove guilt when witnesses wind up dead. But there's something else, too, Hunter, that's been nagging at me." She took a deep breath. "I'm afraid this is nowhere close to being over."

After a pause, he said, "Four Horsemen."

"Right. I've been doing a lot of reading. And the main thing is the text of the Bible is a matter of interpretation. And there are so many theories around it. But the first horse brings death by the sword, pestilence, famine and disease."

"Yes?" He paused to look at her, frowning. "I see what you're saying. We're not even going to need a second horseman. Our

141

first victim was struck through the heart —
she wasn't killed with a sword, per se, but
with a metal-tipped stake. You're afraid
we're going to find someone dead due to
starvation, insect infestation or poison —
and through sickness, brought on by a lethal
disease."

She nodded.

He met her eyes, gaze serious. "And I'm
very afraid you might be right. We need to
move quickly, and that could mean a trip
north up the peninsula — back to what I'm
convinced is a practice victim. And I want
to talk to Dr. Carver again. Knowing more
about our victim might help."

"I'll drive. You call Carver."

He didn't protest and Amy was glad; she
was afraid he was going to be the type who
insisted on driving. She was a good driver,
and she'd managed a few high-speed chases
without causing damage or injury.

She remembered when she'd started out
with John; he had insisted on being the one
behind the wheel all the time. When he'd
hurt his right foot during an arrest, he'd
had no choice but to let her drive.

Then, she thought, lowering her head with
a smile for the memory, he'd decided she
should drive most of the time. But she had
been patient with John; he'd been a father

142

figure in a way. An older man, experienced with the FDLE, while she had been a rookie — even if she had spent four years with Metro-Miami-Dade.

Hunter Forrest was certainly no father figure.

She listened as he spoke to his headquarters. He was speaking to someone named Special Agent Sheila Garcia, and Garcia went off on something of a heated rant when the name Ethan Morrison was mentioned.

Many people seemed to think the man should be in prison, and thus far, law enforcement had been thwarted.

"Sheila, we do our best to uphold the laws — we don't make them," Hunter said, glancing Amy's way.

She smiled. She couldn't hear the rest of the woman's words, but the conversation settled down.

He ended the call, shaking his head, and then smiling at Amy as she glanced his way, waiting.

"Well, you heard some of that."

"Yes. She thinks Ethan Morrison is a scumbag."

"A good majority of Americans do, I believe, but he's a smart scumbag. She did know one thing I consider interesting."

"Oh?"

"Morrison owns a lot of land around here — he's a sugar baron."

"I should have known that."

"Nope. Because he owns the land under another company name." He shrugged. "That's why we have brilliant agents — in the FBI and FDLE — who never leave their offices but sure as hell help solve the crimes. Sheila is the best."

"Does he — does he own the land where the victim was found? I thought it was actually state land."

"Where she was found is state land. But just a half a mile down, part of the old Sweetly Naturally Sweet sugar plantation lines up to the main road. Of course, Sheila also told me Ethan Morrison was seen on national television the day our girl was killed."

"She was killed in the middle of the night or the wee hours of the morning, however you want to look at it."

"He was seen on the news in Texas. It's really unlikely he could have made it out here by then."

Amy shook her head. "We know more than one person killed her. Here's my theory, for what it's worth. He's involved — and I think he may be finding people at the border. Maybe not immigrants, but perhaps the homeless . . . turning them, using them . . . I don't know. But we still don't have identities on either victim."

"I know," he said quietly. "And you know things aren't solved in a day."

"I don't think your 'white horse' is going to take long to act again."

"I agree."

She parked at the diner.

"Be really friendly with Ida," he said as they both got out of the car.

"Oh, you betcha," she said.

Inside, Amy slid into the seat next to Ryan at a window-facing booth and Hunter took the seat opposite. A pretty young waitress came over. Amy noticed a slight frown on the girl's face as Hunter whispered to Amy, "She was working yesterday, too."

"Hi, welcome. What can I get you? Coffee?" the waitress asked. She looked at Amy, and Amy realized that she was slightly put-off, maybe thinking Amy had chosen the seat next to Ryan because there was something between them.

"I would love coffee," she said.

"Special Agent Forrest?" she asked Hunter.

"Coffee here is great," he said.

"So, you two have met?" Ryan asked Hunter.

"Not officially. But you served us yesterday, right?" Hunter said.

"And I must admit, I heard Rabbi David call you by name at some point," the waitress said. She had her very dark hair pulled back in a bun, but little dark tendrils escaped and fell against her forehead. She was in her early twenties, Amy thought, with dark eyes and a quick, slightly nervous smile.

"Oh, well, then, let me perform the introductions," Ryan said. "Special Agent Hunter Forrest and Special Agent Amy Larson, please meet the lovely and charming Miss Kaila Franklin. Kaila knows I've just been kind of waiting around this morning, and she's kept my coffee cup full."

"Nice to meet you, Kaila," Amy said.

"Oh, so, you're a fed, too?" she asked Amy, apparently pleased Amy was one of Ryan's coworkers.

"No, I'm with the Florida Department of Law Enforcement," Amy told her.

"Oh," she said, slightly confused. "Detective Mulberry has been in here, too."

"We're all working together," Hunter said.

"Oh, yeah. It's so terrible! I can't believe it. Things like that — well, they just don't

146

happen around here often."

"Thankfully, they don't happen anywhere *often,*" Hunter said.

"Oh, I meant —" Kaila began, sounding distressed.

"It's okay. We know what you mean," Amy said quickly. "This is such a friendly community. We understand."

"Of course," Hunter agreed.

"Um," Kaila said. "The boss is looking at me. I think the couple in back are ready to order. Excuse me. Please look at the menu. Take your time, and I'll be back with your coffee."

She moved on down the row of booths.

Amy noted Frank was working back in the kitchen; she didn't see Ida.

"So, how's your day been?" Ryan asked them.

Hunter shook his head. "We're getting around, but nothing solid. What about you? Have you learned anything?"

"Yep," Ryan said.

"And what's that?" Amy asked.

"Kaila hates her bosses."

"The owners, Frank and Ida, right?" Hunter asked him.

Ryan nodded and spoke softly. "She says they're all smiles and good cheer to the customers, but they treat staff like inden-

147

tured servants. Staff today is herself and a girl named Jill, who works nights on the weekends, and a guy named Drew, who comes and cleans at closing time."

"Interesting. Anything else?"

He nodded. "She lives in town. Her parents had a small place where they ranched, but her dad got sick, and they lost the ranch. Father passed a couple years ago, and her mother passed recently. She's just trying to save up enough to get out. She wants to live in Fort Lauderdale and go to the community college. She doesn't hate it, but she was an only child and there isn't much left for her around here."

"That's understandable," Amy said.

"I think so, too," Hunter agreed.

"Something else," Ryan said.

"What's that?" Hunter asked.

Ryan leaned closer. "I think she's taking food — hoarding it. Some diners left a half loaf of pumpkin bread. She looked back at Frank, then carefully hid it under her apron. I mean, maybe she's trying to save on groceries, but maybe . . ."

"Maybe she's trying to feed someone who is hiding out?" Amy asked.

Ryan shrugged. "Oh, she loves the rabbi — calls him Rabbi David. He's her favorite. Apparently, priests and pastors meet here often. They're all nice, she told me, but Rabbi David was the best."

"Good to know." Hunter nodded approvingly at everything Ryan had learned.

Ryan leaned back. "Am I driving to Orlando to pick up some things for you, Amy?"

Amy didn't get to answer — Hunter answered for her. "Yes, we're going to be here a few more days, I think. And if you'd stop by my hotel, I'd appreciate it. It shouldn't be much bother. I stay packed."

"Yes, thanks," Amy said, determined to speak for herself. "I'll talk to my friend who feeds my cat for me when I'm away," Amy told him.

"All right. I'll head back after this. Unless you have other instructions for me?" Ryan asked.

"No, but I'll book you a room for tomorrow night, too. We'll need you with us," Hunter told him.

Ryan nodded, smiling. "Thank you!"

Hunter grinned. "You're a good agent, Ryan. You worked this place well. We're going to be glad to have you with us."

"Thanks. So you know, for breakfast, the omelets are great."

"Wonderful," Hunter said.

Kaila appeared back at their table, balancing two cups and a coffeepot. She set the cups down and poured coffee and refilled Ryan's cup.

"Would you like food?" she asked.

"Omelet, please. Cheese, tomatoes, peppers. And a side of bacon," Amy said.

Hunter was looking at her strangely. "Uh, two, please," he said to Kaila.

"Making it easy," Kaila said, and she walked the ticket she had written out with their order back behind the counter to hang for Frank in the kitchen.

"She gets off after the lunch shift, around three," Ryan told them, indicating Kaila. "Ida takes the dinner shift. I guess old Frank cooks all day. I should be back by five — barring traffic. I was going to go to Mass."

"Yep. Good idea," Hunter told him. "Keep in touch, and text me your whereabouts."

"Will do," Ryan said. "I ate already . . ."

"Then get going," Hunter told him, smiling.

Ryan nodded and Amy shuffled out of the booth to let him by. He paused to catch Kaila quickly as he was leaving, saying goodbye. The waitress looked after him for just a second. It was a longing look.

"Poor kid," Hunter said.

"Yes, I agree. Losing both parents, a home — and then stuck in a job working for people who aren't that great. If she's telling the truth."

"I think she is. Let's face it, people put on fake faces all the time. And that's why, sometimes, gut feeling is part of the job," Hunter said.

"Okay. I have a feeling about Pastor Colby — and his daughter. Why would she go all the way to Miami when her father is a pastor? Okay, she could have friends down there — in fact, she probably has friends in Miami. But at that age, she'd be visiting to head to the clubs on the beach, maybe a frat or sorority party at the UM or FIU. Would you really go all that way to go to church, unless you felt that you needed to do so?"

Hunter didn't answer; Amy saw Kaila was coming to their table with their food.

They thanked her as she set down the plates. The girl paused just a moment.

"You guys are really cool," she told them. "Well, not that I know any other law en-forcement agents of any kind, but . . . Ryan is so nice. And . . . well, you guys seem the same. I guess I thought you'd be all serious and . . . cold."

Hunter laughed. "We honestly try to be somewhat warm and cuddly."

Amy decided to take it a step further.

151

"He's right, you know. We need help all the time from people close to a situation. And for that, we must earn their trust. We try very hard to do that."

Kaila nodded. "Well, you three are doing a good job at that."

She smiled and moved quickly away from the table. Glancing back, Amy saw Frank was watching Kaila, making sure she was giving her attention to all the guests.

Or that she wasn't spending too much time talking to them, specifically?

Hunter stood, walking over to the counter. He was going to talk to Frank himself. Amy couldn't hear what he said, but it was obviously friendly. He pointed to her, and she smiled and waved, and Frank waved in return.

Hunter returned to the table.

"Good move," she murmured.

"I want to find Kaila later, when she's off work and away from here."

"Right."

He looked at his watch. "Should be time to see Colby after we eat our omelets. That was strange."

"What was strange?"

"Your order. At least we have similar eating habits."

Amy grinned. "If I hadn't ordered first,

152

you really would have ordered the same thing?"

"I really would have."

She laughed.

Kaila came to the table with refills for their coffee. Amy smiled and asked, "So, what do you do around here for your off time?"

"Well, I used to ride. I had a barrel horse — we were good together. I raced with my gelding, Beau, in Davie, up at the dude ranch, Kissimmee, wherever. But . . . well, I had to sell him. My folks passed away in debt."

"I'm so sorry," Amy said.

Kaila shrugged. "It's okay. I sold Beau to a friend in Kissimmee. When I make the money, I'll buy him back. I'm going to go to college. I'll start with junior college, but I'll get there."

"That's great," Hunter said.

"But now?" Amy asked.

Kaila laughed. "I go home and study! I'm going to get my bachelor's degree in media arts, and I study everything I can get my hands on."

Hunter had his phone out; he gave Amy an imperceptible nod.

He'd found her address online; they'd stop in on her later.

They both thanked her again; no, neither wanted ketchup for their hash browns.

Hunter glanced at his watch again.

"Let's stop by the motel before we head back to see Colby. I want to see if I can get someone into the prison. I want to know about the fellow who apparently managed to hang himself before he could testify against Ethan Morrison."

"We could go ourselves," Amy suggested.

"The prison is too far north. I don't want to leave yet. Gut feeling. Someone is going to give us something." He grinned. "I'll talk to your office — they know that system best. I do trust FDLE officers, you know."

She made a face at him.

He laughed.

They ate, and though they weren't in a hurry, they both ate quickly.

"You don't mind me getting the bill?" Hunter asked her.

"Hell no. A fed is in charge — put it on a federal bill," she said.

He nodded and paid Kaila with his card. Amy noted he left the girl a generous tip. She would have done the same.

Back on the road, he had her drive again; he was putting through a call.

The FDLE agent he was seeking was going to have to call him back, but he would do so shortly. By the time they reached the motel, his phone buzzed.

Amy opened the door to her room, and Hunter followed her in. She heard him speaking to an agent named Carl Winter. And then he listened. And listened. Finally, he thanked the man, ended the call and looked at Amy.

"Well?" she prompted.

"I don't think there's a lawman in the state who didn't think that witness's suicide was a murder. But there was no way to prove it. It happened during a shift change, and the witness, one Samuel Hornby, was out in the yard, but in a corner. And, of course, no one saw anything. He hanged himself from a fence — with strips ripped off his uniform."

"Right. Okay," Amy said, "you want gut feeling? He was murdered. And you want more gut feeling? Ethan Morrison is involved in this somehow."

"And so is someone local," Hunter said.

"On to Colby now?" she asked.

"Yes," he said. "I'll call Dr. Carver on the way. I want to see if any of the toxicology has come back."

Before he could make his call, his phone rang. He stood dead still as he listened to the caller, his face darkening and furrowing into a frown.

"Hunter?"

"We're not going to see Colby now," he said, and looked at her, meeting her eyes. "We have another victim."

"Where?"

"Here. Right here," he said quietly.

7

Seconds ticked by. Seconds that were like hours. Every noise in the quiet woods felt like a thunderclap. His own panicky heartbeat seemed loud.

Sam wondered how he had been so blind, so willing to believe. So desperate that there had to be a better world, where a man cared for those around him and the sick and the elderly. Where color and ethnicity, sex and sexual orientation, all were equal.

How?

They had slid into it all slowly. And he was in love. Jessie had been so determined to leave behind everything she had learned during her upbringing.

She'd been pregnant with Cameron, and she and Sam both wanted marriage immediately. When she'd told her parents, they'd demanded she rid herself of the baby

157

— and Sam. She had been raised to so much more. She had the best education. She had them behind her. She could rule the business world.

Maybe they weren't cruel people — maybe they'd really believed the world they could give Jessie was worth all they asked of her.

And maybe, for some, living life among the elite was something of a religion.

But Jessie, with her generous heart and loving personality, didn't buy any of it.

Despite all that, it hadn't been easy for her. She hadn't finished with the elite education; her pregnancy started to interfere, and she figured she'd have to drop out when the baby was born, anyway. Sam had to work endless hours, which was all right — after those endless hours, he was with Jessie.

But it was somewhere in that time of working, struggling and knowing she could never go home that Jessie became close with an older man she'd met at the park. His name was Robbie, and he referred to himself as Brother Robbie. He told Jess he liked to come to the park, but he lived out in the valley, far from the insanity he sometimes watched in the heart of the city.

Jessie had thought he'd needed help, that he sat on his bench, hungry, but too proud to ask for any kind of handout. She would make sandwiches, go to the park with those sandwiches and convince him she had gotten carried away, and just had too much to eat herself.

He was often there with a gray-haired, middle-aged woman who seemed to be the epitome of kindness. She called herself Sister Sarah.

After Cameron was born, Sarah was a frequent visitor to Sam and Jessie's little studio apartment. She wanted to help; people all needed help, she told them cheerfully. Then Brother Robbie would come along, as well, and as time passed, they talked about their home out in the valley, a place where everyone worked for the benefit of all.

Robbie talked about God, and the way some truly served Him.

Sam and Jessie had both grown up in traditional religions; they had always had faith.

And slowly, slowly, they had been shown the wonder of the community where Sister Sarah and Brother Robbie lived.

It seemed like a paradise. There was land, and the people of the community farmed it. They did so much themselves.

Then Sam and Jessie agreed to go to their

first service in the valley, and they met Brother William for the first time. He was the head of the community, and he seemed so warm and jovial. His teachings felt right. Sam believed that a man's time on earth was short; eternity was — well, eternity. On earth, man was to care for his brother — and leave behind a legacy of love for his children.

Sam was twenty-three when they were set up on their little spit of land, and for a time, it seemed life was beautiful. Every word Brother William preached was good; the community worked together, built structures, grew their own food, cared for the land. They tended to the elderly and cared for the sick.

The sick, Sam thought. *Sickness — that was when he first discovered he didn't agree with every word out of Brother William's mouth.*

He'd been working to repair the roof of the church when he'd overheard a conversation between Brother William and Sister Alma — a woman who was one of the man's cousins.

She wanted to leave. Brother William had wanted her to marry one of his deacons, an older man, and Alma did not want to marry him. She argued with William, telling him the man was too old for her, that she was restless, that she didn't want to farm.

William told her no one left the community.

Alma told him no one else might leave, but she intended to. And he was lying to her; others *had* left. They'd left, and never come back.

Alma might have been planning to go, but she didn't get the chance. By the next week, she was sick, burning up with a fever that wouldn't go away.

Sam thought Alma needed to get to a hospital. Her illness seemed beyond what they could handle in the community. Brother William told the group that if Alma was pure of heart, God would heal her. He was afraid sin weighed heavy on Alma's heart. But by enduring her illness before falling into the arms of the great Higher Power, she could earn back an entrance into heaven.

Somehow, Sam managed not to tell Brother William his words were a crock.

Alma died.

And Sam began to wonder if Alma had been right — if others had left, disappeared, moved away not just from the community but from the county and the state.

Had they really managed to leave?

161

By then, Jessie had taken the indoctrination to heart, and she couldn't believe anything bad of Brother William. He was a chosen leader of God, and their duty was to pray for him, and obey him in all things. He was the Word of God in the flesh.

It wasn't until Brother William turned his eyes on Jessie in a different way that she began to see the light.

They hadn't realized that, even living there as they did, Brother William considered the men to be the Servants of God — and the women to be servants of Brother William. He called all the single women in the community his wives; there were several, and it appeared they were wives in that Brother William cared for them.

But they'd been blind to so much as the first years passed. Sam knew Jessie had so desperately wanted to believe in a world where people always helped each other, where all were equal — where a man with her father's wealth didn't ignore another who was down and out and starving on the streets.

Sam had started to notice the strange whispering that went on, plans that didn't include all the commune's members, and the way that hard work was fine for some while others were part of the whispered plans. He'd liked sharing, and he didn't mind working, and he loved that the people around him seemed to be good and giving. But he'd felt himself questioning the way that women were brought to the compound, some of them young — too young.

While hauling farm equipment one day, he'd also noted a stockpile of arms in one of the warehouses.

Almost as if they were preparing to go to war.

He could remember the day Jessie had walked back into their kitchen, white as parchment. "He told me to come to him tonight. It's my time to serve," Jessie said shakily.

There was enough of himself left in Sam that the very thought instantly infuriated him.

"Don't go."

"He said —"

"And I say you're a married woman. A mother, a wife already. My wife."

Jessie didn't go. And for a while, the matter lapsed.

Brother William had a new wife — a young woman he had recently met and charmed into joining their community.

Her name was Alana. She was bright and cheerful, giving and beautiful. Everyone

163

liked her, and little Cameron had loved her dearly. She wasn't much more than a child herself. She played games, and she helped with every manner of task; she sang and danced joyously at their gatherings.

She also had a brother. Her brother sent police out to the compound. It was wrong that families couldn't communicate with their loved ones.

That day, they discovered that Brother William's deacons were not all about God's scripture; Sam knew they had weapons, and they were ready to use them if things went badly.

Brother William took the police around the compound. He showed them hardworking people who loved what they were doing.

The police might not have liked it, but it didn't appear Brother William and his deacons were doing anything wrong or illegal. People had the right to live the way they chose, even if it meant living so . . . strangely.

They didn't find the stockpile of weapons.

It was the next week that Cameron had stumbled upon Alana. Dead.

Brother William made another alarming demand of Jessie: she would have a week of sleeping alone in the "cleansing" chamber. She and Sam were no more; she would now honor, obey and sleep with Brother William when he chose.

Miraculously, it was Alana's brother — worried when she broke ties with her family — who convinced the FBI that something was very wrong. And an undercover agent from the FBI had come in. They'd already heard rumors about illegal arms being amassed. He and Sam had connected. And they had made their plan to flee, Sam swearing he would tell the courts everything he knew. And there were others, Sam could swear, who would tell the truth about things that happened at the compound.

There were others like him. Disenchanted with the cult, furious with Brother William's Divine Right demands — and yet so terrified for a wife or a child they did nothing.

The plan had been made.

They had run in the deep darkness of the night, ready to meet with their saviors as dawn broke over the hills.

A sob escaped Jessie now. Sam clamped his hand over her mouth, whispering a soft warning.

There was movement before them in the trees.

He prayed then, as he had never prayed before.

And the seconds ticked by.

165

8

Amy and Hunter were on the scene before anyone else. That was because the person who had called Hunter had been none other than their host at the motel, Martin Sanders.

Sanders had called Hunter the minute he'd stumbled upon the body while cleaning up in back. In panic, he had reached for Hunter's card.

Hunter had called it in to his headquarters, who in turn notified local authorities even as he and Amy hurried back to the motel.

The victim was a distance into the rich trees and bracken that grew behind the little patch of backyard. Martin Sanders, white as a sheet and sweating profusely when they reached him, said he'd followed a loud buzzing sound to find her, thinking that he had a dead raccoon or possum back there. The growth had apparently been too thick for the vultures. He reluctantly led them to what he'd found.

It had been a long time since she'd been sick at a scene, but Amy swallowed hard and tried to breathe in a manner that would keep her from retching. She'd had to step closer than she wanted to in order to ascertain with any certainty that the corpse was real and that it was the body of a woman. It was impossible to guess what had killed her; it was almost impossible to see she was naked. She was covered by a swarming hill of ants, and flies buzzed around so thickly they almost appeared to be a blanket.

Amy's first feeling was horror.

Her second was deep and profound sorrow and failure. They hadn't caught the killers; the killers had struck again.

Despite their distance from heavily populated areas, sirens were soon heard. Detective Victor Mulberry was quickly there, alone in his car, but the local forensics department was right behind him. Dr. Carver reached them with applaudable speed, along with his assistants and morgue vehicle. Amy was glad the FBI had taken over and Hunter was lead investigator on the case. He did the talking to the others. Nothing had been moved; they had not touched the corpse.

Dr. Carver quickly went to work, getting help from his assistants and forensics. He needed to capture some of the insects on the body, and get rid of others so he could give it his initial inspection.

While Carver and his team worked, Amy and Hunter stood in a line with Detective Mulberry, watching as Carver inspected the body and the forensic team carefully inspected the area. Aidan Cypress was working the scene, Amy saw, and she was glad. Cypress had grown up just an hour or so south of where they were; he knew the landscape here as few others would.

She stepped back as the team moved in, her movement instinctive as the swarm of flies and other flying creatures took flight at the disturbance.

She and Aidan looked at each other.

"Ants," he said quietly.

"Pardon?"

"I'm not the ME, but I'd bet a bundle they're going to discover that she was killed by some form of army ant. There are hundreds of kinds of army ants, but . . . the way the body looks, I'd say that's what happened."

"There are . . . large colonies of army ants around here?" she asked him.

He shook his head. "No."

"But —"

"I had several classes in entomology at the university, but I also had a cousin who had been traveling, bought a colony of the suckers and forgot to cover their dome one night. Another cousin woke up screaming. A small colony had started feasting on him while he was sleeping. I'll never forget how quickly they did a number on his skin." He hesitated. "I'm not the medical examiner or a detective, Amy, but I'm going to suggest the ants were brought in on purpose. Not that they don't exist in North America — they do. But a colony that could do that to someone . . . wherever they came from, it was planned."

"Pestilence," she said softly.

"Are you all right?" Aidan asked her.

She shook her head. "We . . . we didn't stop this."

"Amy, this corpse — and some of the insects at least — were brought here. I'm going to bet, too, she's been dead for several days. They held her somewhere and had the insect population under their control. They brought her here to let other forest creatures finish her off."

"Last night?" she asked softly.

He shook his head. "I don't think so. I think she'd have been here right around the same time we found the other woman on the cross." He hesitated. "Don't go thinking you could have stopped this. It likely happened before you were on the case."

"Thanks, Aidan," she told him.

She looked over to where Hunter was standing, a few feet away, and caught his eye. Amy thought he had probably heard her conversation with Aidan, as well.

Dr. Carver swatted at a flying bug, left the corpse and approached them. His expression was grim and he had a sheen of perspiration on his face.

"Insects," he said.

"Lots of them," Hunter agreed. "But did they kill her?"

"I'm going to have to get her to the morgue, get her cleaned up enough so that I can do a thorough inspection and autopsy. Honestly, there's been a lot of damage. A form of army ant has been at work on her along with any number of other creatures — worms, flies, you name it." He hesitated. "She's, uh, still being compromised as we speak, so we'll have what's on her now to study —"

"Compromised?" Mulberry said.

"They're still consuming the body," Hunter said quietly. His expression remained hard and dark. Amy wondered if he, too, had thought at first they might have stopped this.

Mulberry made a sound in his throat and turned away.

"She could have been dead before the insects started?" Hunter asked.

"I'll get right on this. We have fine entomologists in the forensics department locally, but any evidence or . . . anything can be handed over to the FBI."

"We're going to need to know, if possible, how she died — and when," Hunter said.

"An exact time is going to be difficult, but the entomologists will help in that area. Even when you have army ants, as you see, there are flies, and larvae, and growth stages," Carver said.

Hunter looked at Mulberry. "You good to stay here?" he asked.

Journalists were starting to arrive. Mulberry's men were keeping the trucks and cameras back on the main road.

"I've got this. Do what you need to do," Mulberry said.

"We're almost ready to get her to the morgue — and keep this from becoming a dog and pony show," Carver told them.

"Thank you," Hunter said. "Amy?"

She nodded, and Hunter turned away from the scene. She followed as he walked

171

toward the motel owner's little house. They had already talked to the man, of course. Sanders knew he would have to give a statement, but Hunter had let him go back to the house since he'd been such a wreck.

Hunter knocked at the door. Martin Sanders answered it, still ashen, still shaking.

"It's . . . it's . . . she's . . . gone?" he asked.

"They'll be heading to the morgue soon," Hunter told him.

Sanders nodded. A woman came up behind him; she had long white hair and a cherubic face, big blue eyes and a look of sorrow and concern on her face. "I'm Patty," she said. "I'm sorry we haven't met yet. I'm in the middle of chemo treatments and I'm afraid I spend a lot of my time resting."

"Patty, good to meet you. We're so sorry regarding the circumstances," Amy told her. "Of course you must rest. That's so important in the middle of chemo treatments."

"You have a loved one with cancer?" Patty asked her.

"Everyone has a loved one or friend with cancer," Amy told her. "But thankfully, you may well beat it."

"That's what Martin keeps telling me. Maybe I will. Martin, my love, let's not leave these young people standing here. Invite them in," Patty said.

Patty might need her rest, but she — or possibly the motel's housekeepers — kept their home neat and clean. Patty asked them to sit at the dining room table and offered them something to drink. Both Amy and Hunter demurred.

"I think Martin needs some water," Patty said. "Or a double bourbon."

"I'm all right, Patty, please sit. Don't let me worry about you, too, now — more than I do already."

They took seats at the table, Martin and Patty facing each other with Amy and Hunter between them.

Martin Sanders spoke, not meeting their eyes, still seeing an image of the dead woman that must have been locked in his mind.

"I didn't do it," he said. "Oh, God, I didn't do it. I couldn't. I could never have done anything like that. I know she's on my property, but I swear to you . . . . oh, God. I didn't do this."

People could lie. They could pull off extraordinary lies — and the best profiler who had ever studied human nature could be fooled.

But Amy couldn't believe Martin Sanders

173

or his wife could have been involved with this.

"Mr. Sanders, we don't think you killed the young woman," Hunter said.

Amy was glad he spoke sincerely. But then Hunter added, "But you do know something. I believe you know more about the missing woman, Wilhelmina, or Billie, than you've been telling us. And I think you're very afraid this might be her."

Sanders covered his face with his hands. Patty stood, coming behind him, curling her arms around his shoulders.

"It's okay, Martin. We should have told them."

"It's really okay," Amy said, setting a hand on his where it lay on the table. "Please, we don't think you're a suspect in this. What we need is your help."

"Tell them. Talk to them, Martin!" Patty said firmly.

He sighed deeply, shaking his head. "She came here — just as I told you. And just as I told you, when I said she needed ID and a credit card, she was disappointed — and she walked away. But . . ."

"But?" Amy encouraged.

"I couldn't let her go," Martin said.

"He's a good man," Patty said, indicating her husband. "He asked me if it was okay,

174

and I said, yes, we must help her."

"So, you did," Amy said. "You are good people."

Martin didn't appear to be as trusting as Patty. He studied Amy through narrowed eyes.

"I told her the heyday of our place was long over. We were never full. I said I wouldn't rent her a room, but I'd give her a key. She was welcome to stay."

"And then?"

"I brought her some dinner that night," Patty told them. "She cried when she thanked me. Such a beautiful soul! I asked if there was anything we could do for her, and she just said we'd done so much already. And she stayed — I brought her food in the evenings — until the day you checked in. Then she was just gone."

"I wanted to reach her. I think she was afraid of someone local. I wanted to assure her you weren't local," Martin said.

Hunter glanced over at Amy, frowning, and asked, "She was afraid of local law enforcement?"

"Oh, no, not specifically. I've known Victor Mulberry for years. He's a good man, and I tried to tell Billie he was. But she begged us to keep her presence secret. I think she was just afraid of anyone being friends with

175

everyone else around here."

"We talked about it, and that's what we believe, anyway," Patty said. She sighed. "She told me she just had to get away, far away, somewhere she could blend into a crowd."

"I offered to drive her. She didn't even trust me," Martin said. He put his hands over his face again and started to sob. Patty hugged him more tightly. From under his hands, he said, "I saw the body. I was so afraid. So afraid." He looked at them, his face red and tearstained. "It's not her, please. I was so afraid!"

"According to the ME thus far, no, it can't be Billie — not if you saw her the day we arrived," Hunter assured him.

"Then it's some other poor girl," Patty said.

"Some other poor girl. Special Agent Forrest, what the hell is going on here?" Martin said, shaking his head.

Hunter leaned across the table and spoke with controlled passion. "Martin, right now, I don't know. But I promise you, I won't rest until we get the people doing this." He glanced at Amy and amended his words. "We won't rest until we discover the truth. I promise you that."

"But there is something we have to ask

176

you," Amy said.

"We want to help," Patty told her.

"I know you do. So, if you hear from Billie, if you see her — please, you must convince her she can trust us, come to us. We can protect her."

"Like that witness was protected in jail, right?" Patty muttered. "That really filled up the news for days on end!"

Amy glanced at Hunter; it would be nice to have an answer to that "suicide."

"She needs to come to one of us. I swear, I would never leave her under the protection of anyone I didn't trust completely," Hunter said. "She won't be in prison. She'd be in protective custody, and trust me, I know the best men — and women — to watch over her."

"If she calls us again or comes back," Patty said softly. "Especially after this."

"Martin, did you go out last night, hoping Billie had come back?" Hunter asked.

Martin sighed. "Yes, and I knocked over one of the big garbage bins. I thought . . . I thought I heard something. Maybe I did. Maybe those bastards were killing that poor woman right beneath my nose."

"No, Martin, like I said," Hunter told him. "The ME thinks she was killed before, that . . . well, he thinks she was killed a few

177

days ago. She was just left to be . . . found recently."

He glanced over at Amy. She knew what he was thinking.

The woman had been left out for the insects to finish consuming her, down to the bone. She was meant to be found, but not in any recognizable condition.

"Are we in danger?" Patty asked suddenly, her frown fierce.

"I don't believe so. You have each other, and if you disappeared, you'd be missed. But another agent will be taking a room here for the next few nights, if that's all right with you. He'll be here tonight, and he'll be keeping an eye on things, too. His name is Ryan Anders. Special Agent Ryan Anders, and I think you'll find him trustworthy, as well."

"We'll get him set up right next to you, Special Agent Forrest," Martin said.

"Maybe on the other side of Special Agent Larson," Patty said.

"Whichever," Hunter told them. He glanced at Amy. "Agent Larson is pretty good at taking care of herself."

"Of course," Patty said. "I didn't mean to imply — oh, yes, sorry. I guess I was."

"It's all right, Patty," Amy assured her. "We all need others to watch our backs."

178

"I'm sure glad she has mine," Hunter said, rising.

Amy followed suit, as did Patty and Martin.

"One more thing," Hunter said. "And please, think carefully. Have you seen anything unusual around the motel?"

They looked at each other and shook their heads.

"I mean . . . Well, I guess we just don't expect things like this to happen and don't spend time watching for bad things?" Patty said weakly, the words a question to them, and herself.

"I do have a rifle," Martin said. "I don't have a pool, but where we are . . . well, I'm prepared for an aggressive gator."

"Or human being," Patty added. "Unfortunately, we don't have an alarm system."

"Even our room keys, as you've noticed, I'm sure, are older than dirt," Martin added.

"You'll be okay. Just . . . stay vigilant. You know, I can call in — get someone to watch over this place, if you'd like," Hunter said.

Patty looked at her husband; Martin held her gaze. "No," he said softly, addressing Patty rather than the two of them. "But, Patty, I'm not worried about me. I worry about you —"

"You think I'm more afraid of those

bastards than I am of chemotherapy?" Patty asked him. "I think I'm going to put my faith is something high." She looked straight at Amy and Hunter and said, "I've had incredible years, and if I'm lucky, I'll get a few more. But I'd trade my old life for that young lady's years in a heartbeat. Don't you worry — Martin knows how to use his shotgun. And he wields it well, with damned good ammunition. You ever try to pierce a gator's skin?"

Amy smiled. "No, I've never tried."

"You tell me if you change your mind," Hunter said, addressing Martin and Patty.

He and Amy took their leave at last. Hunter headed toward the driver's seat and Amy didn't protest.

Sliding into the passenger's seat, she said, "Please tell me you think they're the real deal?"

He smiled. "I do. But remember, we could be wrong."

"He admitted to being out there last night."

"I don't see Martin Sanders for it," he said. "But all avenues remain open."

"Do they? What about Victor Mulberry? Why would anyone be afraid of local law enforcement?"

He was quiet, giving her words thought.

"Again, all avenues are open. Sometimes, people are complicit without knowing it, but Mulberry is an old, seasoned cop, with no suggestion of any form of corruption in his record — no hint there were ever even whispers."

"You know this?"

He nodded, glancing her way. "We have ways of finding things out," he told her.

At her look, he laughed. "Legal ones, I swear. There's no good in catching a bad guy if you wind up losing him in court. Hey, grab my phone and give Ryan a call. Catch him up on everything — make sure he checks on Martin and Patty Sanders when he gets back."

"He'll have to check with them if he wants to get in a room," she reminded him.

"Yes, true, but emphasize we want to make sure they're doing all right, that nothing else has happened in the area or with them."

"Got it."

When she ended her call, Amy glanced at the dashboard clock and groaned. "Look at the time! Do you still think we're going to find Pastor Colby at the church?"

"Yes."

"And why are you so sure?"

"Because news of bodies seems to spread

like wildfire. The press was out there right on the heels of law enforcement. Pastor Colby will be at church, reassuring the frightened and nervous among his flock. Also, he knows we're coming. Young Pastor Karyl will have told him."

"So, he'll be waiting."

He glanced her way again. "Oh, yes. Waiting, and most probably worrying over everything he's going to have to say."

"You're saying a man must be evil if he's rich?" Pastor Jared Colby asked.

Hunter smiled easily. "Pastor Colby, I said nothing of the kind. Those are your words."

Amy looked over at Hunter. "I know tons of wealthy people who are wonderful. I know you do, too," she said.

"Yes, but you've come to me over Ethan Morrison, having heard from someone that I have a friendship with him."

"Well, you do, right?" Amy asked.

Colby sighed. "What does this have to do with anything?" he asked.

"The young women who have died —" Hunter began.

"And you just came from a second murder site?" Colby asked weakly.

"Third, for me, but I believe it's the second to be part of a particular murder scenario," Hunter said. "We haven't been able to identify the young women. Which suggests they could be from elsewhere. Morrison owns several private detention camps for immigrants, and we know paperwork has been sketchy at those institutions, to say the least."

Colby stared at him blankly. "I still don't see what the thoroughness — or lack thereof — of Morrison's office personnel might have to do with this."

Hunter watched as Amy leaned forward, looking at the man earnestly. "Pastor Colby, we've seen your church, we visited a youth group, and I can tell that you are a caring and godly man. Surely, to you, sir, the life of every living soul is of value."

"But —"

Amy continued passionately. "Sir, we believe the women who are dead might be immigrants, young women full of hopes and dreams who crossed the border, wound up in a camp and were then seized and made sacrifices in some *ungodly* agenda."

"What?" Colby looked stunned. He also looked nervous. He sat back in his chair, staring at them both, wide-eyed, as he continued. "No. Ethan would never kill anyone. He might be a capitalist — we are a capitalist country. He likes money. But that

183

doesn't mean he would kill!"

"Do you know him well?" Hunter asked.

"I . . . Yes and no. I grew up near here — I still live in my old family home. And the Morrison family has property in the area. Ethan was here now and again when we were kids. He sees me sometimes, and I try to use that friendship to good end. I point out people who need help. He does contribute to charities, you know. He's a philanthropist! Yes, he makes money, but . . . I believe his detention centers are kept to high standards. I don't believe — I can't believe that Ethan Morrison could have anything to do with this!"

"What is his religion?" Amy asked, looking at him curiously. "Does he have one? I really need to read up on the man," she said, looking at Colby. "Of course we're asking you about him. Because he does own property out here. Almost bordering the first murder site," she said.

"He — he, well, he isn't a member of this church," Colby said. "But he is very generous. I think he's given donations to many churches. His family doesn't go way back or anything like that. I believe his father bought the land, and it was worked for a while — sugarcane. I've tried to renew Ethan's interests in this area. We do need conservation efforts done right — a way to see that the Everglades and water supplies are untainted or polluted. He could help a lot down here. There are tons of rich folks in Miami-Dade, Broward and Palm Beach counties along the coasts, but move inland and . . . plain folk!" he said, his sound cheerful and then the cheer fading as he shook his head. "Another young woman is dead?" he said weakly.

"Another young woman. Horribly murdered," Amy said, and her words were heartfelt.

The murder scene they had just left had been absolutely, stunningly, horrific. They'd have been robots not to have been affected by it, even needing time to emotionally recover. He couldn't think of an agent so jaded they wouldn't have been moved.

But time was something they didn't have.

"How did she die?" Colby asked weakly.

"Horribly," Amy said.

"Yes, but —"

"There hasn't been an autopsy yet and law enforcement is keeping details from the press," Hunter said. "We're already getting tons of tips — sadly, many from zealots who simply want to predict the end of the world."

"Maybe the end is coming," Colby said

on a breath. He looked distracted.

"When is the last time you saw Ethan Morrison?" Hunter asked Colby.

Colby lifted his hands. "Uh, maybe a month ago."

"What does he do when he comes here? Does he stay the night on his property?" Amy asked.

"I doubt it," Colby said.

They both waited.

He shrugged. "There's still a house out there on the property, as I said. And he pays maintenance people to keep it up. But . . . well, it's a house. It's nothing fancy. No room service or maid service. I just don't see . . . I'm not suggesting he's spoiled — he's just accustomed to creature comforts. Although . . ."

"Although?" Amy asked as Colby's voice trailed.

Colby seemed to be looking off into the distance. "When we were teenagers, the Morrisons were already rich. They weren't just into the land, agriculture or ranching or any such thing. They were making big money on the stock market. I believe Ethan is still big into pharmaceuticals, and I guess there's really big money there. But once, with a scout troop, we went on a camping trip. Some of the older kids teased him, and he said he could survive anywhere. He could do anything they could, and he wasn't afraid of creatures great or small. He would survive just fine in a tent and do great with a canteen of water and some jerky sticks. Of course, that was a long time ago now."

"Did his family attend any of the churches out here?" Amy asked.

"I think his mother attended this church. I didn't see him in any of my youth groups, but maybe he came by now and then. I don't think his dad was much of a church-goer." He hesitated. "His father ruled the roost, not his mom." He was quiet again. "Okay, so I guess his dad's god was money. And sometimes, I admit, a lot of Ethan's charity work is done to create tax breaks, but it's still charity. Being rich does not make a man a murderer, regardless of his religious practice."

"Of course not," Amy said. "Committing a murder — or conspiring to commit a murder, ordering one to be committed — that makes a murderer."

"Anyway," Hunter said quickly, "due to the proximity of his property, we wanted to speak with you. As before, if you think of anything that can help us, we'd be grateful."

"Me, too," Colby murmured. "These killings . . . My congregation is going to grow more frightened. I can tell them to have faith, but . . . the first girl. She was killed on a cross. That news is out there. That's frightening. What does it mean?"

"I think it means someone is abusing religion," Hunter said, and he stood, aware Amy joined him almost simultaneously, as if they did have a silent language between them. "Cults," Hunter said. "Most often, they're led by someone using the framework of religion. A charismatic speaker, like Jim Jones, or someone who can appeal to the young and disenfranchised, like Manson. There are still major cults operating around the country, you know. And cult leaders have openly asked congregants to bring assault weapons into their churches. They can convince parents that thirteen-year-old girls — and younger — are being touched by God when they have sex with the leader. The right speaker first lures people with faith and goodness and love and hope — and then any disobedience is seen as an affront to God. Alternatively, there are those who don't really bother too much with religion, but they convince people they have a rite or a program that can make them happy within, strong and ready to move mountains. It's a different kind of faith, but if it abuses the believer's rights, it's no less dangerous."

"Special Agent Forrest, we are nothing like that here!" Colby said, horrified.

"No, sir. Of course not," Hunter said, smiling. "But it's scary just how much of it does exist — out there. Thank you again for your time. And for any help you can give us. We never asked — how is your family? You have three children, right?"

"What?" Colby looked surprised and then wary. "My kids are fine. My wife . . . my wife died young, I regret to say. She was beautiful and sweet, and a good person. And my kids are great. Why?"

"Hunter is just being polite," Amy said, giving the man one of her disarming smiles. "We bug you, but never ask how you're doing, how the family is doing . . . Just hoping you're doing well in the midst of all this. And we do so appreciate all your help and your time."

"Right. I see. Sure. Yes, well, I'm doing fine — or at least okay," Colby said.

"Hey, are any of your children going to follow in your footsteps?" Hunter asked. "Become pastors?"

"Casey is in media. Jayden is in medicine. Chase just started college — he's up north in the state, figuring out what he wants to

189

do with his life."

"Sounds like they're all doing really well," Amy said. "Anyhow, thank you again."

She turned and started for the door. Hunter thanked him again and followed her. In the car, he paused for a minute, determining his next move.

He looked over at Amy. "I want to go to the morgue. It's a drive. An hour at least, in and then out."

"Were you thinking to leave me here?" she asked.

"I'm thinking it's your choice."

"I doubt Dr. Carver will be ready for autopsy."

"But the body, or what's left of it, will be ready for autopsy."

"What exactly are you looking for?" she asked.

He was silent a minute and then said quietly, "A brand."

She turned in her seat so she could look right at him. "A brand?" She seemed confused at how specific that was. "As in . . . the killer's initials?"

"I don't know if it would be the killer's initials. But it would be something that identified the woman as having been . . . his. A sign of some kind, something."

"Is that common in cults?" Amy asked.

He nodded. "It can be. Years ago, there was a cult. It wasn't even so much a religious cult — it was an organization for self-empowerment, to know yourself, become a better person. But it was a bizarre pyramid scheme — one man at the top, getting very rich off the 'courses' they offered. It was huge, hundreds of thousands of people took the classes and became members, many of them recruiters. But they had an offshoot, as well — and to be part of it, women were branded. Not against their will. They were convinced receiving the brand — something burned into their flesh — was a triumph of will and self-power. Same as sleeping with the founder — the act of sex with him lifted you to a higher plane. There was a side organization to his main group, run by a woman. In learning to be true to promises, they were taught a method in which they punished themselves if they didn't do something. The punishment was supposed to be self-empowering. Say, if they didn't get to work on time, they'd make themselves sleep on the floor the next night and then they'd learn to be on time. His second in command — or whatever one might have called her — told her followers they were getting tattoos, but when they showed up, it turned out they were being branded. To make sure they'd go through with it, they'd been ordered to write up notes to family, work or friends that they wouldn't want given out. Then, of course, they were also told they had no will, no self-strength, if they couldn't handle pain to be a member of such a strong group. The founder and his second in command are in prison now. He finally fell to child abuse charges because he decided he was so powerful he could go for underage girls. I don't remember what else they got him on, but at least his power seems to have ended. That's one. It's still very frightening to see how many men like him are in prison, with followers who didn't seem to mind giving their children over to obeying at any cost. And these followers are still out there, worshipping them."

Amy shook her head. "I wonder how . . . I mean, how do people fall beneath the spell of others like that? Willing to do anything."

He shrugged, clenching his teeth, and then spoke. "Charismatic leaders start by appealing to goodness and godliness. They prey upon the young and the lost. People disappointed with the mainstream can fall under that spell." He hesitated and looked her way. "Both Charles Manson and David Koresh were big on spouting Revelation. If you can convince someone they will rise above everyone else when those who didn't seek the right path are wiped off the face of the earth as the end descends, you've twisted young minds nicely. Some people grow up in cults. They learn that doctrine from the time they're born." He turned the key in the ignition. "Sometimes they escape."

There was a heavy pause as Amy considered his words.

She looked over at him. His grip on the steering wheel was tense. When she must have realized Hunter didn't want to add anything, Amy changed the subject. "I didn't sketch this morning. I can't believe it." She looked out the window. "I want to see Dr. Carver — and the corpse. I think I can be most useful going with you. Detective Mulberry is canvassing the locals, and Agent Anders will be back here soon to hold down the fort."

He nodded. "Right."

There were several phone calls to be made as they drove. His first was to Carver; his second was to his home office, reporting to his field director, and then finding out if anyone had gathered any more information on Ethan Morrison and his Florida properties — or on the children of Jared Colby.

He put the phone on speaker, introducing

Amy to Sheila, the agent doing the research. Then Sheila gave them what she had.

"Ethan Morrison spent many years down in your area there," Sheila told them. "His father made the family fortune, dabbling in sugarcane, but hitting the stock market, mainly pharmaceutical companies. He was a heavy investor in a company called Ever-Questing. They're always fighting to keep the cost of their drugs high," Sheila reported. "He likes to drive. A lot of his property is over the border in Georgia, but he's back and forth all the time — per his credit card expenses. Could he have been at the murder sites? Yes, for the woman who was found in Maclamara, Hunter. No, for South Florida — he's been at a convention in Atlanta for the past week. His own convention, by the way. 'Invest and Thrive: Empowerment for the Soul.' "

"All right, thanks, Sheila. Keep me posted on anything."

"He's in Florida right now, visiting his kid at college — North Central Florida."

"Okay. What about Pastor Colby's kids?" Hunter asked.

"Casey, good kid — has a nice business doing websites and web promotions. Jayden will be starting med school — he and Chase are at a Florida school, also north/central

194

part of the state — oh, yeah, this is interesting. Same college where Ethan Morrison's kids are going."

Hunter glanced at Amy.

"How far is the college from Maclamara, where the murder victim was found?"

"Ah . . . twenty miles," Sheila said. "Just twenty miles."

"Thanks. Again —"

"You know it. I'll keep on it, and keep you posted," Sheila told them.

Hunter ended the call, staring straight ahead.

"So," Amy murmured. "Colby's daughter has been going to church down in Miami, and his sons are upstate in college, where Morrison's sons are also in college."

"What do you want to bet they know each other?" Hunter asked dryly.

"We'll be looking into that?"

"You bet."

They both fell silent for a minute.

"You do realize how late it's going to be when we get there, right?" Amy said.

He nodded solemnly and reminded her, "A morgue is never really closed."

9

Carver didn't seem to be surprised they'd come to see the body again; he was glad to tell them she had been cleaned, and the insects and larvae feeding on her had been gathered and removed.

That was . . . a relief, Amy thought. Too late, but good.

"I know you haven't started the autopsy yet, but you've done an inspection. Did you find anything to indicate she had been stabbed, shot, slammed in the head — anything that might indicate a cause of death rather than by —"

"Come on, I'll show you what I know so far — and that included a few surprises."

They followed him into one of the morgue's holding rooms; he pulled out the drawer where the body lay. This time, despite the way the corpse disturbed her, Amy was ready with her sketch pad.

The body was respectfully clad in a sheet.

Somehow, it appeared even more incongruous.

The woman's face had been stripped of its first layer; there was not much left of her mouth.

Amy's pencil moved across the page as if by instinct as she stared at the corpse.

Despite the damage done to her, she thought Hunter was right.

It appeared that horns — demon horns — had been carved into her face. Even with so much flesh gone, some of the tissue and muscle structure remained.

Enough to show the deep gouges.

"Her wrists," Hunter murmured.

Carver nodded. "Yes. She was held somewhere. She fought desperately."

"Was she . . . eaten alive?" Hunter asked.

"Yes and no. At least by my educated guess so far," Carver said.

"How *did* she die?" Amy asked.

"Come, I'll show you."

They followed him into the next room. Lab equipment sat on sparkling clean tables. Smaller drawers here held evidence taken from bodies.

Carver drew out a plastic container. It held a bug — far bigger than an ant. To Amy, it appeared to be a spider, but different than any spider she had seen before.

And it was big. Her first thought was that it was a tarantula, but it seemed too slender. It wasn't moving.

"Him!" Carver said.

"And he is what kind of a spider?" Hunter asked.

"Phoneutria," Carver said with deadly seriousness.

"Oh. Of course. I see," Amy said, but she didn't see at all.

"He's a Brazilian wandering spider, sometimes called a banana spider. They can be found in northern South America, but they're not a regular denizen around here. I've sent pictures to Dr. Levy, Hunter."

"Levy will pin him down for sure," Hunter said. He turned to Amy. "He's based in our Miami office, and he's one of the best entomologists I've ever met."

"One spider killed her?" Amy asked.

He nodded. "You're welcome to come back tomorrow morning when I do the autopsy. I honestly don't think there is much more I'll be able to tell you then. This young woman was held somewhere and she was bitten by the spider. The poison was left to do its work. She was dead, or close to dead, when she was placed out in the wilderness. The ants were then set on her. That kind of ant, well, it stays as long as the food source remains. Naturally, as you know, there were flies and other creatures and critters involved, too." He hesitated. "I'm truly sorry to say her death would have taken time, though once the poison started its work, she wouldn't have been conscious."

Amy felt her fingers jerk as she drew the spider.

"It was . . . on her?" she asked.

"Dead, squashed," Carver said.

"I'd like to see the body one more time," Hunter said.

Amy glanced at him. Dr. Carver nodded, watching Hunter. "What specifically?"

"All right, it looks as if the same slashes were cut into this woman's face as were in our Jane Doe on the cross."

"I agree," Carver said. "But you're looking for more."

"Yes. I want to see our first Jane Doe again, and our second."

"What are you looking for?"

"A brand."

Carver frowned for a moment. Then he nodded. "So much damage to even the first body, but yes, let's go back and see if any of the injuries are covering any kind of a burn or a pattern. You say a brand, right, not a tattoo?"

"I believe we're looking for a brand. I

think this killer — the head of this cult, for lack of better terminology — is borrowing from things done in the past, from things done by cult leaders he admires or wants to emulate because it will make him look like a religious fanatic," Hunter said.

They walked back into the room with the crisp clean metal drawers where the bodies were stored.

Carver called for one of his assistants.

"We'll start with Jane Doe number one," he said.

Hunter nodded.

The body was brought out and wheeled into one of the autopsy rooms, lights flicking on as they went.

The dead woman was then placed on an autopsy table.

Amy kept her book out; with gloved hands, Carver and Hunter went over the body, slowly, meticulously.

"Doc?" Hunter said.

"What? Where?"

Hunter pointed to an area on the woman's inner thigh.

"There's a piece of flesh ripped away there, but . . . a scar. Yes, Hunter, that could have been caused by a burn!"

Only half of it was there.

Hunter went dead still, staring at it.

Yes, flesh was gone, as if had been sheared off by the rough wood of the cross. But something remained. A line . . . and near it and above it, the curve of a backward *C*.

He saw Amy was sketching it, even as Carver asked his assistant to take photographs.

When they were done, Jane Doe number one was returned to her drawer.

Jane Doe number two was brought out.

They didn't have to search as hard this time; Hunter knew where to look. And while the insects had dined on so much of the young woman's flesh, the brand on her was more recent.

A part of the backward *C* could be seen, along with a faint line that seemed to be underneath it this time.

When they were done, Hunter thanked Carver.

"Damned right you'd better thank me — I don't come in at this time of night for everyone," Carver told him. He spoke lightly, but then added, "Any time, Hunter, Amy. This is what I do. I look after the dead, and I try to speak for them. You come any time you think I might be able to make them say more. I want you to stop this."

"I have one more question for you," Hunter told him.

"Shoot."

"So far, we think it's young women. In their early twenties. Anything on their ethnicity?"

"Both are Caucasian," Carver said. "I've seen nothing that indicates where they might have been born. I am checking on something with one of our dental experts regarding X-rays on Jane Doe number one's teeth."

"Could they have come from Central or South America?" Hunter asked.

Carver grinned. "You know, we — North Americans — have a tendency to forget that most of the islands and Central and South America are immigrant places, as well. I know dark-skinned South Americans — and little blue-eyed blondes who speak Spanish or Portuguese as their first language. There were native tribes everywhere, but there has also been a lot of European immigration. Our first Jane Doe was light — light hair, light eyes. I believe this girl was a brunette. I don't know about her eye color — it doesn't exist anymore. Maybe tomorrow I'll be able to answer you. My dental expert is going to compare her fillings with those I have seen in some of my deceased patients from South American countries."

Hunter nodded. "Thank you."

"Are you heading back out to the motel in the boondocks?" Carver asked.

"We are," Amy told him.

"I'm going home — ten minutes away. And I'm going to start on Jane Doe number two first thing. I swear, I'll call you the minute I have anything." Carver looked at Hunter and managed a smile. "Please, go. Get some sleep. It's been one hell of a long day."

"It has. Amy?"

"I'm ready," she assured him.

They left the morgue. He was accustomed to driving, but he paused, looking at Amy. "Sorry, I don't mean to be taking over. Did you want to drive?"

"No, something is bugging me. I want to review my drawings while we head back."

"There's a plan," he said.

They rode in silence as he started out west. She had a penlight, and kept it close to her notebook as she went over her drawing, perplexed.

Hunter must have noticed her expression. "What is it?"

"I'm just trying to figure out what I see. I think I almost have it." She glanced up for a minute, grimacing. "Like something on the tip of your tongue, you know?"

"I do know. I was looking at it and I felt

that I should know . . . that I *do* know. But it's in the back of my mind somewhere."

"Maybe initials, or a symbol that is initials . . ."

Her phone started buzzing and she winced and looked at him. "Sorry," she murmured. "It's my brother."

"How many siblings?" he asked her.

"One," she told him, covering the phone. Then she spoke into it. "Linc! Hey, how are you?"

Hunter smiled. Amy made a face.

"Good, good. I'm just checking up on you!" her brother said.

"Lincoln, I'm fine."

"And you're working that bizarre case?"

"Yes, I'm working the case."

They worried about each other. It was natural that he had called.

"And John?" Lincoln had met her partner — and liked him.

"Believe it or not, he's been a good patient. John is doing great. His family is with him."

"But you're working without a partner."

"Don't worry. A case like this — you know that I'm not working it alone. Half the officers of every department in the state are working on it." She smiled, glancing at Hunter and shaking her head. "I'm not

204

working alone at any time, Lincoln. I've been paired with an FBI agent."

That, apparently, mollified her brother.

The call ended and she glanced at him apologetically.

"Older brother."

"What does he think of you being an investigator?"

"He's with the police in Richmond, Virginia," she told him. "He moved north for love — my sister-in-law is great. Our father was a Miami-Dade detective."

"Ah, a law enforcement family."

"Yep. What about you?"

He shook his head. "My dad is a writer. My mother is an artist, and teaches art."

"Cool. What does Dad write, and what does Mom draw?"

"Together, they do children's books."

"That's — that's great." She frowned. "What do they do separately?"

He laughed. "Oh, he writes all kinds of stuff. And she draws what she sees that she likes. They live in a little town in Maine."

"Nice."

"And your folks?"

"Retired — and right now, thank God, they're on an eco-trip in the Amazon."

"Thank God?"

"I'd be trying to get my dad to remember

that while I value his opinion in all matters, I can't just stay on the phone with him questioning everything."

Hunter nodded and looked ahead, and Amy followed his gaze to the dark road beyond the windscreen.

The good thing about it being very late at night, Hunter thought, was that there was no traffic.

The negative part of the drive was the complete and utter darkness.

It made it possible, though, to understand how people could have been out there — how they could have slammed a heavy stake/ cross into the ground and driven a spear into her heart without being seen. And the body had gone several hours without being discovered.

"Did you grow up in Maine?" Amy asked him.

"Not really. I was born in California. I spent some time here, though."

"Here? In this area?" she asked, surprised.

"Went to middle school in Broward County."

"Oh!"

He grinned at her quickly. "Learned to drive here."

She laughed. "Okay, so did I. We're both

defensive drivers."

He grinned and was surprised to realize how much he really liked her. He'd acknowledged she was attractive. Even with her hair pulled back and her staid suits, he found her huge eyes stunning. She had a knack for knowing when to be gracious — something he could be better at.

And he was so impressed by her drawings.

"Hey, when we get back, I'm going to snap a photo of your drawing. I'll study it while I drift off to sleep. Maybe whatever is burning at the back of our minds will come forth."

They arrived at the motel. The office was dark, but the nightlights fell over the parking lot.

Ryan's car was there, and Ryan was up. His door opened even as Hunter shut down the ignition.

"You didn't have to wait up," Hunter told him.

Ryan shrugged. "I couldn't sleep, anyway. AMC was showing one of my favorite old movies. Did you get anything else?"

"We think the women were branded," Hunter said.

"Branded? Like cows are branded?" Ryan asked.

Amy walked over to him with her sketchbook. "The bodies were . . . well, the flesh wasn't all there. This is as much as we got."

"Mean anything to you?" Hunter asked him.

Ryan shook his head. "I'm sorry."

"Did you get anything today?"

"I did get back in time for Mass and chatted with Father Brennan after. I enjoy talking to him. He says he's been thinking about Revelation since . . . since this began. In his mind, people use Revelation to try to scare others. Anyway, he came to the diner with me. He's not married, being a Catholic priest," he reminded them. "And we ran into Rabbi David. He was telling me if the world went by the Old Testament all the time, a good portion of people walking around might have already been stoned to death. Many things were punishable by stoning at one time. There were the laws of God — and the laws of man. The two of them were very philosophical — got a little heavy for me. But I can tell you this — they were both deeply disturbed about the second murder. Don't worry, I didn't give them any details. Oh, and when I got here, I checked in with Martin Sanders, and about an hour ago, I went to see him and his wife, and all was well."

"Good, thanks," Hunter told him.

"I think I'll just walk around and check the outside of their little house," Amy said. "See if they're still awake for any reason."

"I brought your bags," Ryan reminded them. "They're in my room."

"I'll get your things and set them in your room," Hunter told Amy, waving as she started to walk to the far end of the motel and skirt around the office.

"Thanks," she called back to him.

He didn't realize he was staring after her until Ryan said with admiration, "She's something, huh? Good for FDLE — they know how to recruit."

"Yes, she's an impressive agent," Hunter said. "Come on, it's late. We might as well try to get some sleep after the day we've had."

Sleep. Hell yeah.

They needed sleep. He knew he needed to close his eyes — for a few hours at least — and not see their Jane Does in his mind's eye.

They needed to be fresh; they needed their minds to be sharp.

They headed to Ryan's room and Hunter grabbed both small bags, asking Ryan if he'd had any trouble.

"None at all. You were already packed, and when I got to Amy's place, her friend was there. She timed everything so she could feed the cat and meet me, and all I had to do was grab the bag."

"Thanks."

Hunter headed out with both bags.

"Hey, I can help," Ryan said.

"I've got it."

Ryan still lingered just outside his door. Hunter headed into his room and set his bag down, then entered Amy's room, setting hers at the foot of her bed. He paused and went to the window and looked out.

Ryan was still outside, waiting.

There was no sign of Amy. But Martin and Patty might have been awake; she could be reassuring them.

But the fact that Amy hadn't walked straight back bothered Hunter. Gut reaction.

Not that she wasn't capable; it's just that what was happening here raised red flags at every turn.

It was past midnight; the older couple probably went to bed long before that time. Martin opened the office up early, so they had to be early risers.

Hunter went out to the parking lot. Everything was quiet. He walked over to Ryan. "I'm going to see what's up."

"Well, hell, then I'm coming with you,"

Ryan said.

Hunter paused. "Right. Good idea. You head to the front door. I'm going to cut to the side and watch. Knock, and see if everything is all right."

"And if it's not —"

"Like I said. I'll be there. And, Ryan?"

"Yeah?"

"Be ready for anything."

Ryan drew his gun out of its holster, but eased his arms around his back, so it wasn't visible. "Ready," he said.

Gut feeling.

Hunter drew out his Glock, as well.

Yep, gut feeling. Ready for anything.

"Please!"

The word was barely a whisper.

Patty Sanders was trembling so violently Amy feared she'd hurt herself on the knife blade at her throat before any harm could be purposely done to her.

But Patty Sanders did have a knife at her throat, scraping the flesh, causing a tiny trickle of blood to flow.

She stared at Amy, desperate pleading in her eyes.

Fear, one of Amy's instructors at the academy had told her, was an instinct, natural to most living beings, and it was a good instinct — it could keep a human being from falling into dangerous situations.

Letting fear become panic and overtake rational thought was when the fear itself became something dangerous.

Amy had always tried to act and react with those words in mind. But fear for *self* was one thing; this was another.

No matter how much she wanted to shoot the smug look off the young bastard's face.

Patty hadn't been the one to open the door after Amy, seeing that lights were on, had tentatively knocked.

"Come on, come in! Please, come tell Patty that you're back, and all is well!" Martin had said. "She's lying down. If you'll just come with me."

He'd seemed fine, though now Amy could see he was shaking, too.

Because once she was inside, Amy saw that Patty was being held with a knife at her throat and that a second assailant had a shotgun pointed at Martin.

Now, of course, the gun was on Amy.

The most bizarre thing about the picture, Amy thought, was the age of the two assailants — and the fact that she knew who they were.

Two of the teenage boys from Karyl Vine's youth group, the kid with the lock of dark hair that fell over his forehead and eye, and the blond young man who was still wearing the rock band T-shirt.

"You want her to live?" the boy holding the shotgun demanded.

Amy was confident with her own weapon; she was fast and accurate. But she had also been taught to weigh a situation, and at this moment, the lives of the hostages were at stake. She couldn't take down both boys at once, and she really didn't want to shoot the teenagers unless it proved there was no other choice.

They might also be part of something bigger and could lead Amy to where her investigation needed to go.

"What do you want?" she asked.

The dark-haired boy — wielding the shotgun — smiled at her. "You," he said.

"Really. Why?"

"Because you need to be cleansed. So you're gonna give me your gun, and we're leaving through the back. Now."

"We can't work it that way," Amy said. "Because if I give you my gun, I have nothing — and no guarantee you'll leave these people alone."

"I can shoot you right now," the dark-haired boy said.

"Hank, they want her!" the blond said.

He wasn't as cocky or assured. In fact, he seemed nervous. That was good and bad. His hand shook — and he had his knife against Patty's flesh.

"Me? I'm flattered."

"You should be," the blond managed to sputter.

Patty whimpered. Her eyes never left Amy's face; they were filled with terror.

Hunter and Ryan were out there, Amy thought. When she didn't return they would want to know why, and they would come check.

But how long would that take? The situation here was explosive. These young thugs were obviously new at this game, and that could make them more foolish — and more dangerous.

"All right, how about I kill one of them to show you what I mean, and leave the other?" the dark-haired boy — Hank — suggested.

"No," Amy said flatly. "No one dies here. Hank — that's your name, right? Let me think. I bet I'm a second choice. I think you believe Billie has been here, that she might have still been here, and she's the one who is really wanted by your great leader."

"Don't you mock the Divine Leader!" the blond cried. "He is trying to save the world, save all of our souls. For you . . . there will be pain, but the pain will cleanse you, and he'll save you, too."

"You just can't be that fucking crazy," Amy said flatly.

The kid gasped.

His hand still shook.

"Artie, shut the hell up!" Hank said.

He was staring angrily at Artie. Artie was glaring back at Hank.

It was her chance . . .

Suddenly, there was a knock at the door.

"Kill her, Artie. We'll just kill them both!" Hank shouted.

Amy acted; pitching herself in a roll toward Artie, she drew out her Glock.

Artie flew backward.

Hank took aim at her.

10

Hunter flattened himself against the side of the house, nodding at Ryan.

Ryan nodded in return and tapped at the door. "Martin! Hey, Martin, you guys are still up, right?" he called.

Hunter heard shouting; they couldn't wait. He burst past Ryan, throwing his entire weight and strength against the door.

It gave.

As he moved through the doorway, a shot rang out.

He surveyed the scene.

A blond kid was slammed against the wall; Patty Sanders was on the floor, sobbing hysterically. Amy was on the floor, too; she was the one who had fired, and a dark-haired boy was bleeding, but taking aim at Amy with a shotgun.

Hunter had a clean shot, and he took the boy in the shoulder, causing him to spin around without firing, screaming out in pain.

Amy was immediately on her feet, her Glock in her hand. "Patty, see to Martin!" she said firmly, walking toward the dark-haired boy.

Hunter recognized the kids; they had been in Karyl Vine's youth group that morning. Amy stomped toward the dark-haired boy, kicking the shotgun out of the way as she approached them. "I told you there were FBI agents here, you jerk," she began. "Now we are going to get you to a hospital and then you're going to tell us — stop!" she shrieked. "Hunter, stop him —"

The kid had reached into his pocket with his good hand and stuffed something into his mouth.

"No!" Hunter exclaimed, dropping down by the kid and reaching into his mouth.

Whatever he'd taken, it was gone already. And the kid was staring up at him, laughing.

"I'll rest among the clouds, with the Chosen! I'll have Eternity in beauty while you rot in the putrid fires and ashes of hell! They're coming, they're coming . . . all the Horsemen, they're coming!"

Hunter heard Amy swear; she lunged toward the blond kid, who was already trying to get his hand to his mouth.

Luckily, he was shaking too badly.

Amy was able to wrest the pill he was about to swallow from him.

The blond hadn't wanted to die.

"Artie, you're a wuss! Worse — a betrayer of the Divine Leader! You . . . you won't see Eternity, you won't . . . you'll rot in the fires in the deepest bowels of hell!" the dying kid screamed. "You . . . you spawn of the devil! You —"

His words were choked off in a cough; he was foaming at the mouth.

Hunter dialed Emergency, even though he knew it was too late.

But they had the blond kid, Artie. Amy had pocketed the pill she'd grabbed from him. He was obviously deflated and terrified now — because they had him, or because he was going to the deepest bowels of hell, Hunter didn't know.

Still, Amy was cuffing him, dragging him to his feet, while Ryan helped Patty up. She flew to her husband, who reached out his arms to her, white and shaking so badly that the two had to stumble to the couch and crash down on it.

Patty sobbed; Martin held her.

Hunter looked at Amy, a question in his eyes.

218

"I'm fine," she assured him. "But I must say, you two had impeccable timing. Thank you."

The sound of sirens filled the night. Emergency response teams arrived along with the van from the coroner's office.

Hunter called in to his supervisor; Amy called in to hers. They'd both discharged their weapons, but no one had been killed with them. Still, someone had died, and there would be paperwork to fill out. He knew they had responded by the book.

But there had been a death.

By then, they had Artie out in the back of Hunter's car. Hunter had tried to talk to him, but the boy had clammed up completely.

Amy had a softer touch, so Hunter had left her to it, but so far, all the kid had done was cry.

His ID showed that he was Arthur Claymore. He was eighteen, so it wasn't necessary to reach his parents before he was questioned.

To Hunter's surprise, it was Dr. Carver who came out with the response teams. His first words to Hunter were dry.

"Really? Tonight?"

"What the hell are you doing out here? The county has other medical examiners."

"I asked to be sent out on anything to do with this case. The powers that be agreed. Figure I'll get a break when this is solved. You do plan on solving all this, right?"

"We won't stop until we do," Hunter assured him.

"It's a shame. This kid."

"He meant to kill Amy, and yet, you're right — it's a shame. He was a kid. What did he take? Cyanide?"

"That would be my guess. You can smell it," Carver said.

"We have one of the pills. The other kid didn't manage to get his in his mouth," Hunter told him. "It's in an evidence bag."

"Well, we'll get it to the lab," Carver said. He looked at the dead boy he'd bent over just moments before. "And we'll get him to the morgue."

"How the hell do these kids have cyanide pills?" Hunter asked, shaking his head.

"I'm not the detective or the investigator," Carver said, "but even I can speculate that adults — with finances to pull this all off — are behind it."

"Pharmaceuticals," Hunter murmured.

"What?"

"If you have big money in pharmaceuticals, I guess you can get what you want. Anyway, I have to report in, and Amy is going to have to report in, and the paperwork is going to be endless. I'm hoping she's getting something from our suspect. I've been ordered to take him down to our Miami offices, where he'll stay held until charges are determined."

So much for a few hours of desperately needed sleep.

Patty and Martin were barely coherent, but even in that, they thanked Hunter, Amy and Ryan, certain the young people would have killed them.

"Maybe not the blond kid. I don't think he knew it would go so bad," Martin said. "But that dark-haired boy, he was like . . . possessed!"

Patty sobbed again. "We're alive! We're alive!"

Victor Mulberry arrived, a little late to the scene, looking a bit rumpled and bleary-eyed. "I might as well move out here. What the hell is going on? People all seem to have lost it!"

"Letting someone convince you that killing is a way to reach God . . . it's hard to understand," Hunter told him.

"I won't lie," the detective said, watching Carver instruct his assistants on securing the body of the dead boy. "I'm scared of

221

how far this might go." Mulberry then turned to Hunter. "All right, then, I've got this. You do what you need to do."

Ryan walked over to Hunter.

"Mr. and Mrs. Sanders have asked if I can stay for the rest of the night."

Hunter nodded. "Fine. Amy and I will get Artie down to Miami."

A few minutes later, he was finally in the car with their bags. Artie remained hand-cuffed in the back seat.

Amy was still sitting next to the boy. "I think I'll just stay back here for the drive," she said lightly.

Hunter glanced at her, wondering if she'd gotten anything from him at all. She didn't speak, and he knew they'd have a chance later to talk. He nodded.

Soon after they started out, the boy wailed, "I want to die! I need to die. Why was I such a coward? I'll never reach the clouds, the heavens — I'll never come to divinity. I'm going to be caught in the fires that are coming, lost forever, burning, hurt-ing . . . I'm such a coward!"

"You're not a coward. You're a sensible young man," Amy told him. "Artie, in your heart, you know all this is wrong. You didn't want to hurt Mrs. Sanders. You were just more afraid of Hank than you were of me

— of us — of the truth."

The boy started sobbing.

Hunter kept silent. Amy had built up a rapport with Artie. He meant to let her build on what she had started.

"Artie, whoever has been telling you all this is lying," Amy said.

"No, no, because . . . because what Hank promised me came true before. It will come true again," Artie said.

"What came true? What did he promise you? Was it Hank, or someone else?"

Artie shook his head. He was silent for a long moment. Then he blurted, "I'm not a Hank . . . an anybody. I never had . . . girls don't . . . And then there was a woman. I . . . Love is life. Being with someone, that's part of love. On my own . . . when I vowed to help Hank . . . I didn't know . . . I mean, I didn't know that it meant killing. I wasn't there before . . . I knew, yeah, Hank was there, that he helped. He said it was beautiful, that the heavens opened to take the girl's soul . . . the one they called Lady Liberty."

"Artie, Lady Liberty . . . she was the young woman on the cross?"

He started sobbing again. "She . . . yes. She was . . . with me. She came to me at night. Then Hank told me she had been

223

chosen. That she was so lucky. She would face the pain and the sacrifice that would allow her to soar up and sit on the highest clouds and know nothing but love and grace and happiness for eternity. And now I . . . now I will burn!" he whispered.

Amy snapped at him firmly then. "Artie, that is bull — pure, simple bull! That girl died in agony, and it was cruel and brutal and horrible. And she didn't die for any reason — there is no divine human being, no Divine Leader. Hank fed you a total crock of bull!"

Hunter wondered at her logic — suddenly becoming so fierce and firm when she had been so sweet.

But she might have pulled it off just right.

"Really? Do you think —"

"Artie, you were brainwashed. It might be hard for you to see it, but you were brainwashed! And you're young. You're a handsome boy. There will be a girl out there, sometime. You know in your heart that killing is wrong! Think of the Ten Commandments. Thou shall not kill!"

Artie started to sob again.

"You didn't kill anyone yet, Artie. That's what you told me. You said Hank was there, though. At least for the young woman on the cross, the woman you called Lady

Liberty. Artie, do you know who was there with him? Did this 'Divine Leader' take part?"

"He leads us in the way of righteousness. We listen, and we obey, because he is the Divine Leader."

"Artie, that's all over. There is no Divine Leader. There is a man out there telling you things, preying on your weaknesses, convincing you that you will have both earthly desires and a cloud in heaven. But, Artie, it's all lies. So, help us — help us stop the horror of killing. Do you need pictures of Lady Liberty on the autopsy table? I'm sure we can get them to you."

"No, no, they couldn't have . . . they said she would rise, know happiness forever, that she would be loved and live in grace . . ."

"Artie, no. They murdered her, brutally."

He began to cry again.

Hunter glanced back; Amy had set an arm around Artie's shoulders.

"Artie, we need to know — please help us! We need to know who else was there when she was killed. Who killed the woman we found today?"

"Hank and the Brothers from the north."

"Hank was the only one you know who was involved?"

"I know Hank was there. He told me he

saw her soul rise to heaven, that he saw her laughing. The great Brothers, apostles of the Divine Leader, came, and they commanded he needed to witness."

"Why weren't you invited?" Amy asked him.

"I am too raw, too new. Only deep believers, accepted believers, those who wear the sign of the Divine Leader, can take part."

Hunter briefly caught Amy's gaze through the rearview mirror.

She was going to stop for the moment, he knew. Artie was far too weepy to make any more sense. He'd be held overnight, and then they'd start in the morning.

An agent was waiting for them at the entrance to the facilities in Miami.

The agent took custody of Artie and studied them as he gave Hunter a set of keys. "It's not far from here, in Coconut Grove. It's our house for times such as this. Stocked with everything you'll need. You two sure as hell look like you could use some sleep." He grimaced. "Sorry. You know what I mean. Get some rest. We'll see this young man is safe and looked after."

Amy told him, "Thank you."

"Thank *you*. I understand we're working tightly on this one with FDLE and members of the local forces around the state. Hell of

226

a case, from what I've read, from the briefings we've been given. And a big state to cover, so it seems."

They both thanked him and headed back for the car. Hunter knew exactly where the little house was — down the street from a police station.

Hunter unlocked the door and followed the alarm instructions on the key chain. Amy entered and looked around.

It was an old place for the area, a small but charming Mediterranean house with a barrel-tile roof, probably built in the late 1920s or early 1930s. There was a large living room with a handsome mantel carved out of coral rock. A dining room led to a nice-size kitchen, and a hallway led to bedrooms to the left of the entry.

"The bedrooms are down that way," Hunter advised her.

She smiled at him. "Cool. I'll take the first room."

She paused, looking at him.

It was just a moment.

It struck Hunter that it was probably a good thing for them both that they were keeling over with exhaustion. Because he looked back at her. Her eyes appeared almost luminescent in the sparse light falling on them from the hallway.

The way she stood enhanced the sleek length and beautiful grace of her body, and even hinted at the curves that lurked beneath.

He thought of her hands, the length of her fingers.

The way she spoke, the way she moved.

In that minute, he imagined . . . the two them, simply dropping everything, and him sweeping her off her feet into an embrace . . .

She gave him a crooked smile. The moment broke. He wasn't sure if he turned, or if she turned. Or if maybe, just maybe, she had envisioned the same thing, and the fact of who they were and why they were together swept in. Just his imagination, of course. All in his head.

And yet, in that moment, he wondered if they hadn't shared their thoughts, as they sometimes seemed to do . . .

She headed down the hall. He heard the bedroom door close.

Despite the fact that the house was an FBI holding and had a top-notch alarm system, Hunter still checked the back door that led out from the kitchen, and then the front door again.

He was beyond exhausted, and he still feared he wouldn't sleep.

He told himself he'd be thinking over the events of the day, thinking about the brand that had been seared into the flesh of the dead women, thinking about the horror of the half-consumed corpse that had been the center of the day.

Thinking about bursting into the house that night, just in time . . .

Amy was a damned good agent. She could hold her own. But thank goodness he'd gone to check on her.

He headed into the second bedroom, realizing his footsteps slowed as he passed her door. He forced himself to keep going.

The bedroom was fine, simply furnished. The sheets on the bed were fresh and clean.

He crashed down on the bed.

Awkwardly, he realized he had to set his gun holster by the side of the bed, shed his shoes and jacket at the very least.

He stripped down.

The bed felt wonderful. His body craved the comfort.

His body also craved something else.

No, he needed sleep. Let the sweet act of falling asleep interact with the subconscious mind, make use of the night and the rest . . .

And his mind remained awake.

But he realized he wasn't attempting to reason out the case, sorting information into the compartments of his mind.

He was thinking about the woman who slept so near him, the light in her eyes when she was passionate, when she laughed, her wit, reason, humor . . . The empathy she showed. How she faced the things they'd already been through together without falling apart.

He *liked* her.

Admired her.

Wanted her.

He had known her just a few days.

It was . . .

Not good.

They were partnered up for this — a professional partnership.

They were working together to catch a brutal killer. And it might well get way worse. *Eye on the prize,* he reminded himself.

But it wasn't easy. She slept just feet away.

Thankfully, he didn't dwell on that thought; he was physically and mentally exhausted.

And in less time than he had imagined, he slept.

Hunter was already at the dining room table with coffee. He had his computer out and was studying the screen intently when Amy came out of her room, showered and ready to face the day. She had slept deeply, and she was glad she'd set her alarm — otherwise, she'd have still been sleeping deeply.

She was surprised because she'd thought, as tired as she was, she'd have a hard time falling asleep. There had been that strange moment between her and Hunter in the hall . . .

And she had thought maybe, just maybe, there would be a tap at her door; she would whisper he should come in, and then . . .

She'd imagined all kinds of things she probably shouldn't.

At least she had slept well once she'd slept. She knew it was in part because Hunter had been so near. He had her back, and she could let down her guard.

And now it was morning. They had a witness to interrogate today, a witness who would most probably be charged with a federal crime: Artie had taken part in holding Martin and Patty hostage.

But she didn't think, in the end, the young man could have killed anyone. That wouldn't matter legally; he had aided and abetted Hank in his plans.

While Amy was not nearly as experienced as a man like John Schultz, she had worked vice and homicide for Metro-Miami-Dade.

231

She'd spent two years with the FDLE. She'd seen bodies on the beach, and bodies in barrels, encountered those with the drug cartels who had executed another in the blink of the eye.

She'd learned something about people.

If she was any judge at all of human beings, Artie wasn't a bad person. She even wondered if, had she not been able to get his pill away from him, he would have gone through with suicide. But they would talk to Artie again this morning. Possibly, there was something he could say.

"Morning," Hunter said, looking up. "There's coffee. There's sugar, fake sugar and powdered creamer, if you like."

She smiled. "I used to like cream in my coffee, but then there were too many times it was nonexistent or going bad in the station when I first started working," she told him. "Black is just fine. What are you studying?"

He looked up at her and he was quiet for a minute, and she wondered again if he, too, hadn't thought a little bit about her.

"I think that I know who is behind this," he told her.

"Oh?" she said.

Uh, no. He had his eye on the prize.

He hesitated.

"Okay, I don't have anything to back this up yet, but I believe Ethan Morrison is the 'Divine Leader.' "

"Okay," she said slowly, sliding into the seat next to him. "I hate, loathe, passionately despise everything the man has done and gotten away with, but we can't jump to an assumption like that, Hunter."

"I listened to Artie last night when he was speaking with you. Artie was a kid who couldn't get a girl, and Hank convinced him that if he followed the Divine Leader, he'd get a girl. I'm puzzled because — if what he was saying is true — our first victim went to have sex with him before she was murdered. She was brought down here by someone. We might be looking at trafficking, too." He shook his head. "We needed Hank alive. Once I shot him —"

"Once you shot him, you saved my life," she said.

"You were doing okay on your own," he told her.

"Thank you," she acknowledged. "And thank you again for having my back."

"It's a good back to have," he said, and then he managed a rueful smile. "Sorry, that didn't sound the way it should have —"

"It's all right!" she assured him. "We know Ethan Morrison wasn't at the murder sites."

"But according to Artie, it was the 'Brothers,' or acolytes, or his main band of followers, who carried it out. We'll get more on Hank today from Dr. Carver, but we know he took a poison pill — a death pill. Followers must all walk around with them. Think of the depth of that brainwashing! It's terrible. When you put the need to believe in something together with a person who feels down, perhaps unloved and unwanted by the world, it's a playground for a person who knows how to manipulate others."

He closed his computer.

"They have an interrogation room ready for us. Artie will be arraigned and transferred after we've spoken with him. I'm afraid we're not going to get more out of him than what you already managed to get in the car. Artie was a teenager more downtrodden and mixed up than your average teenager. Hank promised him sex with a woman — something he probably believed he'd never have. Sex, heaven, a life where he was loved . . . He was easily manipulated."

"I — I almost feel bad for him."

"So do I. But if we're lucky, he'll help us stop this thing from going any further, and prison might be the thing that saves him,"

Hunter said.

She smiled and he arched a brow.

"I was just hoping that my feeling bad for him wasn't a mistake," she said.

He shook his head. "No, empathy isn't a mistake. It's a good human quality."

"Well, let's get started on this, shall we?" She stood and went over to the counter, where there were paper cups next to the coffeepot. "I'm taking along a coffee. Can I get you one, too?"

"Yeah, thanks. I'm going to grab my things. Your bag ready?"

"On the bed."

"I'll get it."

"Thanks." She started pouring the coffees and, thinking aloud, said, "It's a good thing we travel well. I'm starting to think we've slept together over half of the state."

Her words came out entirely wrong; she turned to stare at him in horror.

But he laughed.

"We do it well," he said lightly. "We do it well."

11

Fall 1993
Sam

Time. Seconds stretched out. All life was a matter of seconds.

Seconds became minutes, minutes became hours, and then days . . .

And finally, in the end, a man's life would be measured.

Sam found himself praying; he no longer knew what he believed, except that there was a higher power, and he knew now, with crystal clarity, that a man's life was not measured by riches or power but by his actions and reactions — and his common decency to his fellow man.

Nice realization to make while he stood here, holding what was most important in life to him, his wife and his child.

And praying.

If I am going to die, that will be fine. I've been a fool. I knew there was something wrong, but I understand too clearly how Jessie felt, as well. We needed something different in life. We stumbled upon a really wrong different, and now . . .

We're both aware we might die for our mistakes. But please, God . . . Save the life of our child.

There was another whisper of movement in the leaves.

Jessie looked at him, her beautiful eyes filled with fear.

He brought his fingers to his lips, warning her. "Stay still! Just stay still. We have to wait and watch," he breathed into her ear.

Someone was coming, but he hoped it was the agent who had slipped like an eel into their commune — and slipped out just as easily. The man who would be their savior.

For a moment Sam worried he'd been tricked. That the man who had identified himself as an FBI agent was really just a plant, someone to find out who might betray Brother William and his core of deacons. His . . . *henchmen.*

The movement in the trees continued.

Sam strained his eyes to see. There was someone there. They weren't clad in the casual everyday clothing of the members of the commune.

It was a hunter, he thought.

237

Except they were on federal land. He didn't believe hunting was legal here, and yet the man moving through the trees ahead of them was in forest-camouflage pants and jacket, a tan baseball cap on his head. Sam held a small camera in his hand. It was all they had taken with them. Their clothing, Cameron's toys, *everything* had been left behind. That was the only way to escape.

He had managed to secretly get the camera. The main members of their colony — as Brother William called it — didn't have personal equipment like cameras. Technology was a distraction from work and from the love and togetherness they shared.

But on one of the rare supply runs into the nearest town, Sam had managed to buy a little point-and-shoot camera and a roll of film at a drugstore. He had taken pictures of damning evidence against Brother William, shots sneaked quickly in the office of letters — people swearing that they will not leave the colony. And even once during a gathering when Brother William had been choosing a young — underage — girl to be "honored" by his touch.

More than that, he had images of some of the paperwork that showed the vast amount of money that Brother William was making off his followers: investments, assets, all handed over to the colony. And payments to his henchmen and others. Those who carried out Brother William's dirty works received great rewards on earth, as well as those promised in heaven.

If they were caught, the camera would mean a horrendous punishment for them. For him and Jessie and for Cameron. He knew now that Brother William would kill them.

He had risked their lives for this. Jessie had known all along. She'd agreed. Cameron wouldn't have understood, although Sam thought his son was special, smart, even at his young age.

Cameron was suspicious of those they were supposed to obey and follow. When another young girl had been punished for not doing her share of work in the fields, Cameron had rushed forward, saying he would pick up the slack. He'd even volunteered to take the seven stripes on the back that were the child's corporal punishment. The memory made Sam flush with pride and anger all over again.

Sam barely dared move, but now he looked for a place where he might secrete the camera.

God, he thought, *if nothing else . . . if*

You're there, I beg of You, spare the life of my son.

He managed to twist slightly and ease the camera into a thicket where the black case was hidden completely by vines and brush.

Movement again . . . Closer now. *Someone was there.*

A savior, offering them new lives?

Or a murderer, bringing death?

Sam strained his eyes.

"Sam?"

He wasn't sure at first whether it had been Jessie who said his name so softly.

Not Jessie.

She, too, was staring at the man who began to emerge from the cover of the trees.

A man carrying a gun.

12

Artie looked somewhat better than he had the night before.

He was in an orange jumpsuit, but he'd had a shower and washed and brushed his hair.

They met first with a Dr. Kashi in the hallway before they went in to speak with Artie. Dr. Kashi had seen the young man the night before; because of the circumstances of his arrest and his state of mind, Dr. Kashi recommended that he be on a suicide watch.

"This kid has suffered from anxiety disorder for a long time. He has trouble focusing. He was horrified when I first suggested he take pills to calm down and focus on a conversation, but then he wanted to try. He looked at me so hopefully. I have a feeling he comes from a family, perhaps a society, where anything that is perceived as a mental abnormality is ignored or frowned upon.

Any use of drugs is forbidden. I'm not for pushing pharmaceutical intervention — we did go through a time when it was too easy to think every problem could be solved by popping a little white pill. But some people seriously benefit from medication and Artie is one of them. But now, he's anxious — almost excited — about seeing a therapist and maybe having a life. I'm not a judge or a jury, but I hope they go easy on this kid."

"We're hoping that, too," Amy told him.

"He's able to have a conversation, right?" Hunter asked.

Kashi nodded gravely.

Ten minutes later, they were seated in one of the bureau's interrogation rooms, facing Artie. He was calm, and he managed to smile at Amy.

"I know I have to pay a debt. After that . . ."

His words faded. "I don't know what I'm going to do. My parents thought I'd graduate and just stay on — we have a small cattle ranch. I wasn't going to college — no money. Please, don't get me wrong. My parents are good people. And now I can tell you how sorry I am. I knew Mrs. Sanders. I didn't want to hurt her. We weren't supposed to hurt them — Mr. or Mrs. Sanders, I mean. We were just supposed to wait and

242

ambush you, Special Agent Larson, and sneak you away. Now I know that was a lie. It would have been necessary for us to kill them both, because we couldn't leave witnesses behind."

"Artie, we know you didn't *want* to hurt anyone — that was evident," Amy said.

"But I did. I hurt her. I cut her neck."

"She's going to be all right," Hunter told him. "But we still need your help. Artie, there is no reward in life or death for serving anyone who wants you to commit murder."

"Oh, we weren't supposed to kill anyone," Artie said. "I mean, I wasn't supposed to have to kill anyone. That's what Hank told me. We were supposed to hold the Sanderses as hostages, knock Special Agent Larson on the head and bring her to an old shack that's in the Everglades a few miles. Used to be, people could have little hunting shacks out on that land. The law did something where they were grandfathered in, but when the owners died, they were supposed to be removed. But mostly, no one really cared, and lots of the cabins were just left to rot. Then we started up on those 'great python challenges' and people were going out to find constrictors loose in the Everglades, and whatever cabins were still left up kind of came in handy for the python hunters. Anyway, that's where we were supposed to take Special Agent Larson." He looked at Amy apologetically. "Hank said you were a girl — that we wouldn't have any problem taking you."

Hunter glanced Amy's way. "I guess she proved to be a problem. Artie, where is this cabin?"

"There's an old work road about a mile before you reach the diner," Artie told them. "You just take it west until you come to the canal. At the canal, you hop in a canoe. An airboat would be better, but Hank told me we were just to use canoes, as airboats were hard to come by. My dad has one and lots of people out here own them, but an airboat is . . . I don't know. Too high-tech?" Artie asked dryly. "Anyway, we were to use the canals. South along the water. The shack is visible from the canal. At least that's what Hank told me. I've never been to the shack. Hank has. Hank *had* been." Artie sighed, shaking his head.

"Does anyone else know about any of this, Artie? Were you Hank's only recruit?"

"That I know about. All I had to do was take care of Special Agent Larson. Then we could leave home. I could be an apostle. We'd move up north in the state and join the True Brotherhood. I would never be awkward or unloved again or made to feel stupid. I'd have a position of power, and when I wanted a girl, I could have one. The women in the Brotherhood know how to serve." He paused, a pained expression on his face. "The worst thing is, I wanted to believe Lady Liberty had really welcomed her sacrifice, that she was high above with angels and the Lord and everything beautiful. I wanted to believe it so badly. I don't think, deep down, I did. But Hank told me, when he recruited me, it all had to do with empowering oneself and carrying through with promises. He . . . he made a video of me naked . . ." His voice trailed and he looked acutely uncomfortable.

"It's okay, Artie. I've heard just about everything there is to hear," Amy assured him. Again, she had the sense that this boy had gotten mixed up in something he barely understood.

"Okay, okay . . . Well, he recorded me playing with myself."

"Masturbating?" Hunter asked.

Artie was a dark shade of red as he nodded.

"He said me doing the video for him was a commitment. It was powerful and strong and part of the Brotherhood. He'd erase the video. He said it wasn't being mean or threatening — it was so I could find my inner strength. I mean, he laughed, too, and told me I looked like a crippled giraffe trying to get a hard-on." He winced, closed his eyes and opened them again. "He could be funny. Hank could be cool and funny. That one was at my expense, but he had me laughing. And then . . . I cared about her — she was my first girl ever. She was great. Lady Liberty, I mean. Strange, though, something I didn't think of back then."

"What's that?" Amy asked.

"I was talking about rewards in heaven — gibbering, really. She was beautiful. My mind wasn't working. She told me her rewards were going to be on earth."

"Artie," Hunter asked. "Did Lady Liberty have an accent?"

"Yes, a beautiful accent."

"Was it an accent that someone who spoke Spanish as their first language might have?" Hunter asked.

"Maybe. Lots of my friends are Cuban or their folks come from South America, but most of them were born here and talk like me, so . . . it was beautiful. Her words were beautiful."

"Did she call you by any pet or special names?" Amy asked.

"Yeah. I thought she was calling me a whore at first, like a male whore! As if. But she was calling me *mijo*. It means —"

"That you were a dear one. It's a term parents often use for children," Amy said.

"She must have liked you," Hunter said. "You're a likable kid — when you're not holding a knife at someone's throat."

"I'm so sorry . . ."

"We know you are," Hunter assured him. "And we're going to talk to the authorities about you, let them know how much you're helping us. Tell me honestly, right now, are you all right if you stay here?"

"Sure. Dr. Kashi is nice. I am going to jail, though, right? A real jail. I . . . what I did was against the law."

"District attorneys and the federal government are figuring that out right now. You're eighteen, so it can't be juvenile court, but you've also admitted your part in taking Mr. and Mrs. Sanders prisoner, and you're being cooperative in an investigation. You're all right here, though — it will really be protective custody right now. I don't want anyone who has anything to do with this knowing you weren't killed right along with Hank."

Artie nodded slowly. "Thank you. You know, I wish I'd met Dr. Kashi years ago."

"He seems like a good guy," Amy said.

"He is, and yeah, I'm fine here. I have a little room to myself. Okay, it's kind of a cell, but it's mine, and the bed is even comfortable. And out in the exercise yard . . . everyone out there seems to be as scared as me." His eyes brightened. "Can I keep seeing Dr. Kashi?"

"I believe that will certainly be possible," Amy told him.

"Artie, can you tell us anything else at all? Was there anyone else Hank might have been talking to on the side?"

"He had a thing for Casey Colby — the pastor's daughter. But Casey thought he was a kid. Hank was older than me by a few years, but younger than Casey by a year or two. She doesn't like him. I heard she saw him throwing rocks at a dog one day and that was it for her." He shook his head. "But I don't think Casey was in on anything. I think Hank thought that, you know, while we were all seeking heavenly reward, he was going to get Casey on earth." He shook his head. "He was the only one I talked to and knew. When I finished my first task, I would have been brought north. And then I would have met the accomplished members of the church."

"Thank you, Artie," Hunter said. "Sincerely, thank you. And be strong. We'll see that Patty knows how sorry you are."

"Thank you," he said. He looked right at Amy. "Agent Larson . . ."

"Yes?" Amy asked him.

"Please be careful. You — you didn't ask me why they wanted you."

"I know why they wanted me," Amy told him. "They wanted me to die. They were probably going to inject me with a deadly disease. They don't have me, so they'll find another victim. Don't worry, I'm pretty tough."

"You could still be in danger."

"And I also have someone even tougher at my back," Amy said, grinning at Hunter. "Thank you, Artie. We are going to hope for the best for you."

Hunter nodded.

"Amen," he said, and then added, "We've got to get going, kid. We have a lot of ground to cover before nightfall. You take care."

They left after speaking with the area supervisor in charge; he would look after Artie, seeing they moved carefully on filing charges and considering Artie a cooperating witness who needed to be protected.

Then they were out of the office at last.

The skies over Miami were almost a

crystal blue that day.

It could be a pretty city, warm and welcoming.

Like any big city, it had shadows and danger when the sun wasn't shining so brightly.

Still, Amy wouldn't have minded being in the city a bit longer. But they couldn't stay.

Amy looked at Hunter. "If we're going out to a cabin in the Everglades, I have a friend I want to call."

"Aidan Cypress?" he asked.

She nodded. "I can have your back, you can have my back. But out in the Everglades, I'd sure like to have Aidan, too," she told him.

He grinned. "I agree. Call him. I'll drive."

He hesitated, hand on the car door, looking at Amy.

"What?" she asked.

"They wanted you."

"They didn't get me."

"You might want to take yourself off the case."

She shook her head stubbornly.

"I want on this case more than ever. I have a vested interest in making sure these people are stopped — and that they face the full extent of the laws of the state and the country." She was quiet for a minute and

250

then said, "Hunter, please. This is my case. Yes, FBI has the lead in the investigation. But I want to be there when we get him, them, whomever. And I believe I can help, I know my state. Please! Don't suggest to anyone that I be removed."

He was smiling.

"What?"

"Wow."

"Wow?"

"I love that passion about you. And I was just asking. I'd be remiss if I didn't give you an opportunity to stay as far away from these monsters as possible."

"And where would that be? Hunter, we have no idea where they might strike next. We're even struggling to investigate the murder sites."

"Well, let's get moving. This cabin may give us a lot. If we can find it."

Two and a half hours later, they had Aidan Cypress with them, and they were rolling down the old work road off the highway.

"I'm glad that kid told you which dirt road — there's more than one, you know. There were years when this was nothing but sugarcane, for miles and miles," Aidan said. "Before that, surviving out here, many of my people were pumpkin farmers. Don't see a lot of that around here."

"Ah, there has to be some. Seminole pumpkin bread is awesome."

Aidan grinned at her from the back seat. "Yeah, my mom's is the best."

"Well, you might have offered me some."

"I will. Next year. If you're still working in the state next year."

"Where would I be?" Amy asked.

"I think the feds like you," Aidan told her.

"Hey!" Hunter protested. "We don't poach people. Often."

Amy lowered her head, smiling.

She was glad Hunter really did seem to think she was good at her job.

"What do you think we're going to find in this cabin?" Aidan asked. He hesitated and then said, "What happens in this car stays in this car, right?"

Amy saw Hunter frown and gaze back at Aidan through the rearview mirror. "Unless you killed someone, or caused someone injury . . . What the hell, Aidan. Speak up."

"I went out to the old Morrison place, the derelict house on the Morrison property," Aidan said. "I figured it was a matter of time before we got a search warrant."

"You think he's involved, too?" Amy asked.

"Let's see. He's a white supremacist. He's

a hateful bigot who thinks women should be subservient. Also hates anyone disabled. And anyone gay. He's a despicable human being."

"Which we all believe, but that doesn't —" Amy began.

"Make him a murderer, I know. And you two have already been telling each other that, right?"

"Correct. Aidan, the thing is, if you'd come across evidence of anything illegal at the house," Hunter said, "we could have lost everything in court."

"You're forgetting who you are talking to — one of the best forensic experts in the state, if I do say so myself," Aidan said. "Trust me, if I'd found something, I would have found a way to make you guys get a warrant — fast."

"What did you find?" Amy asked.

"Nothing! Yes, someone has been there lately. But there was no blood, no tools, no Dade County pine to make a cross out of, no drugs of any kind . . . nothing."

"So, maybe we'll find what you were looking for out at this hunter's shack," Amy said.

"I'm hoping," Aidan said. "There may be a way to nail him."

"If he's involved in this. Just because a man is detestable —"

"Yeah, yeah, and bull," Aidan said flatly. "I know you both suspect the bastard."

"There's the canoe," Hunter said, drawing the car close to the embankment.

Aidan laughed. "I can manage the canoe. But a friend of mine has an airboat, just south. Let's take that."

"You might have mentioned that fact," Hunter said, turning the key in the ignition again and shaking his head.

"Hey, you asked me along for a reason, and not just my forensic kit," Aidan said, grinning.

They pulled up another two hundred feet; as Aidan had said, an airboat was waiting by the embankment.

"And who owns this?" Hunter asked.

"My cousin James. He does airboat tours — he has a business off one of the exits on I-75."

"And he just managed to leave it here for you?"

"Yeah. Takes less time to get where we need to be."

"But . . . where's your cousin, then?" Amy asked.

Aidan laughed. "He owns more than one airboat. Another cousin picked him up. We're good — they'll come back and get it tomorrow. You don't have a problem with it, do you?" Aidan asked them.

"Hell no," Hunter told him. "I wasn't into the idea of rowing for miles."

"Keeps you out of the gym," Aidan said, grinning. "But, hey."

"I like the gym. It's air-conditioned," Hunter told him.

"It's not even a bad day — we're lucky," Aidan said. "Come on, hop on. Trust me. I know what I'm doing."

"Didn't doubt you for a minute," Amy assured him.

In a few minutes they were all settled on the airboat. Aidan had taken over, directing them to the bench in back. There was a higher seat just above it; Aidan took that seat, finding the key that had been secreted into a niche in the flooring.

They rode south and west, into the Everglades. The air blowing past was fresh and clean; the sun was out and the sky remained a beautiful blue. The temperature was hot, but eighties-hot, and the feel of the wind and the spray of water that dashed up and touched Amy in tiny droplets felt good.

She glanced at Hunter; whatever else, he, too, was enjoying the ride. They passed herons and cranes and other birds, and two alligators sleeping on the embankment.

Hunter's eyes met hers. He smiled.

"Great blue heron!" Aidan shouted, pointing to one of the large birds on the shoreline.

"I'm not seeing any vultures," Hunter said.

"No. Nothing dead around here — not right now," Aidan said.

They passed another two alligators. The creatures did not look up; they were accustomed to the whir of an airboat. As they passed, Amy noticed that one of the gators was enormous.

"That's old Methuselah! Been holding down that area of the embankment since I was a little kid," Aidan told them. "Don't go near his territory, and he won't mess with you — he's about thirteen feet of pure terror when someone threatens his realm. Too bad we might be after locals who probably know that."

She thought about the injuries the murdered women had suffered, the agony they had endured before death had taken them from the pain.

Maybe those who fed a woman to bugs deserved to be a meal for an alligator.

She winced; she enforced the law. They were not judge and jury.

And whoever was doing this had knowledge regarding the area. They would know to avoid the territory of an alpha alligator.

Or a female guarding her eggs, a creature just as fierce, if not more so.

"Hey, guys, I don't know this cabin. I need help looking!" Aidan shouted.

"We're not there yet," Hunter said. "Hey, wait. There! I see it just ahead, through the trees — over there!" Hunter told him.

Aidan slowed the motor, bringing the airboat in so they could step off without hitting too much muck. He grabbed his large black case, his face grim.

As they approached the rickety cabin, Amy and Hunter drew their guns. Neither of them believed they would encounter anyone, but they were not taking any chances.

They crept around the shack surrounded by bracken and long grass, and each took a side of the door. Hunter nodded at Amy; she would cover him. She nodded in return.

He kicked the old door; it gave way easily. He stepped inside and she followed.

It was one room.

"Clear!" Amy called back to Aidan.

They stood in the entry for a minute, their eyes adjusting to the dim light seeping in through the doorway and chinks in the wood.

Amy felt something cold trickle down her spine.

They'd found the murder site. Scuffs on the dirt on the floor showed where someone had been held and possibly dragged.

But the scuffs weren't what made her heart skip a beat with pity.

It was the table in the center of the room. The table where flies buzzed incessantly over pools of dried blood.

Amy knew; this was where the women's faces had been slashed. Where their wrists had bled while they were being held down. It was probably where the spider had been set on Jane Doe number two in order to deliver its deadly bite.

It was where they had let her writhe in pain, probably screaming in agony, her cries going out to the creatures of the Everglades, unheard by human ears other than those of her torturers, her tormenters.

Her killers.

13

Hunter's first action was to call in what they had found.

There was no body, so Carver wouldn't have to be called out. Aidan's crew would come, along with Detective Mulberry.

There was little they could do after surveying the room, though Amy had her sketchbook out. She worked, and Hunter marveled at the way her eyes seemed to stay on the condition of the room, assessing details, while her fingers seemed to work on their own.

He called both John Schultz to keep him apprised of the day's events, and then Ryan to tell him that they'd be back soon.

"What's the next move?" Ryan asked him. "I mean, we know where they set the young women up for killing — where they tortured them before murdering them — but does it give us anything else? What about the kid — Artie?"

"Well, we found the shack thanks to Artie. They're keeping him in protective custody now. The attorneys are going to have to decide if he'll be charged. He's seeing a Dr. Kashi down there — maybe he can be confined in a facility for a while. Kashi seems to do well with him. Artie needs to be deprogrammed. He's already better than he was last night."

"But did he give us any names?" Ryan asked.

"According to him, Hank was the man in this area. The plan was to kidnap Amy, then Artie would have been allowed to meet others in the church. Artie was an easy mark for someone like Hank, who promised him a place to be loved and appreciated. It can be frighteningly easy to take over the mind of someone who has felt ignored and mocked their entire life, unloved, so to speak. We don't know much about his family or Hank's family. Detective Mulberry is going to be speaking with the families, finding out what he can through them."

"Okay, do you want me to stay on top of that? I like Martin and Patty, but . . ."

"You're tired of babysitting."

"I just think I could be more useful."

"Let me talk to my superior first."

Ryan thanked him and he ended the call.

He immediately called Charles Garza to bring him up on the latest events regarding the case, and let him know that he wanted to head north again.

"Why do you think they 'practiced' on a woman up there, and then came south with their next victims?" Garza asked.

Hunter told him, "I think they chose this area — and the north — because Ethan Morrison has property in both places."

"You really suspect he's behind this?"

"I do."

"You're talking big money here. Huge money. And influence."

"Yes."

"Don't make any mistakes. Don't let us look like fools in court."

"No, sir. I'll only hit him if I see him with a weapon in his hands about to commit murder."

"Hunter —"

"Sir, I know. Sorry. But . . . none of this could be carried out without connections. Victims who have no identities . . . easily could have come from a private detention center. Hank killed himself with a suicide pill — Morrison has massive pharmaceutical holdings. He has a reputation for being a white elitist and a womanizer."

"Right — so how do you become a Divine

Leader with that reputation? I know you can explain this, and you know far more than I do."

"Easy. You find people who feel the world is against them. Those who welcome the concept of rewards, because they feel like lesser people and want to be the chosen ones."

"But why would a man like Morrison even want to do this?"

"He craves power. The right to do whatever he wants. Any time anyone kills at his command, it's a tremendous lift. This is what I believe. Now the way to him, of course, is paved with followers — like Hank. Ready to die for their cause because they believe the rewards that await them will be great. Sir, you know as well as I do how many cults there are in existence today, and they have massive numbers of followers. Some are collecting weapons, and training their members as potentially violent forces, and so we have them on our watch lists. Most people do have a faith they adhere to. Some take it to the extreme because someone craves power."

"Follow your nose, then, Hunter. Close this one. Details have been kept out of the media so far, but the news has wind of the women who have been killed and we need to get this stopped, now."

"Yes, sir."

"Call in for any help you need — even in the wilderness."

"Special Agent Ryan Anders is proving to be quite an asset."

"Then keep him working."

"We may wind up with something big going down. We may need a small army."

"And you'll get it."

"Right now, sir, I need a way out of here. When we learned about the shack, we asked for help from forensics expert Aidan Cypress. He's busy right now."

"I'll see they send a local officer with an airboat out to get you. Leave Mulberry and his people and the team to gather what they can."

"Yes, sir."

Hunter finished with his call; he saw that Amy, too, had been speaking with her immediate supervisor.

"We're good with FDLE," she told him. "Well, not that you need to be good with FDLE, but I do. They've promised plenty of help when needed."

"So, we'll leave this to the experts here," Hunter said. "Our drive north is about six hours."

"Ready when you are."

As they stood there, her phone rang. She glanced at the caller ID and looked at Hunter as she studied the number, frowning, and then answered the call.

"Larson," she said.

After a second's pause, listening, she covered the phone's microphone and whispered, "Artie."

She listened gravely, and then thanked him.

"What is it?" Hunter demanded. He chaffed a little; he was officially in charge of the case. But then again, he'd been glad Amy's talents included setting up a rapport with victims, and those involved as criminals, as well.

"He said he was talking to Kashi, and Kashi got him to remember everything, how Hank had gotten him into this all from the beginning. At one point, he remembered he told Hank he was worried about the cops. Hank told him not to worry. He says he's been going crazy, trying to remember if Hank meant they'd be too slick for law enforcement, or that law enforcement might be involved."

Hunter weighed her words.

Detective Victor Mulberry?

He'd known the man and known his reputation.

Mulberry couldn't be involved with any of this. It seemed impossible.

But they couldn't take chances. He nodded and called Ryan.

"All right, Ryan, we're driving up to Granville today. I'll have you come, but I'd like you to stay here about another twenty-four hours or so. You can meet with Detective Mulberry at the diner for dinner. I'll set it up. Make sure you know everything he knows. Keep a look out for our still-missing woman — Billie, or Wilhelmina. I think she may be getting food from the waitress at the diner — the young lady you're flirting with so well. See what you can come up with. We know Martin and Patty were helping Billie, but if she moved on or was seeking help somewhere else, too, it's possible you can discover something by being your charming self at the diner. Remember, we need to take extreme personal safety measures around here. Trust no one."

"I'm on it," Ryan swore. "So — here, at this moment, I'm the agent in charge?"

"Yes, Ryan, here, at this moment, you're the agent in charge."

He ended the call, smiling. He liked Ryan, and believed he had the right stuff to become a strong agent, and he was an agent

265

who could follow through with Hunter's unit.

"So, Ryan holds down the fort here and we're heading north."

"As soon as we check with Aidan Cypress — see if he has anything more he can give us."

Amy nodded gravely. She smiled. "I told you we needed Aidan."

He laughed. "Hey, we both knew we needed Aidan."

Their smiles faded as they looked at one another; it was good *not* to be in the shack. The tinny scent of blood was strong; heat had done a number on the place, and it was difficult even to stand near.

Aidan emerged. "We'll get everything we can. Reports will be sent to the sheriff's office, FDLE and the FBI," he said. He studied Hunter. "So, what happens if I find something that shows I'm right — that Ethan Morrison is somehow involved?"

Hunter said, "He is a person of interest, you bet. But I've been warned, and I'm warning you. We are going to need proof, and we're going to have to go by the book. The man employs an army of lawyers, so we need every move we make to be within the law."

Aidan hadn't followed the law when he'd

investigated on private property. Aidan knew it. But he was also aware many people had no idea that the Morrison house was still on private land — the area was a mishmash of state, federal and tribal land, often with blurred lines that made little sense. "I'm processing this scene perfectly by the book," Aidan promised.

"And as you said, please make sure everything and anything winds up in the hands of every law enforcement agency involved," Hunter said.

"Yes, sir." He glanced around. Only Hunter and Amy were outside with him. "I shouldn't have said anything to you about the Morrison family holdings. I put you in a bad position. I swear, I will follow the law to the nth degree as we move forward." He let out a breath. "I've been at this for years. It's just . . . what was done to those women! And why — what the hell is this man trying to make happen?"

"An apocalypse," Amy said. "It's possible he's trying to start something around the country. Florida was his place to begin. He owns land here, where he can get away with anything — with murder, he thinks."

"Get us what you can from that shack. A solid fingerprint would be nice," Hunter said. "Amy, an officer is coming to get us back to my car. We should head down to the embankment, be ready for a quick turn-around."

Not thinking, he slipped an arm around Amy's shoulders as they walked back toward the canal. The *incorrectness* of doing so struck him immediately, but Amy didn't seem to notice. She was deep in thought.

"We've never spoken with Casey Colby," she said. "Do you think she might know something? We're heading upstate — should we try to find out where she is?"

Hunter released her and pulled out his phone again.

"You're going to call her?" Amy asked.

He smiled. "I'm calling my tech magician, Sheila," he told her.

He put through his call. Sheila suggested he just stay on the line.

"I started pulling up info on just about everyone you've met down there — and Casey is easy! She is constantly on social media. She's a bit of a rebel, but on the other hand, true to her teachings. She wants to respect everyone — and every faith. And . . . oh!"

"What?"

"She's near you."

"How do you know that?" Hunter asked warily.

268

"She just posted a picture. Like, just a minute ago. She's at a diner, a few miles down 27 from where you are now. The name —"

"We know the diner. Thanks, Sheila!"

He ended the call and looked up; an airboat was arriving. An officer in a county uniform was at the controls.

It was tricky maneuvering getting out to the boat. Aidan's crew and Mulberry had also arrived via airboat, and the dry area of the embankment had been filled up.

Amy easily leaped onto the flat-bottomed vehicle and he followed suit. They introduced themselves to the officer who was happy to help them, and shortly they were back at Hunter's car.

"Let's hope she's still there," Amy said.

"For where we were, we moved pretty quick. Hopefully, she just ordered. Even fast food takes time."

"Kaila," Amy murmured.

"The waitress — what about her?"

"She and Casey must be close in age. I'm willing to bet they're friends."

"Possibly. So, you think they're both helping our missing Billie?"

"I definitely think it's possible."

"Well, then, be your charming self," Hunter said. He exited the car; Amy did the same. She led the way in.

Kaila Franklin was working; she was delivering sodas to a table against the window when Hunter and Amy entered.

Hunter smiled and waved.

"Sit where you like," Kaila said.

He noted a young woman with long honey-brown hair sitting alone at one of the booths. Amy saw her, too, and headed straight for a booth that was just in front of Casey's.

But she didn't sit; she looked straight at the young woman and asked, "Casey Colby?"

The girl started, almost spitting out a swallow of the tea she had been drinking. "Yes, hi, I — do I know you?"

Amy managed a brilliant move, sliding into Casey's booth across from her, and saying quickly, "May we?" And not waiting for an answer.

She hurried on with, "We know of you! We've been to your father's church. I'm so sorry — I'm Amy Larson and this is Hunter Forrest."

Kaila Franklin had hurried over and said quickly, "Casey, yeah, these are two of the guys — sorry — two of the agents working on the murders."

"Oh!" Casey said, her eyes wide.

By then, Hunter had slid into the booth, as well, taking the seat next to Amy.

"Your father seems to be a great guy, and the church is really nice," he said.

Casey leaned back, looking at them, and then at Kaila, and then them again.

"My father is a great guy," she said passionately.

"Right," Amy said, frowning slightly, seeming unsure where Casey was going with this.

Casey lowered her voice and said, "If anything, my father is too good a man."

"They're okay, Casey. Honestly, I've been telling you." Kaila said the words quickly, and then moved on to respond to a man by the window who had lifted a hand to summon her, ready to give her his order.

"So, you're okay," Casey said dryly, studying them. "FBI — Big Brother. But you're okay."

"He's FBI. I'm FDLE," Amy said. "We're trying to catch a murderer. What happened here was brutal, cruel and beyond horrible."

"My father wasn't involved. I know you've been to the church. You need to know my father wasn't involved."

"Your father does appear to be a good man, an upright citizen," Hunter agreed. "But then, you have Artie and Hank — two

271

young men from one of the church's youth groups — holding an older couple hostage. They're thought to have been answering an apparent call to arms for the Apocalypse."

Casey leaned back. She shook her head, saying again, "It's not my dad. My dad is a good man. I get scared, though. I . . . I need Kaila!" she said.

Hunter saw that, behind the grill, Frank was pretending to work — while watching them.

Amy reached across the table and took the young woman's hand. "It's okay," she told her. "Casey, do you know a girl going by the name of Billie? We think she's in trouble."

Casey leaned forward, words tumbling from her lips. "This is true — whatever it is, my dad isn't involved. And we don't know what's really going on — we just don't know! We met Billie. We met Billie because Patty and Martin were helping her. Sometimes Kaila helps out at their motel, cleaning rooms. They told Billie that she might be able to get food at the diner when she needed it. And so Kaila would slip food to her, and we were always so careful! She was afraid of everyone. And after the first dead woman was found on the cross . . . she was more terrified than ever."

"But terrified of who?" Amy asked.

Casey shook her head. "She didn't know. She's from Mexico. She and her family were caught trying to get across the border. She didn't know exactly where. They were split up and sent to different facilities. Then she was put in a van with other girls and taken somewhere in the woods where they were promised that they'd be safe. There was a preacher, and he talked about how being part of the group would protect them, and then they were asked to have sex with strange men. They were given — or forced to take — 'happy' pills and they were told that brought them closer to God, and then they'd be safe forever and loved in the community. The community would hide them from the evil people who would come to throw them back into their countries."

"Why didn't you call the police and get help for her?" Hunter asked.

"She begged us not to. She begged us just to hide her," Casey said desperately.

"But the police, or the FBI —"

Casey shook her head. "She was so nervous about any member of the police. And I don't know if it's because . . ."

"Because?" Amy encouraged.

"Because of me." She lowered her voice still further. "I had my own doubts. Because

273

of Hank. His father is dead, and I always wanted to feel bad for Hank. I'm sorry to speak ill of the dead, but Hank was just . . . I don't know . . . born evil. Or maybe his horrible alcoholic father made him evil. He used to beat Hank something awful, but he had him brainwashed, too, because the cops would go to his place sometimes. Hank would say he'd tripped or done something stupid, and his dad just kept on beating him. Hank always kind of had a thing for me. Like I said, I was sorry for him, but . . . he was scary! He said he was high on the chain of humanity, that the people who treated him badly would get what they had coming to them, one day. He . . . cornered me outside the church one night — my dad's church. He told me I'd be lucky to call him mine and didn't know what I was missing. He said maybe he'd show me. I told him I'd scream. He started laughing and told me to scream away — the law wasn't going to stop him, no one was going to stop him. The law, he told me, well, the law wanted to be better, too. We get some highway patrol out here now and then, but we mostly don't see the police. Detective Mulberry has come around through the years. But he just basically checks on people. He worked the case when Barney Hough fell in his barn, but it was just an accident. I mean, Mulberry has always been a good guy to all of us, so . . .” She paused, taking a deep breath. “I didn’t know if Hank was trying to scare me, or if we do have corrupt cops anywhere.”

“I swear to you, we’re on your side,” Amy told her. “Where is Billie now?”

Casey didn’t answer. But Kaila came to the table and leaned over it, saying, “We don’t know. She hasn’t come around. She hasn’t been at the motel, and she hasn’t come here for food. We’re scared. She is the sweetest, most innocent and most vulnerable woman we’ve ever met. One thing — she was bright enough to know someone wanted something very bad to happen to her.”

“What do you think has happened to her?” Hunter asked. “We know the girl who was killed first — Artie called her Lady Liberty — was apparently willing to do whatever was asked of her. Hank used her to bring Artie into the group. He basically gave her to Artie for his first sexual experience, with the promise of a home, community, friends and respect to go along with everything. But I’m afraid we don’t know anything about the second victim.”

“Please . . . I pray it wasn’t Billie,” Casey

said in a whisper.

"I don't think it could have been. She was evidently being killed when we arrived here, when we discovered the first victim," Amy said.

"I don't know . . . I don't know," Casey said.

"Kaila, when we were here before, Ryan saw you hiding food. Was that for Billie?" Hunter asked.

"It was," Kaila said.

"But you couldn't find her?" Amy asked.

Kaila shook her head. "We should have called the cops," she said dolefully.

"If something does happen to her . . ." Casey murmured.

"No, don't go that route," Hunter said firmly. "You two were her friends. You, Martin and Patty — you helped her. And we don't have any answers yet." He hesitated and looked at Amy. "Do you think you could sketch a likeness of our Jane Doe number two's face, as she might have appeared in life?"

Amy stared at him for a minute. Could he read her mind? *Her face was eaten — I'm not a magician!*

But he kept smiling at her; others didn't know the circumstances of the woman's death.

276

"I can try."

Amy pulled out her pad and worked. Kaila looked nervously around.

Amy created a pleasant image of a woman with long dark hair, dark eyes and a smile.

Casey looked at the image.

"No, not her," she said.

"How do you know?" Hunter asked.

"Billie has light hair. Lighter, dirty-blond hair and pretty eyes, a soft, soft brown, like an amber or yellow. And her hair is short — like curving around her face, just about chin length. She chopped it off when she started running."

Amy and Hunter exchanged a quick glance; they hadn't known much about the second corpse, not from the way the body had been all but eaten. They did know she'd had long dark hair.

"When did Billie start running?"

"When they brought her down here."

"When who brought her down here?"

"The men with the van. They brought her and a few of the other girls." Casey paused, taking a deep breath. "Billie said the men in the van — there were three of them — brought down three girls. So, from what you're telling me . . . well, Billie knew the women were transported here because they were supposed to serve men — and were

277

convinced it was a holy mission. She escaped from a cabin somewhere and made her way out through the brush and the snakes and whatever somehow. From what I've seen on the news, and what I've learned from my father, and now you . . . I think the girl killed on the cross was one of the girls Billie was with. I guess the other girl — the second woman you found dead — was the third. Because that's not Billie you sketched," she said, looking at Amy. "I mean, I don't think it can be."

Amy nodded and reached across the table to squeeze Casey's hand. "It's not Billie."

"Not that the murders are any less horrible," Casey said.

"Excuse me, people think I work here," Kaila muttered, moving away from the table to pick up an order of food Frank had set out. Then she put on her waitress smile and went and checked with her customers.

As Kaila headed to a booth, Frank left the kitchen and came around the counter. He spoke casually to a few of his customers while making his way to them.

Hunter watched him, speculative.

"You have to find these killers," Frank said, smiling as if he pretended for anyone watching that he was just discussing his recipe for French toast. "We haven't figured out what the hell is going on around here, but two girls are dead. It's bad for this town. Bad for business."

"That's what we're trying to do," Hunter told him.

"We don't know what you know, but we know Artie was arrested, and Hank is dead. That boy never stood much of a chance, but still. Sometimes I think there just might be an evil seed and some folks are born with it."

Frank straightened as the door to the diner opened. Agent Ryan Anders had arrived, ready for his meeting with Detective Mulberry. Time had been ticking away — they'd started early that morning interrogating Artie, driven back here, taken an airboat out to the shack and made the bloody discovery there.

Yeah, it was dinnertime.

And if they wanted to get up to Maclamara tonight, they had a good five-hour drive ahead of them.

"Hey!" Ryan said, surprised to see them there.

"Hi!" Amy said.

Frank moved away from the end of the table. "Are you joining this crew here?" he asked.

"I, uh, for a minute, sure. I'm meeting

279

Detective Mulberry for dinner," Ryan said.

The open seat was next to Casey. He and Casey hadn't met yet.

Hunter quickly performed the introductions.

"Please, sit," Casey said.

"Back to work for me. Some of us don't get dinner breaks," Frank said, and walked off.

Casey turned back to Amy. "Billie wouldn't just leave, not without a word to us. She was grateful and sweet and . . . we were idiots. We should have done more. She should have . . . trusted cops, I guess," Casey said. "They have her."

"We think we know where they have their main group," Hunter told her. "And we're heading that way."

"You're leaving?" Casey said worriedly. "I admit, I'm afraid. For me, for my dad . . . My brothers are safe. They're up at college, though . . . I don't know! I worry about them, too. I swear to you, my father is a good man. But he thinks he can bring that billionaire Ethan Morrison into the fold, and that if he can do that, he can convince Morrison many of the things he does are wrong. My dad always wants the best in life — he wants to see the best in people. He believes every man can be helped. My dad

280

thinks he can fix a man like Ethan Morrison.

"I worry sometimes my brothers think he's cool — that the media has lied about him, and all he's trying to do is save humanity, researching drugs that can cure cancer, that kind of thing. He scares the hell out of me, but . . . I love my brothers. Anyway, that's not the here or now, but . . . I'm scared of what's going on here."

"I'm staying at the motel," Ryan said firmly. "If any of you need me to help in any way, you make sure you have me on speed dial. I'll come running."

Hunter nodded. "And Detective Mulberry will be close."

He slid out of the booth. "Amy, you and I need to get going. I don't believe Billie is here anymore. I think they found her. They might even know we were closing in on them and got the hell out. I don't believe you're in danger, Casey. But we'll make sure you're protected. And we'll do everything in our power to find Billie."

Amy also stood as Kaila swept back by, anxious.

"What's happening?" she asked.

Amy smiled at her. "Ryan is staying."

"Oh!" Kaila was either relieved, or pleased. Hunter hid a smile. He looked at

Ryan; the kid was going to be a good agent.
And they needed to get going — nothing
else was going to happen here.
Their lead, Billie, was gone.

14

Fall 1993
Sam

Walking toward Sam was Special Agent
Dawson, the man who had slipped into the
commune undercover, who had offered him
this chance.

Sam didn't think he'd ever seen a more
beautiful human being in his life. Dawson
was making his way across an open patch of
ground, where the forest gave way to low
shrubs, in between him and where Sam's
family was hiding in the deeper woods.

"It's all right!" Sam said. "It's all right!"

He heard Jessie let out a soft sob.

She looked at Sam, relief and hope mingling in her eyes. She hugged their son and
said, "It's all right, Cam, it's all right! We
can go to him!"

Cam knew the agent; Dawson had spent
time with them all. Young himself — in his
late twenties — he'd been assigned to watch

the children during his undercover days at the commune.

Cameron looked at both of his parents, questioning.

Sam nodded. "We're right behind you, buddy!" he told his son.

Dawson stepped closer, and at Sam's gentle push, Cameron started to run to him.

The sudden explosive sound of a shot rang out.

Terror flooded Sam. His son, his beloved boy, was out in the open.

If they had somehow gotten Cam, he prayed that death would take him quickly, too, because he'd no longer be able to endure life.

But Cam barely faltered as he kept running. Then Sam saw other men, all in camouflage, come out of the woods behind Dawson. Five of them, Sam counted. Other agents. And it was one of those agents who had fired, who still had his gun pointing at Brother Colin, who had stepped from the woods to their left to take aim at Cameron.

"Down!" Dawson shouted, throwing himself on top of Cameron and bearing them both to the earth. Sam put his arms around Jessie, dragging her back into the trees.

More gunfire crackled. In the silence a few long moments later, Sam saw agents moving toward the direction from which the shots had come. Dawson stood, and helped Cameron to his feet, as well. Sam started running to them, pulling Jessie along at his side.

Dawson kept Cam's hand in his as they came together. Jessie fell to her knees to hug her son.

"There were two of them out here. I guess they thought they'd chase you down and get rid of you easy enough," Dawson said. "Looks like Brother Colin is dead. Think that's Brother Anthony who was behind him, and we'll get an ambulance for him. We'll get the three of you out of here, and then we'll be going in — today."

"Thank you — I don't know how we'll ever thank you," Sam told him.

Dawson grinned. "No, Sam. Thank you. We need your testimony because we're going to try to bring them in, clean out the whole hornet's nest."

"You have my testimony."

"And mine!" Jessie said, standing. "This has all been my fault. I fell into something far worse than what I thought I'd been leaving behind. I was so stupid!"

"Jessie, don't beat yourself up. You and Sam at least saw the truth. You knew Brother William was using people, sucking them dry

285

— and killing them, as well. You did the right thing. Not everyone has that kind of courage."

"We couldn't have done anything without you. You saw what they'd do. They'd have killed us. They were going to shoot Cameron, shoot down a six-year-old boy!"

"But they didn't get me," Cameron said, looking up at Dawson in admiration. "They didn't get me, because of you guys!"

"They're the good guys," Sam said, setting his hands on his son's shoulders. "They're the good guys."

"But there is still danger," Dawson warned them.

"We, uh, have money. We haven't touched it. Brother William knew Jessie's father died, and he left everything to her. He was figuring a way to get her to transfer everything over to him, but thank God you came along. Again, thank God — we do have that to fall back on. We can go somewhere," Sam said. "Somewhere far away."

"We need you to testify, and after that, well . . . What I'd like for you to do is enter witness protection. They can set you up with identities that will let you lead new lives. Cam can go to school . . ."

"Witness protection would be great," Jessie said. "Sam, we can start over. We can

286

be new people and let Cameron have a normal life."

"Let's get out of the woods here first, eh? And get through the operation we have planned for today."

Sam, Jessie and Cameron were taken to a safe house in Los Angeles.

And the operation did happen that afternoon.

An ATF team went in along with a contingent of men and women from the FBI.

Brother William had been stockpiling weapons illegally.

He ordered his followers to take suicide pills when he saw the law coming. But happily, most did not. Instinct kicked in with most people.

They wouldn't kill their children.

Brother William was cornered in his office; he didn't take a pill himself. He swore he'd be judged innocent in court, that he'd done nothing wrong.

But there were others besides Sam and Jessie who testified he'd taken them for everything, and he'd ordered the murder of a young woman and attempted to murder them, as well.

Brother William tried hard. He claimed his henchmen had worked on their own.

Brother Colin was dead, but Brother

Anthony protested and turned witness himself. The case was federal — he wanted to avoid the death penalty.

Brother Darryl disappeared; they were never able to find him, which made witness protection even more appealing to Sam and Jessie.

After the trial, it was time to start their lives again.

Special Agent Dawson introduced Sam to Special Agent Barry Clooney, the man who would set up their new lives.

"Naturally, we have to create identities for you," Clooney told them. "For your new names, anything you want to avoid, or anything that comes to mind?"

"Forrest," Sam said. He looked at Dawson. "This man saved us when we were in a forest."

"Connie. Connie Forrest!" Jessie said. "I always liked that name."

"Al. Alfred Forrest," Sam said. He smiled at Jessie — now Connie, his beloved wife by any name.

"And what about this young man?" Dawson asked, bending down to Cameron.

Cameron had a serious look on his small face as he looked at Dawson. "I thought you were a hunter — you saved my life. I want to be Hunter."

"Hunter? Hunter Forrest?" Jessie asked.

"Hunter," Cameron said stubbornly, and Sam laughed.

"A hunter in the forest saved us. Jess, that's what he wants. It's a good name, a strong name, and the name he wants."

Jessie looked at Dawson.

"It's a great name," she said.

From that day on, they were the Forrest family.

Al, Connie and Hunter.

And the names quickly became more real than those they'd been born with. And a new life, created with love and intention, became real, as well.

They became . . . themselves. Connie was able to retrain and become an art teacher. Al was able to write, and he was published.

They moved a few times, just to be safe. But the memory of their time in the commune faded through the years, though it always remained.

A nightmare that teased now and then . . .

Every day was a gift; the sun always burned a little brighter.

It scared Connie and Al a little, of course, when their son wanted to go into the military. But they didn't stop him; he had really grown into a fine young man.

And they weren't even surprised when he

wanted to join the FBI. They'd been given the gift of life; in the end, they were proud when their son wanted to do whatever he could to give that gift to others.

15

They took turns driving, heading for I-75 quickly, stopping for dinner — which, they both realized, they could have eaten at the diner. But they were quick, taking only thirty minutes for food and time to refuel.

As they drove, Hunter told Amy they'd stay in Micanopy. While a small town itself, Micanopy had a few good hotels.

"Have you been there?" he asked Amy after they had eaten and were back on the way.

"I've been through, visiting friends who went to school in Gainesville," she told him. "I can't say I know it well. It's an old town, right?"

He nodded. "Very old. One square mile, right in the heart of a rural area. The population is well below one thousand, though when you head southwest down to Maclamara, the population goes down to just a few hundred. Micanopy, though, is charming — rural, of course. Micanopy is the oldest midland town in Florida — dripping moss, narrow streets, pretty. Anyway, I still have a room at a historic inn there. It's an old Victorian house that has been adapted. It's a small place, but the inn does a good business what with college students and their parents and visitors."

"You still have a room there?"

"I never checked out when I headed south. I was on my way the second I heard about your victim."

"Ah."

"Anyway, it's a suite on the ground floor. You can have the bedroom. I'll take the sofa."

"I don't mind a sofa."

"I'm sure you don't, but trust me, I don't mean this in any chauvinistic way — I will be miserable if you don't take the bedroom. Can't help it — my mom raised me to be courteous."

She smiled. "I don't care where I sleep as long as I get a shower. I still feel as if I smell . . . like that cabin."

"Me, too," he agreed. "Showers. Even if we do get in at one or two in the morning."

When they arrived, the night-lights that glowed around the place showed the charm of the Victorian building, with the large

292

porch and its fine columns and the balconies above. The surrounding trees were all dripping moss beneath the moon.

Hunter used his key to enter the house and they paused in the old entry. The office — on the ground floor, right across from what was called "the Faulkner Suite" — was closed.

A curving staircase led to the rooms on the second floor. There was a parlor immediately in front, with the hall to the suite just to the side of it. The parlor had been decorated with Victorian furniture, fine upholstered chairs, a love seat and a "fainting" couch.

"This place is lovely," Amy said approvingly.

"The suite is nice, too. These people did a great job renovating."

They headed down the hall where he used his second key to open the door to the suite.

"Believe it or not," he said, "within my federal budget. That's what small-town life will do for you."

She smiled, looking around. The suite didn't offer a kitchen, but it had a wet bar with a microwave and little refrigerator. It was separated from the parlor area by a counter; the parlor had a sofa, wide-screen TV and small occasional tables, along with a dining table that would seat eight.

"Cool," Amy approved.

"Hmm. Didn't notice it before, but I don't need the sofa — there's a Murphy bed against the far wall. I'm all set."

"You take first shower," Amy told him. "That way, we can both settle in. I want to see what made the news — if the murders are still on national TV."

"As you wish."

Hunter headed into his room, and dug into his overnight bag.

A clean T-shirt and boxer shorts would do for decent sleep attire.

He showered quickly; it was late, and he knew they both needed sleep. Cops and agents went home sometimes; they split shifts. They slept.

They didn't have to be on this the way that they were, going 24/7.

Well, he thought, maybe he did have to be on it the way that he was.

Amy didn't. But she wasn't a complainer, and she didn't want off the case.

Despite his hurry, he scrubbed his hair. There had been a feeling the blood and tragedy of the cabin had lingered on them, as if it had been in the air and settled into them.

So he scrubbed, and scrubbed hard — but quickly.

Amy was in front of the television and she looked up as he entered the room.

"Nice boxers," she noted.

"Hey, I'm a fan of the Marvel empire," he told her.

His good boxers featured the Hulk. No wonder she was grinning.

She turned serious. "The murders are still on the news. It seems they've been attributed to cult activity, whether details have been kept back from the press or not."

"We'll go to Maclamara tomorrow. There's one bar there — we should stop in, see who is hanging around and if there's a chill wind in the town," he said.

"And from there? How will we go about trying to find Billie?"

"There are a few nearby college students we'll need to see. But I'd also like to explore. There's one main road. The bar is between here and their Main Street. Outside of that, you have a lot of ranches. They raise horses here, almost like an extension of Ocala. Cows and other farm animals, too. It's Alachua County and the county folk are fine, but if we determine we need a search warrant, we'll still go the federal way. But if we need instant help, well, they're good."

"Okay."

Amy stood and grabbed her bag. "Should I set an alarm?"

"One of us will wake up without one," he said dryly. "And if we don't, well, we'll get a late start. Nothing seems to happen by day. It's the nights we need to worry about."

She nodded and headed into the bedroom and the shower.

Hunter took her seat on the couch, staring at the television.

The news paused for a weather break. They were looking at a full moon tomorrow night.

A full moon.

He closed his eyes for a minute, trying to sort out the cabinets in his mind. His eyes sprang open as a young anchorman started speaking again with his partner, a well-dressed, slim, middle-aged woman.

"What happened when you requested an interview with Ethan Morrison? He surely must have some comment on what is happening down there," the anchor said.

The anchorwoman laughed softly. "I'm afraid his comment was 'no comment.' While Mr. Morrison does have vast holdings in the state of Florida, a representative from Morrison Enterprises informed us Mr. Morrison hasn't been to the south of the state in months. He's no longer involved in the sugarcane business and he only holds on to his property for sentimental reasons. It was one of his father's first purchases as a poor young man starting out. I can't say I'm surprised the man doesn't want to speak with the media — he was cleared in court, but suspicions follow him endlessly."

"Well, it's a pity he won't speak. With his resources, he could certainly help out."

"The FBI and local authorities are not giving out many specifics, but one of my sources tells me that a young man's suicide — after a botched kidnapping attempt — gives credence to the fact we're looking at something pretty bad happening, and we can only hope law enforcement gets it together to get this solved before there are more deaths. And excuse us, folks, we have to take a commercial break here."

Hunter closed his eyes again.

Pictures ran in his mind.

He saw the brands again, both on the bodies and imagining Amy's sketches.

Then he knew; he knew as if someone had smacked him in the head with the truth.

The curves, the lines and the curves . . .

They formed a double *P. PP.*

People's Paradise.

He flew off the sofa, heading to the bedroom, flinging the door open.

"Amy!"

He froze. He should have knocked.

She was just out of the shower. The door to the bathroom was open, and she was just tying a towel around her body. Her hair was free and flowing softly in waves around her shoulders.

She was still damp from the shower and the steam.

"I — Sorry."

"It's okay," she assured him, knotting the towel. "It's something important, I take it."

He nodded.

"Are you . . . going to share?"

"What? Yes, of course. I'm so sorry. I —"

"It's okay. Really," she said. "What is it? Please tell me."

"Your sketches . . . the brands. I know what they are."

"You know — from my sketches? What?"

"The brands are double *P*s," he said. "They stand for People's Paradise."

She looked at him, frowning. "People's Paradise?"

He nodded. Of course she wouldn't know about it. More than a quarter of a century had passed since the day when he had stood, a terrified little kid in the woods.

"They were active almost thirty years

298

ago," he said. "They created a commune in California. It was run by a man known as Brother William, who turned out to be a William Bayer, a stockbroker who liked to play with other people's money. He preyed on those who were horrified by the costs of medicine and the war vets who were left homeless in the streets. He found people who were looking for greater equality among everyone, and he found those who were . . . disenchanted by modern society and anxious to find a different way of life by working the earth. He preached community and giving . . . and everyone gave their incomes to him, any property to him. He kept preaching poverty — and making himself richer and richer. The FBI and the ATF and others shut him down."

"But could this be him . . . now?"

"Not him," Hunter said. "He went to prison, where he was eventually killed by a fellow prisoner in a fight."

"Then —"

"People who were part of the cult — part of the upper echelon of the cult — got away."

"And you think one of them is the head of whatever is going on here?"

"It's possible."

She came toward him, pausing just a few

feet away.

"Do you — do you want to study the sketches again?" she asked.

"It can wait until morning. I'll get hold of the main offices, too, and see if they can trace anything for me and . . ."

"And?"

"I still think Ethan Morrison is involved somehow. I think there must be a connection. The man's father bought the property in South Florida. I want everything that can be found on him."

"Okay."

She took a step closer to him. He realized he'd been speaking in full sentences, even making sense.

But he'd been watching Amy, studying her — her eyes, her face. Her form beneath the towel.

He wasn't sure what made him do it. He took a step closer to her.

And then she took a step closer to him.

She smiled. He felt a flush of heat at her look. They had come to a place where it seemed they could read one another's mind. He took her into his arms.

She seemed to flow into them.

He met her eyes. Beautiful eyes he'd come to know so well, changing with laughter, passion, determination, empathy, like prisms in their beauty.

He hoped he had come to read them well.

He lowered his head and found her lips; she returned the kiss with a sweet fever, lips soft and sure, parting, welcoming, moist and warm.

The towel fell from her body.

He could feel her naked breasts against his chest, pressing against the soft fabric of his T-shirt, and the vibrant heat and curve of her body against his boxers.

He should have been telling himself that this was entirely wrong.

Instead, he was telling himself it was right, that it had been coming. They were deeply involved in so much together, in a case they'd both see through, work tirelessly at, and they were, in a strange sense, connected.

Logic didn't matter. Wanting her had been growing in him explosively. It wasn't that he didn't have control; he did.

This was a fully conscious decision.

Her fingers slipped up under his shirt and trailed down his back, nails a soft but erotic brush against his flesh. He cupped her head and let the kiss intensify, his free hand running the length of her back.

They moved backward, a motion oddly synced, and fell upon the bed. He shrugged off his clothing, then rose above her, cradling her into his arms and drawing them side by side, holding fast to the kiss at first, then easing his lips from hers, letting them fall over her throat and shoulders and breasts. And below.

There was nothing like her touch in return — the sweeping caress of her fingers, the lightest whisper of her breath against his flesh. Every little movement seemed to heighten the raw hunger and desire between them; they played and touched, kissed, tasted, dove into the sweetest intimacy, until the agony of being separate overrode the soaring ecstasy of each of those touches, and he thrust deep within her, finding a new explosion of sensation so rich it seemed to rock the room.

She was a fluid wave beneath him, and he felt her every surge and writhe.

Their lips met again as they savored the wild sweep of the storm that had come between them, long awaited, and yet so sudden.

Wild as the ride was, the climax was evermore combustible, not just an explosion, he thought whimsically when thought returned to him, but the demolition of a city block.

Finally, he lay at her side, bringing her to curl against him, amazed at the time it was taking him just to breathe normally again.

"Um. I swear, I didn't plan that," he said after a while.

She raised on an elbow to look at him, amused. "Really? I have to admit, I have been trying to figure out how to plan something just like what happened."

He arched his head back, studying her face.

"I kind of thought you didn't like me."

"I guess I wasn't really a team player at first. I didn't know . . . that the case would get worse and worse."

"You're an incredible team player," he assured her.

"And you mean that how?"

He laughed softly. "In several ways. Right now, I'm damned glad that you're my partner."

She smiled.

He stretched, and then started to get out of the bed.

"You're not seriously going to go sleep on the sofa now, are you?" she asked him.

He smiled. "No. I did something against the grain. I left my gun out there."

"Oh," she said. "Maybe that's why we shouldn't —"

"Nope. I told you — this wasn't a plan, it was just a moment of . . . wow," he finished softly. "When I figured out what the brand was . . . all that went through my mind was telling you. I'll be right back."

He secured his gun, double-checked the doors and the windows and returned.

She was waiting, and swept her arms around him. He met her eyes, her beautiful, crystal, ever-changing eyes.

"Should we sleep?" she asked.

"Soon. Not quite yet," he told her.

They made love again. It felt like the most natural thing in the world.

And then they slept.

When morning came, with coffee on, with them both dressed and ready for the day, he knew soon it would be time to explain to her just exactly why he knew so much about the People's Paradise.

Amy met Pete Perkins, owner and operator of the Dixie Inn, when they were leaving. Hunter introduced her as Special Agent Amy Larson of the FDLE, and she realized the man knew Hunter was here on a case.

"Glad to have you here. There's nothing down in Micanopy. I mean, we are a small town here, but a normal small town. Old South, yes, and some people have old-fashioned ideas, but we're mostly law-abiding and straight arrows. We have a nice ability to agree to disagree when we have different notions about stuff. Now down in Maclamara . . ."

"Isn't the town a bit of a rural extension of this one?" Amy asked.

"Lord, no," the man assured her. He was a pleasant-looking man, about six-feet-even, gray-haired and lean. "No, I . . . we're mostly conservative, sometimes liberal, but . . . normal. Those guys down there . . . well, it doesn't surprise me a poor young woman was murdered. Have they got any more on that, Mr. Forrest?"

"We're working it. That's why we're back here."

"You think those murders down south are connected."

"We do."

"You be careful. There are a lot of guns down there. Why, there's a preacher down there, says his folks need to bring their guns to church. Guns — in church. Godly men need to protect themselves, their children and their faith, and if that means guns, then each man should have his and know how to use it. And there's no law against it. So . . . anyway, I'll just stay here. We may not be the best people in the world, but we're surely not the worst — and we're normal. You two take care, you hear me?"

305

"We will, and thanks," Hunter told him.

Hunter's hand came to rest on the small of Amy's back. She didn't mind the touch. She wouldn't have minded it before last night; it was nothing more than a hint they needed to politely disengage and get moving.

Except now, this morning, it was a reminder of their touches the night before.

She couldn't remember when she'd last felt so good, so complete.

She cared for Hunter. Liked him, respected him, more.

Maybe it was natural with all they'd been through? Maybe it was just about circumstance, and when this was all over . . .

No. She would still like him and have tremendous respect for him.

And possibly *want* him every time he walked into a room.

Maybe that part would be dealt with easily; maybe she'd never see him again.

For now, they had their work. And from now on, she determined, they could have their nights together.

Even if that night for them was short.

"Amy?" Hunter murmured.

"Thank you, nice to meet you, Mr. Perkins. I love the inn — you've made it absolutely charming," Amy told him.

Perkins seemed to glow along with his smile. "Thank you!"

They headed out.

"We're going to the bar you've talked about?" Amy asked.

"Yep." Hunter cast a glance her way as he turned the key in the ignition. "And let's see that forewarned is forearmed — there are indeed a lot of guns down there. Let's be way above wary, okay?"

"Absolutely," Amy promised.

"The place is called Bikes and Brews," Hunter said. "They do get bikers. They get clients from Maclamara, of course, sometimes people from Ocala, Micanopy and even Gainesville."

"You've been in there already?"

"Yes, but just as a customer. I didn't announce myself. I wanted to take a look at the place and the clientele."

"Of course. That's why we're dressed as we are?"

He'd asked that morning that she wear something casual. He was wearing jeans and a T-shirt and sneakers; she had opted to do the same, but her shirt had a slight V at the neck instead of being flush to her throat. She hated clothing that came right to her throat, but her T-shirt was still quite a respectable one, the design of it being that

307

of a popular cartoon character.

"That's the reason," he said.

"You think someone might approach us?"

"Maybe not, but it's possible. Oh, by the way, you don't believe in any kind of gun control. And you think we need major reform on most of our policies as a nation."

"I do?"

"Today you do." He glanced her way. "What Pete was saying is this — Micanopy residents may manage to get along and respect one another, despite differing beliefs. But when you get down to Maclamara, you're entering a den of white supremacists."

"Ah," Amy muttered. "Understood."

"Let's get all our calls made. You get in touch with John, I'll work my end."

She pulled her phone out and called John. He was home. His son, Johnny Jr., was with him for a few days. Then Brenda would be back.

He was behaving, being an excellent patient, he promised her.

Amy told him about the shack — though he knew about it because he'd already read Aidan Cypress's reports. She told him about their meeting with Casey and explained why they feared Billie had been taken north somewhere — possibly to Maclamara —

and they were on their way there now. She also shared what he didn't know — Hunter was convinced he recognized the brands on the dead women, that were double *P*s, and the situation might relate back to someone who had been involved with a cult a quarter of a century ago.

John thanked her for the call, and she hung up.

"John's doing okay?" Hunter asked.

"He sounds as if he's being a good patient and not even driving those around him crazy."

"That's a relief. John is a good agent for Florida — and a good man."

"He is. And a good partner. Oh, and you're a great partner."

He grinned.

"Hey," she said. "You didn't like me at first."

"No, I didn't know you. I just thought you were . . . young."

"Young doesn't mean bad," she said.

He was smiling as he looked ahead at the winding road. The country they traveled now was rich with tall oaks, and all those oaks dripped moss. It was a beautiful drive, though the road hadn't been repaved in years.

"Young can mean all kinds of good," he

told her. "Not far now . . . we should be there in about five minutes."

"Five minutes? Shoot. I hope you have time to tell me why you think this is related, why you think you know so much about the People's Paradise."

He looked over at her, slowing the car, then looking at the road again.

"Because I lived at the commune as a kid. I was a member of People's Paradise."

16

Hunter had thought he owed it to Amy to tell her about his past. It just wasn't going to be as easy as he thought.

He had studied so much at college, and he had spent time speaking with his parents, of course.

They were good, normal people.

So how had they gotten mixed up in it all?

All that he had learned about behavioral sciences still left him at a loss. He tried to understand; on the one hand, he did. He knew the logic and he knew there was usually a progression in "brainwashing" an individual. It was still harder than he thought to go back.

He pulled into a parking space on the dirt-and-pebbled drive in front of the biker bar.

He turned in his seat and looked at Amy. "When I was six years old, my parents were instrumental in bringing down the leader of

People's Paradise. But they were members when I was a small child, and while I didn't understand everything going on, I knew they revered Brother William, and then they had come to fear him. When we got out, we were put into the witness protection program. My parents are still in it and will be until they die. The feds got most of the people involved in the higher echelon, but there are a few of his acolytes, if you will, or enforcers, who were never found. The assumption was that they fled to Mexico."

"Oh," Amy said.

"We'll talk about it more later, if you want. For now, we should go listen and observe in the bar."

They got out of the car; Hunter's phone rang.

Caller ID showed him it was his boss, and he paused. "It's Garza. I have to take this."

"That's fine. I'll head on in," Amy said.

Hunter watched her go. Inwardly, he shook his head — at himself. He was really falling into frightening territory; he was enchanted with the sway of her hips as she walked. Her jeans seemed to emphasize the fact that she had long, long legs.

"Hunter?"

"Yes, sir. Is there anything you've discovered?"

"We've checked out records. Colby's son Jayden was in a fraternity at school, and then Chase was accepted into the same one. But they left several months ago — left the fraternity after the first year, choosing to live on their own in an apartment."

"Jayden is in premed, from what I understand — about to graduate with his bachelor's degree. Chase just started — he's a freshman," Hunter said.

"That is correct. We also discovered Morrison's two sons — about the same ages — were also members of the same fraternity. And left the fraternity house to live in an apartment just about the same time."

"So, you think —"

"I don't think anything. I'm just giving you the information."

Hunter hesitated. "Sir, can you get Sheila to research something? The general perception out in the world is Ethan Morrison's father was a dirt-poor farmer who worked to the bone to start the empire Ethan turned into billion-dollar businesses. I think we need to know more about his father."

"The man is dead, but we'll do the research that we can."

"Ethan Morrison is a comparatively young man for his riches, right?"

"Forty-four," Garza told him. "Had children young, divorced the first wife. Who was going to go to court against him, but she was never able to do so — she passed away from natural causes."

"How convenient for Morrison."

"It was an aneurysm."

"Right. I'd like to know about the medical examiner who had the case."

"It was almost twenty years ago."

"Hell, I would dig her up."

"If you did and it was proved she was murdered, you'd never pin it on Morrison — not this late in the game."

"People do have an alarming tendency to die around him."

"We're doing what we can."

"I know. Please, this may be important. Ask Sheila to use her most amazing digging talents and see what she can come up with."

"I will. Happy to follow any lead you throw at us." He paused. "I know you're the right man for this, Hunter. But make sure you don't let your past sidetrack you."

"Yes, sir. The Morrison sons' names, by the way?"

"Ezekiel, known as Zeke, and Aaron."

"Biblical."

"Yes. Take care. Should it become necessary, I can send more agents."

"And when we're ready, I will call on

them," Hunter promised.

Garza was quiet for a minute. "You know what it's like, when we reach the point and have witnesses or facts to move on. You're a hell of an agent, Hunter, but you know damn well you're going to need help. As in maybe a SWAT team."

"Yes, of course. But we don't really have anything yet. I know there's a cult at work here, but I can't say who is involved, though I have a suspicion. And whoever is the head man, he has six or more trusted helpers. The men who came down in the van, for one, bringing the victims to be killed in the south. Right now we're trying to check out the friendly folk of Maclamara. We're at a bar on the northern edge of the town —"

"I know where you are. We're tracking your phone."

"Good."

"Keep me apprised of every situation."

"Yes, sir."

"Oh! One more thing," Garza said before Hunter could ring off. "Special Agent Roger Dawson, retired, called in. He heard about the murders and assumed you were on the case. He says he may be retired, but he's available if you want to ask him questions about the past, about anyone concerned."

"That's great — Dawson was my hero. I'm

always happy to talk to him. He helped me forget the past. Now maybe he can help me remember when it might be important."

Hunter ended the call and stood, thoughtful for a moment.

Dawson *had* been his hero, the reason he'd become an FBI agent, and the reason he'd been so determined to make his life count.

He could still remember standing in the clearing on the California hillside.

Hunter hadn't been involved with any of the trial; he'd been a six-year-old. But he had known Brother Colin died in the gunfight. Brother Anthony had gone to prison and died there, as had several others. But the man known as Brother Darryl had disappeared.

And Hunter could remember Special Agent Dawson talking to his parents, warning them they couldn't go back — only forward, only under witness protection and only as their new identities.

Because revenge was something that could possess a man.

17

Through the relative gloom of the bar, Hunter could see Amy was seated on a stool. A tall man in his early thirties with neck-length, dark, curly hair and light eyes was leaning against the bar at her side.

Flirting, obviously.

Amy was laughing at his words.

The man was wearing black jeans and a black T-shirt with a motorcycle insignia.

Just a biker — or was he more?

Hunter walked casually up to the bar to join her. She turned, her smile still in place. "Hunter! There you are. I'd like you to meet Phin Harrison. He lives just about a mile or so down. He has a motorcycle repair shop."

"How's it going?" Hunter said, offering the man his hand.

"Uh, hey," the man said, shaking hands with Hunter, studying him, assessing him.

Phin appeared to be perplexed; apparently, he had thought Amy was alone.

"Motorcycle repair, eh?" Hunter said.

"You have a bike?" Phin asked.

"No, I've had bikes and I've been thinking about getting one again. I'm weighing the pros and cons of the different ones on the market now."

"Well, come by the shop. I can show you a few."

"People here are so nice, Hunter!" Amy said, enthused. "They're having a big barbecue at their city park, sounds really cool. Phin invited us."

"Really? That *is* nice," Hunter said. "But is it like the whole town is invited? And, of course, if we're coming, we'd need to bring something —"

"We do it every few weeks," Phin said. "And we never ask newcomers to bring anything. People just get together. They make plans with each other sometimes, things they're going to do together between barbecues. Oh, we have some preaching, too, but we have it on a Sunday and we're kind of a God-fearing place here, so we're all happy to have our church out in the park. You're not against church, are you?" Phin asked them.

"No!" Amy said. "I'll be happy to hear a preacher."

The bartender, a big man, about six-foot-five, both heavy and muscled, came up, and Hunter ordered a beer.

The bartender eyed him suspiciously.

Just because they were newcomers? Or did someone know the law was heading back to their little town?

The door opened, shedding sunlight into the dimly lit bar.

A young man came in and looked in the bar for a minute, his eyes perhaps adjusting to the light. The bartender lifted a hand to him, and Phin Harrison said, "Hey."

They appeared to know him. He looked to be college-age.

Sandy hair, six feet, medium build. He moved in to take a seat at the stool closest to the door; the bartender moved on to help him.

Phin turned his attention on Hunter and Amy again.

"You two a couple, or what?" he asked.

Hunter and Amy looked at each other.

Hunter laughed softly, setting his hands on her shoulders. "Yeah, we're a couple. Definitely," he said lightly.

"Well, think about the invitation. Like I said, we're God-fearing people around here. We take care of each other. So, are you just passing through?"

Hunter decided to take a chance. "Actu-

319

ally, we were thinking about maybe settling in this area."

Amy glanced quickly at Hunter but didn't miss a beat. "It's so beautiful. I grew up in the city — so seeing the trees here, wow! The way the moss falls from the trees and the trails just streak off the roads, I'd sure consider it."

"Well, we do like places that feel like neighborhoods," Hunter said. "Where people help one another, where they do things for one another. And we have been looking for the right church to join. She was raised Catholic, and I'm Baptist. We're looking for something . . . different."

"You'd love our pastor," Phin said. "And we do have something special and unique here. Think about it hard, because if you don't believe you're right for really loving your neighbors and pitching in, you're not going to like anything about this place. No one is an island here — Micanopy isn't big, and the next biggest thing, well, you have to go all the way up to Gainesville or all the way down to Ocala if you need something and you don't know your neighbors around here. Not that far in miles, maybe, but in an emergency, well, we all need each other."

"So true," Amy said.

"So, where is this barbecue?" Hunter

asked. "Where is the town park?"

"About five miles down — you won't be able to miss it. There's a welcoming sign that's always up. The outdoors is our church around here, though we do have a church. Anyway, like I said. Give it some thought. You're welcome to come by."

"Thanks." Hunter finished his beer and set the empty bottle down. "Honey, let's get back to the hotel. I'm going to call in about the horses, make sure the vet saw Red after we left."

"You horse people?" Phin asked.

"Right. That's why we need property," Hunter told him.

"Nice to meet you — and I'm sure we'll meet again," Amy said.

Amy slid off her bar stool and Hunter took her hand, ready to lead her out. As they reached the door, she whispered, "Go on out."

He did, but remained by the door, not sure what she was planning. But as she headed back in, she called out, "I think I left my sweater."

He waited.

A minute later, she emerged.

He caught her hand and they smiled at one another and laughed, aware someone in the bar could be watching them.

When they were in the car, Amy explained, "I knew the bartender was talking with the kid who came in, and I had a feeling they were talking about us."

"Saying?"

"When I was heading back in, he was saying he'd been warned about a pair of agents on the case down in the south, and they shouldn't be fooled by us. I guess going to the barbecue as a couple of folks seeking a new home is not going to fly. We won't hear anything, anyway."

"No, they'll be watching us like hawks," Hunter said. He looked at her as they drove out. "I'd still like to go to that barbecue."

"We can get a satellite image of the area. We can park a car and see what we can find from the outside looking in," Amy suggested.

He nodded. "Good. Right. And I'll let Garza know just in case there's trouble."

"I'll talk to my people, too."

"And we'll check in with Detective Ellison."

"Ellison?"

"He called me when they found the girl here — before I headed south to be with you. He's a county man, detective, and a good one. We were in a behavioral training class together and worked the murder of a young waiter, maybe five years ago. He's still investigating the woman who is, to me, the first in this series, even if she was killed as practice so they'd know how to kill when they started murdering people for their Apocalypse scenario."

"I don't think I've met him," Amy said. "I've been around a lot of the state, but I haven't met an Ellison."

"Bo Ellison. He might even have something for us, though Bo would have called with anything important. He's been getting reports, of course. But I also want to let him know I believe something more is going to happen here."

"You don't think they're planning something at the barbecue, do you?"

He was quiet a minute. "I've started to wonder about Ethan Morrison's sons — Aaron and Ezekiel."

"Because they're his sons?"

"Well, that. And maybe because I believe he's been a controlling father. But not just for that reason. I don't necessarily believe that the sins of the fathers fall to the sons. But Morrison has been in the news often enough and he's often seen with his sons. It might be natural that they'd be his loyal lieutenants. They might have been among the men in the van, the three men who came

323

south with our victims, Lady Liberty and Jane Doe number two. If not, Colby's boys could be involved, Jayden and Chase — and maybe all four of them. This operation is tight, and loyalty is key. Loyalty among family members can be fierce. We know Hank either helped commit or was privy to the murders. Whoever recruited Hank knew something about him — knew about his past, and he'd be easy prey for them. That makes me believe — along with Casey's concerns — her brothers are involved. They might be at college now, but they grew up back south and they knew Hank."

"We'll need to recognize them when we see them," Amy said.

"Yes, we'll get photos sent to us. Back at the inn, we'll work on contacts and a plan for an hour or so, get some satellite images and head back."

"All right," Amy agreed. "Food along the way, please." She flashed him a smile. "I don't usually drink during the day, and certainly not in the morning. But Phin wanted to buy me a drink, and you said we needed to get friendly with the locals, so . . ."

"Let's get something to eat," he agreed.

There was a sign that welcomed them to Micanopy. The sign explained that Micanopy means "head chief" and that it had been awarded to the famed leader of the Alachua Seminoles. Hernando de Soto had been in the area way back in 1539.

Maclamara, he knew, was a township named for the rich man who'd once been the only landholder in the area — he'd owned a plantation that had encompassed it all. The place still had only about twenty families that called it home.

Amy asked, "Where was she found?"

He knew she was referring to the victim in Maclamara.

"About half a mile back, not far off the road. Right at the border between Maclamara and Micanopy."

"Can we go back?" she asked.

"We need to watch our time."

"I won't need much," she said.

He pulled the car in a tight U-turn and drove back the other way. There was a small part in the trees and a narrow, leaf-laden trail that led to the clearing in the woods where the young woman had been found. Hunter drove onto the shoulder of the highway, and they got out.

A few strings of crime scene tape littered the ground, but it had rained, and there was no evidence that remained to show just where the body had been.

But Hunter remembered, and he showed Amy.

"They had a swarm of forensics experts on her, from the county and from the FBI. They combed the place, and they talked to everyone over the age of three, to the best of my knowledge, in Maclamara and Micanopy. No one saw anything. No one knew her."

Amy looked around.

"It's just like in the south." She started walking back from the site and paused. "You're right, this was practice. What is frightening now is we've had the sword and the pestilence."

"Famine and plague are next."

"They could be starving their next victim to death."

"Or they have a biological weapon. And they're planning on mass casualties — not just one murder." He paused. "Or the first horse, the white horse, is the conqueror — and these murders are to show us the conqueror has come. And the conqueror is showing us he has the power to do what he will with widespread dominion. He carried a bow, but no arrows. He is a warrior and can fight, but first, he's just taking over. Money, maybe even diplomacy. 'And I saw, and behold a white horse: and he that sat

326

on him had a bow; and a crown was given unto him: and he went forth conquering, and to conquer.' "

"It's so confusing. But I still think he's going to kill again with famine and disease," Amy said. "Unless we can stop him."

"Could be . . . the red horse is next. He brings war. By the time he's done all this killing, there will be a war, even if it's a war between law enforcement and his following."

"There are dozens of interpretations regarding the Four Horsemen. Maybe this guy has his own interpretation, as well. Maybe he's convinced his followers that the Apocalypse is on us — many rational people think we've brought the world to that point. Anyway, let's get going. We can get satellite imagery on our phones, but a computer will be better."

They walked back to the car. Hunter paused on the trail. It was so quiet. It didn't seem as if the birds and the creatures of the forest were moving, almost as if recent events had caused them all to hold their breath.

"What?" she asked.

"I was just wondering how many places there are like this, places distant from civilization, from people, where this kind of murder can be carried out."

"More than we can count," Amy said.

They reached the car and he drove again; they were both thoughtful.

"It's a good thing you came into the bar when you did," she said as they neared the inn.

"Oh?"

"I might have carried on flirting with Phin. And then, maybe, go to the barbecue with him after pretending I didn't know you."

"Amy, this isn't a solo gig —"

"I know. But I didn't know, not until I went back in, that we were going to be under suspicion. Someone called up here to warn people about us. Hank is dead. Artie is being held. It wasn't the two of them. And as far as it goes, everyone we came close to claimed they were being secretive, but that's because they were trying to help Billie."

They reached the inn. As they drove up, Hunter saw a vehicle just off the drive that hadn't been there the night before.

It was a paneled van.

He looked at Amy.

"Be ready for anything," he told her.

Amy was ready, even as she stepped out of

the car. The sight of the van and Hunter's warning had put her on high alert. She had a hand on her gun holster.

She was ready to drop behind the protection of the car.

An older man stepped out of the van; he had a rich headful of snow-white hair, stood very tall and straight and appeared extremely athletic.

To her amazement, Hunter cried out, not in alarm, but with pleasure.

He hurried forward, greeting the man with a warm hug. Then he turned back to Amy, smiling, his pleasure at the appearance of the stranger evident.

"Amy, this is Special Agent Dawson," he told her.

"Retired," the man said quickly, and then frowned. "She knows?"

"She's my partner."

"She's FDLE."

"She's my partner. Amy, come meet this guy," Hunter said. "He saved my life — used his body to shield me from bullets."

"He was six," Dawson explained as Amy walked over to shake his hand. "He was six, and by throwing myself down on him, I brought us both out of the path of any bullets." He looked at Hunter. "No one knows your real identity, except for Garza. And we all thought it best —"

"In this, Amy needed to know," Hunter said.

Amy was surprised and touched. She knew, without anyone saying, the information he had given was nothing to be shared. But he had shared it with her.

Of course, they'd shared a lot more. But this . . .

Somehow, it was more intimate.

"Let's get inside, shall we?" she suggested.

"Sure," Dawson said. "We can talk better away from any prying eyes."

"It's great here — are you staying, Agent Dawson?" Amy asked him. "We have a suite and . . . we don't need the Murphy bed."

"I've got a room, thank you, but if you have a cool suite, we'll talk there," Dawson said. "And I'm retired, so just call me Roger. Let me get my things, and we'll talk."

"The town is having a barbecue in Maclamara today and we were invited, while being warned they're all God-fearing people who look after one another," Hunter told him.

"God-fearing white supremacists," Roger said. "So, you're going?"

"No, we're going to watch," Hunter told him.

Roger Dawson nodded. "All right, let's

get in, and we'll talk quick."

By day, the front door to the inn was unlocked, and they were greeted by their host before heading across the parlor to the suite.

Inside, Hunter went straight to brew coffee, asking Amy to bring up a satellite view of the area on her computer.

Roger Dawson sat down at the table and opened his folder.

They both joined him, Amy with her computer, and Hunter after having set the coffee to brew.

"Okay, first thing, I know you have Sheila searching. I'm going to show you what I believe." He produced a picture; it was that of a man of about twenty with a shaved head, in jeans and a hunting jacket, carrying a rifle.

"Brother Colin," Hunter said.

"This is someone from the People's Paradise?" Amy asked.

"I still remember him so damned clearly, the way he looked when he was determined to shoot down a six-year-old. Me," Hunter said. "But, Roger, he's dead. We saw him die."

"Right." Roger produced another picture.

"Darryl, Brother Darryl," Hunter said.

"Right."

Amy studied the picture. This man was young. Maybe late twenties or early thirties. His hair was buzzed, as well; he was wearing a hunting jacket, too.

"Now look at this picture."

This photograph was different, probably taken about ten years ago. The man had a salt-and-pepper beard and was balding, and his hunting jacket and boots looked new and expensive.

She frowned, studying it.

"Oh, that's Morrison, isn't it? Not the current Morrison, but his father, I think. There was a huge magazine write-up on Ethan Morrison when he was acquitted, and he said he'd face any court battle, that his father had fought his way out of the dirt to riches."

"Now, look at them together. The old Morrison had a beard and a lot of graying hair, but . . ." Roger pointed out.

Hunter looked at Roger. "I knew it. Damn it, when I figured out the brand was a *PP,* I knew something had to go back to the California cult. So, Darryl probably managed to escape to Mexico, as we believed, and created a new identity."

Roger nodded. "There are a lot of ex-pat criminals doing that kind of work." He went on. "Ethan Morrison would have been twelve when the compound was raided, but there was no sign of the child found, either. Darryl's wife was dead. Suicide was the best they could conclude. Forced into suicide, or on her own, no way to know. She might have been too much baggage for the man. I don't have proof for any of this." Roger sighed.

Hunter interjected. "A number of people killed themselves during the raid, I heard. It's still so tragic."

"You never knew him when you were a kid?" Roger asked.

"Not that I know of," Hunter said. "We were separated from other kids. Little people talk — maybe they didn't want us talking too much."

"Well, if you go into any records, you'll see the father, who called himself Sebastian Morrison, was born on the Florida/Georgia line, and his mother, Mildred, died in childbirth. You'll see Sebastian bounced around. He was homeless until he got a job on an old sugar plantation and worked his way up to manager, saved his money and invested . . . and there you have it. At eighteen, Ethan Morrison went to the best schools money could buy. He was a good student, smart. He took all the right courses. He owns fifty-one percent of one of the biggest pharmaceutical producers in the country. In short, through business, through legal machinations, through the face he tries to give to the media, he's just a good old guy, maybe old-fashioned and conservative, but a good man, one to admire."

"The White Horseman," Amy said.

"You got anything else?" Hunter asked him.

"Well, you can get them online, but I brought you pictures of Aaron and Ezekiel Morrison and Jayden and Chase Colby."

He brought out more pictures.

Amy tapped one.

"That's the kid who was talking at the bar."

"That's Chase Colby — shouldn't be in a bar. He's just nineteen. I guess there are places where that doesn't matter," Roger said.

"Or maybe there are places where your name matters more than your age," Amy said.

"Do you have a map up?" Hunter asked her.

She turned the computer screen to face him, showing the satellite image of the town.

"There's a turnaround on the road here, overgrown, but hey, it's a turnaround," Hunter said. He looked at Amy. "We'll have a quarter-mile walk through the woods."

"I have my sneakers," she assured him.

"I'll drive down that way. Be on speed dial if you need me. I'd go with you —" Roger began.

"Ethan Morrison was one of the 'big' boys when I was in People's Paradise," Hunter said. "He might remember you."

"He might remember you," Roger told him.

"I doubt it. My hair is darker now, and I was a scrawny kid . . . and we're not dropping in for lunch. We're lurking in the woods. With you lurking behind. And I'll call Detective Ellison — this was his case. He called me in. I owe him."

Roger nodded.

Hunter excused himself to call the local detective. Roger Dawson looked at Amy, friendly curiosity in his eyes. "So, young lady, you're FDLE?"

She nodded.

"You should consider the FBI."

She smiled. "I might, but I do have a real partner. I mean, Hunter and I are partnered right now, but John —"

"I know about John Schultz," he said.

"Of course. You're FBI."

"Retired."

She laughed. "Okay, retired. You're still FBI!"

He shrugged. "They say that about the marines. Well, I guess that's me. I was a marine, too. Hunter followed me too far, I think sometimes. I would have loved to have seen that kid just have a safe and happy life." He hesitated. "He found the girl, the girl the cult had killed. He cared about her, and he went to his parents. His dad told me the kid would do something if he didn't. Kid had too many balls right from the start. But don't worry. We saw to it he was trained right, too. And his dad? That man is a warrior with a pen now."

"We do what we choose to do," Amy told him.

"Were your parents happy with your chosen path?"

"They're okay."

"Right. Your dad was a cop. Your brother is a cop."

"You really are FBI," she said lightly.

"Easy research," he told her.

Hunter came back into the room. "Ellison is going to be close on hand, too," Hunter told them.

"All right, then. I'd say the barbecue is underway. Shall we?" Amy asked.

They headed out, Roger Dawson striding to his van and Amy and Hunter getting in the car.

Amy waited until they'd been on the road a few minutes and then said, "He's a great guy."

"Roger? Yes. Don't let him fool you — he's a hero. He saved our lives. He came into the compound undercover. He's the only human being who ever successfully slipped out. He stayed friends with my family, checked up on us and had a huge influence on me."

"Obviously."

He grinned. "My dad did, too, and my mom."

"How did they . . . ?"

"Wind up in a cult?" he asked flatly. He shot her a quick glance. "My grandfather — a man I never met — was extremely rich. And he looked down on anyone who was having a hard time. Ungenerous. My mother couldn't deal with it. She was looking for something else — for people who cared about other people. People who didn't worship money. My dad loved my mother. And in the beginning, they believed that, okay, maybe this religion was the way in because they were finally somewhere where people did help others."

"How did they . . . figure it out?"

"Two things. The leader decided he wanted my mother. There was a commune divorce, something made up by Brother William, because the other laws of the state didn't mean anything to him. My mother was devoted to my father. Still is. The idea of being forced to be with Brother William was too much. And then . . . then they killed Alana."

"A friend? Because she tried to leave?"

He nodded. "I found her. At the bottom of a ravine. They didn't even really try to bury her. Maybe we were all supposed to see her. They'd try to tell the authorities she had fallen. But we all knew the punishment for sin — which included turning away from Brother William — was death."

"I'm so sorry," Amy said.

"That was all long ago. I survived, and my folks survived. Some didn't. And it did make me what I am, for better or worse. But at least I'm determined to spare others that fate."

"My life was easy in comparison," she said.

"Hey, you became a cop, and you joined FDLE. That was a hell of a journey."

She grinned. "It was one step after another. And though they check on me, which is great, my family has been supportive."

"Mine, too," he said. "That is something. Not everyone gets support."

"Is that the turnaround?" she asked.

"It is. I'll pull off and park here." He eased the car to the far right of the road, almost into the trees. He looked at her for a moment.

She loved his face, more so now that she knew what had built the character into his cheekbones and jaw.

"We have to trek through the woods," he reminded her.

"What's not to like about woods?"

"In Florida? Number one, mosquitos," he said. "And you can't gain anything even by trying to shoot the little buggers."

"I won't be trying. I've survived the bastards before."

Grinning, they got out of the car. Roger Dawson pulled his van off the road behind them. He waved his phone at them, and then pulled out a newspaper.

They started walking.

It was cool enough and dry enough the bugs weren't so bad. A startled blue jay gave Amy a moment's pause as it nearly flew in her face, but she refrained from both a gasp and drawing her gun on the bird.

Eventually, they heard voices; they were near the town park and the barbecue.

Hunter motioned to her he was moving to the west.

She nodded and went on forward, coming as close to the gathering as she dared and finding a spot behind a very old and gnarly oak.

She leaned against it, watching.

Metal barbecue pits had been set up in the center of the grassy slope; there were picnic tables around the pits. People sat in groups at those tables, drinking from paper cups, talking to one another.

To one end of the park, young children were playing a game of kickball. Near them, an older boy was running with a few younger children, trailing a large kite.

At the other end, a lone singer with a guitar was playing. Church music, Amy thought, but they weren't tunes she recognized, nor were any of the words familiar.

It could have been a Norman Rockwell painting of small-town charm.

Amy gave her attention to the singer. She listened fully to one verse.

"And so the time is coming nigh,
"A time for you and I
"For disbelievers must adhere
"The godly need not fear.
"We give our all, we give to thee
"And hear your voice,

340

"The messenger we hear and listen dear
"The leader of your divine choice."

Many people were deep believers, she told herself. But the song was frightening; the young woman's rapturous voice as she sang was frightening, as well.

Her song ended. A horn blared.

"The righteous and virtuous, the beauty of woman, young and sweet!" someone shouted with a microphone.

Everyone stopped what they were doing and applauded.

Then, from the church just across the street from the park, there came a procession.

It was of young women, all dressed in white with garland crowns of flowers on their heads.

The guitarist played a joyous piece. The young women in the procession smiled as they made their way toward a podium set up just behind the barbecues.

There was a man standing on the podium in front of a microphone. He was wearing robes that weren't really priestly; they were more like something an old druid might wear.

She strained to see his face. His robe had a hood.

She started to inch around the tree, just a bit.

That's when she felt the nose of a gun in her ribs. She heard the sound as the gun was cocked.

She hadn't heard a thing; not a single crinkle of leaves, nothing. Then again, she'd been listening to the singer, paying heed to what was happening in the park . . .

Still, she should have known better; she should have been aware!

"So, you decided to come. But not to join us — to spy on us!"

She knew the voice. It was Phin Harrison. The friendly, flirtatious biker from the bar.

"You just won't believe what we do to gun-toting spies around here," he added.

18

Hunter saw Phin Harrison as he moved in on Amy.

He was afraid to let out a shout and alert the man; these people weren't rational — he might well shoot Amy before being shot himself.

He moved with all the stealth — and speed — he could muster, coming up behind the man, determined that he would disarm him with surprise. He'd shoot him if he had to, but the fear remained that neither he nor the bullet could move fast enough.

Hunter was on him, his Glock just about at the man's back, ready to demand that Phin drop his weapon, when Amy moved.

She had been staring at the man, probably sizing him up. And then she made her move, slamming his gun arm with a sudden slicing movement of her own; Phin let out a yelp of pain and surprise.

His gun slipped from his fingers.

Hunter leaped to retrieve it lest the man recoup quickly. Phin made a lunge for Amy, but Hunter was there, and only too happy to slam him back against the tree with a tight grip to his throat.

"You just threatened an FDLE agent, Mr. Harrison. You're under arrest," Amy said.

She had cuffs out; Hunter released the man before he could do damage. They both had weapons now, and Phin didn't.

But they'd been seen from the park; Hunter was aware that man in the robes at the podium had beckoned to a group of men behind him.

The entire populace of the park was turning to look into the woods.

Phin Harrison knew that.

He smiled. "Another spy!" he said quietly. "On my land. Stand your ground, buddy. This is my property right here — I own this land, and I have the right to stand my ground when someone is trespassing and might be dangerous. But screw the law, guys, you're badly outnumbered."

"No, he's not."

Hunter smiled; it was Roger Dawson who had spoken. He had followed behind the two of them.

"Phin Harrison," said another voice. Detective Ellison.

Ellison continued with, "Threatening a state and a federal officer. You will be coming with me."

"You have no right —"

"We saw a threat of fatal danger. We have every right," Ellison said.

Amy clicked the handcuffs onto Phin Harrison; Detective Ellison reached for him.

The crowd in the park was still.

Hunter looked at Amy; with a nod, she indicated that he should look behind him, behind Detective Ellison and retired agent Roger Dawson.

There were at least eight armed agents from the FBI coming through the trees.

"Take me in — you go on and take me in. And then I'll be suing your asses and having your badges. You are on private property. *My* private property."

"We'll let the courts settle it all," Hunter told Phin. "Feel free. This is private land? We'll go on down to the park and see about that barbecue."

Phin stood silent. Hunter moved past him, handing Phin's gun off to Dawson, a "thank you" in the nod and smile that he gave him.

He started through the remaining trees and down the embankment that led to the road and the park.

But as he moved, the robed figure backed

off the pedestal. Hunter started to run.

A woman thrust a small boy of three or four in his path. He swerved. The whole population of the park was moving, intent on blocking his way.

He reached the barbecue grills and was met by the bartender from the biker bar.

"Hey, man, what's your hurry? How about a few of the best barbecue ribs this side of Memphis?"

The figure in the cloak, the leader, was gone.

The girl with the guitar had also disappeared.

Hunter noticed the kid from the bar — the one who had really been too young to be in there ordering a drink. Chase Colby.

Next to the tall, beefy bartender, he was very small, and looked very young.

"Told you — he's an FBI goon. They just don't let law-abiding citizens alone," Chase said.

"I am with the federal government, and I think everyone should be concerned. A woman was found not far from here, brutally murdered," Hunter said.

"Yes, and you should be out finding her killer, not disturbing peaceful folks at a barbecue," the bartender said.

"She was killed in this town," Hunter said.

"By an interloper — like you!" Chase told him. "And you'd better let Phin go. He was just protecting what was his. And that's our right — we protect what is ours."

The crowd had dispersed. The girls with their flowery crowns and white gowns were gone, having hurried back to the church.

Hunter could see that the group of young men who had been about to rush up the embankment to come to Phin's aid were backing away, as well — across the park in the opposite direction.

But he'd gotten a look at them.

And he was certain he'd seen Chase's brother, Jayden, among them. Along with Ethan Morrison's sons, Ezekiel and Aaron.

There was nothing more that he could do here now. It had been a town barbecue, nothing illegal in that.

He smiled at Chase. "I know your dad. And your sister. Good people."

Chase frowned; he hadn't expected to be recognized.

"Yeah, my dad is a good guy. And you've been harassing him, too. And the church."

"Your dad *is* a good guy — who offered to help us in any way that he could. I know you feel the same. I know you all feel the same. We're here to catch a killer. And we will. Anyway. Excuse me, folks. Sorry to have disturbed you."

It felt terrible, turning to walk away, exposing his back to Chase and the bartender. But he knew that Amy, Roger and a half dozen sharpshooting agents were watching everything.

As he walked back toward the others, he could feel the way he was watched. It was — ridiculously, perhaps — like dozens of fiery needles shooting at him.

He reached Roger and Amy waiting in the woods.

"Ellison has Phin Harrison," Roger told him. "He says he can hang on to him for twenty-four hours. He doesn't suggest pursuing charges now. The law can be iffy . . ."

Harrison probably would be released, if it proved to be his property where they'd been standing, even if he *had* threatened Amy — and Hunter, for that matter. They had no warrant, and they had been on his land.

"Right. *If* Phin owns this land. He may not — someone else may own it," Hunter said.

"You're thinking Ethan Morrison," Amy said.

"I am."

"Well, we can talk to Phin."

"And we will. I want to shake the hands

of a few agents before we go. They sure made a timely appearance."

Amy grinned. "You have one hell of a boss, your Garza. Roger told me he's had tech on the satellite imagery. The agents were geared up, down the road, and ready."

He nodded.

Sometimes things worked out. Except that their plan hadn't worked completely. They hadn't seen whatever ceremony had been planned for the young woman. They had never seen the faces of the men in the strange robes. But they did have Phin.

"Come on, let's say thanks and follow Detective Ellison to the station."

Hunter made his way back through the woods; the contingent of FBI agents were waiting by the road. He greeted their team leader, Special Agent Monroe, and the whole group; Amy and Roger did the same.

"More than happy, Special Agent Forrest, to help where we're needed, when we're needed. Though it seemed you were good without our firepower —"

"There was no fire because you were here," Hunter assured them.

"And we'll be here. Count on us," Monroe told him.

"We'll be in touch," Hunter said.

He and Amy and Roger started down to

the road to their cars; there was no more reason to use the trees as a shield.

The ride to the county station took about twenty-five minutes. As they neared their destination, Amy sighed. He glanced her way.

"Civilization! I've never loved it so much."

He smiled.

"Thank you," she said.

"For?"

"You really had my back. You're a hell of a partner."

"Amy, you had him. That was an impressive move."

She shrugged. "I have some moves. We're taught, as you know, that thinking strategically can make up for size and strength. I had him disarmed, but if I would have made it to his gun before he clocked me — I don't know. Thankfully, I didn't have to find out."

Hunter smiled, nodding. "You are a damned good agent."

"Thank you. I'll take it. Hey, is Roger following us?"

"Yes, but he won't come in on the interrogation."

"He won't?"

"He's retired, remember? Doesn't mean that he won't be listening in."

Ellison had Phin Harrison in an interroga-

350

tion room, waiting. He was cuffed to a bar on the prisoner's side of the table in the room.

Amy and Hunter took seats across from him.

"This is ridiculous," Phin sputtered.

"Is it? I'm sorry," Hunter said. "But I'm trying to remember your words. Something about Special Agent Larson and me getting to see what you did to spies in your town."

"You were spying on us."

"We were watching a ceremony in the park," Amy said. "If you recall, you invited us to the barbecue."

"Right. You should have just come to the barbecue. You would have been welcomed. Even though the kid knew who you were. Even if you're going after a community full of good people, instead of searching for whatever drifter dumped a body here," Phin accused them.

"Someone in your group of good people has to know something," Amy said. "Phin, you're far too smart not to realize that! What happened here, well . . . all this property that's owned by all these good people. One of them has to know something."

Phin was silent.

There was a tap at the door.

Detective Ellison, bald with just a fringe

351

of tidy gray hair and a well-maintained mustache and close-cropped beard to complement the look, entered. "Mr. Harrison, I interviewed you myself regarding the murder. You spend half your time at the biker bar, and you see who comes and goes. You claim that you all keep a watchful eye, so tell me, what the hell happened?"

"I told you — some damned drifter," Phin said.

"Sure," Ellison told him. "Oh, and by the way, I just checked. You don't own that property. It's owned by Ethan Morrison."

"And I'm his property manager!" Phin protested.

"Well, it's going to be interesting to see how this plays out," Ellison said.

"I think I'll do a little legal investigation," Hunter said, rising and looking at Amy, and hoping that she understood. He wanted to see how Phin reacted to her alone. Phin was cuffed to a steel bar. There was nothing he could do to her, beyond threats. But Hunter wanted to know if he would threaten her.

"Amy, ask him about the girls."

Amy met Hunter's eyes and gave the tiniest of nods. She understood what he wanted.

"Right. So, Phin, what was the ceremony about? Had the girls graduated from classes or something like that?"

Hunter headed toward the door; Ellison stood, as well, when he saw Hunter's intent.

Once the door clicked behind them, Ellison asked, "You think that he'll sing a different tune, alone with Amy?"

"He's a macho supremacist — yes, let's see what he'll have to say to Amy."

"What is the story with the girls?" Amy asked Phin.

"What do you mean, what's the story?"

"What was the ceremony about — those pretty girls all coming out of the church. What kind of a church is it, anyway?"

"It's nondenominational. We don't think one thing. Everyone has a right to an opinion. We know that God gives us leaders and that the leaders show us the way. We may be lost and floundering, and they lift us up. You people are jaded, and you don't understand faith — you're so busy ripping people to shreds that you don't understand community and protecting those you love from others."

"Why do you think people need to be protected?"

He lifted his hands in a huge, expansive gesture and stared at her as if she was insane.

"Look where I am! We were having a friendly barbecue — and you waltz in to spy on us as if you've a right to tell other people how to live."

"You didn't answer me — what was the ceremony about? Who were the girls?"

He leaned forward, as if he was incredibly clever, and therefore amused at her stupidity. "Pretty girls, lady. Good girls. The kind who know how to be girls. You know, you've got the look, Miss Special Agent. I thought you might be someone who was really special. Pretty thing . . . but I was wrong. You're a tool. You're used by a society that doesn't care about you or support you. You could know something better. What it's like to be loved. Really loved."

"What was the ceremony?"

"An award ceremony — they completed classes that our church has for young ladies."

"I see. I guess they learn to obey the men in their lives."

He arched a brow to her. "And that's a bad thing? Women who make their men happy keep them. We don't have divorces. It's biology, idiot — sorry, lady, but you are an idiot. Biology teaches us that the male is the stronger of the species. He's made to protect his partner, and to protect his

354

children. She is made to bear those children, and to be a fine example of living."

"Women are built to serve," Amy said, keeping her tone sweet and pleasant. "And when they serve well, they are rewarded with love."

He shook his head at her again and then leaned forward. "And what? You can't charge me with a crime because we believe in the natural order of the world. Yes, we believe that men are to earn a living, to support their families and to protect them at all costs. And women, yes, they keep the home. They cook."

"The bartender from the biker bar was barbecuing," Amy said.

"Barbecuing is a man's business."

"Does everyone in town think and feel the same way?"

He shrugged. "You saw. The whole town was out. Yeah, that's right! You saw the whole town enjoying a barbecue, some beautiful religious music and a ceremony to mark some of the young women with special rewards and honors for completing classes."

"Run by a man in a hooded robe."

"You're mocking me? You're probably from one of those faiths where the priests or whatever wear robes. We have leaders and ceremonies. Yes, there are ceremonial robes."

"How much of your money do you give your great leader?" Amy asked.

"Divine Leader."

"How much of your money do you give him?"

"Money is a material thing. We live, knowing that there is a place where there is no pain, where we are all rewarded."

"So you turn over all your income," Amy said flatly. She leaned back, laughing. "And that's okay, because your beer is free at the biker bar."

"I haven't done anything illegal."

"I'm a state agent. You threatened me at gunpoint. But you also threatened a federal agent. That's serious."

"Standing my ground!" he said.

"But it wasn't your ground."

"I am paid to protect that ground."

"Is that a job that's written down on paper?" Amy asked.

He leaned back again, and tried to fold his arms over his chest, apparently forgetting that he was cuffed, and the cuffs were attached to the bar on his table.

He leaned toward her again, pure venom in his eyes.

"You don't have anything on me. And I

know what you want. You want to tear down something holy and beautiful, because you don't understand it."

"I think I do understand it. Let's see . . . this was probably always a religious community. But agriculture went bad about fifteen to twenty years ago. There was a cold snap back then, I think. A Florida cold snap filled with frost and freezing temperatures. I remember when it even went to freezing down in Miami when I was a little kid. The rest of the state was way worse. Orange groves were affected by the freeze, and other agricultural industries were hit hard, too. One bad year can make or break farmers. The town would have been pitched into poverty. I'm suspecting that, here, the change was subtle. Everyone spent a few years suffering and when a new preacher came to town and things got better — well, it had to be because of that leader, a charismatic speaker, someone who convinces you that he or she has been ordained by God, and that by following him you'll have rewards in heaven and on earth."

He stared at her. "I will be rewarded. Here. On earth. They'll set me free. You have nothing. And you'll never understand the beauty and peace that you might have had. Does our town have faith? Yes. You see, years ago, a seal was broken. And when that seal was broken, it was the beginning. Only those of us with faith will survive what comes. A quarter of the earth will perish. You could have been one of the saved." He leaned back. "I think I'll wait for my lawyer now."

Amy stood. That was it; that was the law. She was done.

"All right. Well, thank you for your information."

"I didn't give you any information."

She smiled sweetly. "Yes, you did. So much!"

She turned to leave the room. He shouted after her angrily. "You could have been exalted! You could have had so much. Now, you will die in the sin of the disbeliever!"

At the door she turned to him. "Is that another threat?"

"That is simple truth," he told her.

"Your truth," she told him.

She knew that she had to get out; he'd asked for an attorney. She stepped out of the room, closing the door behind her.

Detective Ellison was standing by with Hunter and Roger Dawson.

"Nice guy, huh? Bet he gets all the girls," he said.

"If he gets them, it's because he serves

the Divine Leader so well," Hunter said. He looked over at Dawson. "That language. This is something based on Brother William and the People's Paradise," he said. "Ethan Morrison's father had to have been the missing Darryl. Here's what bothers me. Maclamara is small — population around two hundred, maybe? With the People's Paradise, Brother William found land that he could sweep up in the valley, some 'bequeathed' from followers he found when he began his quest. He brought people in. Somehow, he — I'm going to say it's Morrison, because I truly believe it was Morrison — came into town and took over. Small town, good religious people — but probably with a tendency to white supremacy and a dislike for any immigrants. And then Morrison settled in, taking over. But even in a community this small, there would be someone who disagreed." He looked at Amy. "I think that you nailed it in your conversation with him. But what bothers me now is not just what is going on and how we stop it, but what happened to those who didn't fall into his fold?"

"You think that he murdered anyone who disagreed?" she asked.

"Dawson?" Hunter turned to his mentor.

"It seems likely," Dawson agreed.

Amy remembered that very few people knew that Hunter hadn't been born with the name he now carried.

Ellison muttered beneath his breath, "And this has happened in *my* county."

"Detective, it's so subtle sometimes, so hard to see — until a takeover is complete. But I still believe that the Divine Leader has an agenda. And that this is only the beginning."

"Where do we go from here?" Ellison asked.

Before anyone could answer him, a well-dressed man with slick dark hair and wearing an expensive suit came walking toward the interrogation room.

"This is laughable. You're laughable. And on top of a ridiculous arrest, you've been interrogating my client without his lawyer present."

"Your client didn't request an attorney until about two minutes ago," Ellison told him.

"Trumped-up charge. I'll have him out of here in another two minutes," the attorney said.

Amy couldn't help herself. "I'm impressed. Mr. Harrison can afford an attorney with an Armani suit!"

The man ignored her. "I will see my client now."

Ellison opened the door for him. "Knock yourself out."

"I'll have your badges," the attorney said.

"You don't really want them. They would play havoc with that suit," Amy said.

He went in, pulling the door firmly behind him.

"What now?" Ellison asked.

"Hold him for the time that you can, pending charges. If he wants his freedom by claiming that he's working for Ethan Morrison, we're going to want a paper trail for it," Hunter said. "You hold on to him, and we'll get back to the drawing board."

Amy thought that they were ready to leave, but Hunter hesitated and turned back to Ellison. "If they were getting rid of people who didn't fall into their fold, they won't have buried them on their private land. They would have been killed in a way that could appear natural — something like a fall, being crushed by a felled tree. Or they'd have simply disappeared. If you can think of any state or federal land where we might find remains, well, there could be a connection there. Or any unresolved missing persons files. Anyway, we'll keep all information circulating. I'm convinced that they are holding at least one other woman hostage. We have to find a way to save her life, because she's going to be next."

"My entire force is here for you."

Amy, Hunter and Roger left the building, heading out to their vehicles.

"What now?" Roger asked.

"Back to the drawing board," Hunter said. He grinned at Amy. "But you nailed it. Phin Harrison couldn't possibly afford the lawyer who just went in to see him. His arrest must have been reported to the Divine Leader, who might have been the man in the robes. We need to find out if Morrison will claim to have appointed Phin Harrison as his property manager. If he does, I'm sure that Phin will walk out of that police station. And we need to know who is paying for that lawyer. I want the paperwork. If Morrison disowns Phin, well, the man might be ready to talk." He hesitated. "I'm going to have Garza get into a few conversations with Amy's superior in Florida and with the county department down here. I think that there are going to be some bones in the woods. If Ethan Morrison learned all that he knows from his father and Brother William, then he knew to get rid of dissenters during his takeover."

"Back to the inn?" Roger said.

"Back to the inn," Hunter agreed.

"This is all so unbelievable," Amy said when they were in the car. "I mean . . . it's really hard to understand. How do people allow their friends or neighbors to be murdered?"

"They don't think of it as murder," Hunter said. He was looking ahead as he added, "Do you think that the regular citizen in 1939 Germany really wanted to see an entire part of their population gassed to death? The regime sure as hell didn't start out by saying they'd fix everything with mass murder. No, you seep in, and you take charge. You blame misfortune on others, and then you turn those others into scapegoats. Rationality may remain, but by then, fear is such a factor that the moral people remaining are terrified to speak up. They know what will happen to them if they voice disagreement."

"Politics and religion. They can both go too far." She was thoughtful for a moment. "You do realize that, even if with all you know, we're still not sure what we're looking for? I've read the King James version of Revelation, the People's Bible version and a few others."

He nodded. "Here's what we have that they all share. Four Horsemen. Exactly how

363

all the methods of death align, we don't know. But I think that the Divine Leader is seeing the fall of the People's Paradise as the breaking of the Fourth Seal. The rest . . . well, he's playing by ear. We could see them imitate something that is a death by a 'beast,' or in a way to simulate disease, or even by starvation."

"Starvation takes a long time."

"Not if —"

"What?"

His brow furrowed into a pained frown.

"Not if you remove a victim's stomach."

Amy winced, shaking her head. "You think that —"

"I think that anything is possible. With the many different interpretations, they could kill by 'beast.' They could have had one of their victims mauled by an alligator. There are all kinds of possibilities out there, but the thing that scares me most is that this could go on a long time. Even if we manage to . . . stop things here."

"What do you mean?"

"It could reach farther than we're imagining. There are cults out there — not running around murdering anyone that we know about — that have a global influence. Like everything else in the world, the underlying foundation is usually power and money." He sighed. "We haven't always performed spectacularly — the FBI has made plenty of mistakes. Even with the best intentions. When there's a lot of firepower in play, people get hurt. People die. But you can't go into a den of hornets without firepower. And any time something goes wrong, the government looks worse — and cult leaders have more 'proof' to fall back on."

Amy was silent and so thoughtful that she jumped when her phone rang.

She glanced at Hunter and answered it quickly.

"Larson," Amy said.

"Amy?"

The voice on the other end was Casey Colby's.

"Are you all right?" Amy asked quickly.

"I'm fine, I'm fine. Have you found Billie?" Casey asked anxiously.

"I'm so sorry, not yet. Is everything all right with you?"

"Oh, yes, I'm okay. I was hoping that I could speak with you. In person, and alone."

Amy frowned. "Casey, you're about five hours south of me —"

"No, no, I'm almost in your area. I'm heading up to stay with a friend who owns a horse farm in Ocala."

"Casey, we had Agent Ryan and Detective Mulberry looking out for you."

"I don't need to be afraid. If my family is involved, they would never hurt me. But please, I need to see you. I can meet you at a little diner called Sal's Stopover. It's just north of Micanopy, heading toward Gainesville. Say, tomorrow morning, about nine?"

"Of course. But, Casey," she started, but hesitated. "I've seen your brothers. They're with a group of questionable people in a little town called Maclamara."

"They're not bad people, I swear. Please, I — I need to see you, just you. I have a ton of thoughts and questions and things rushing through my mind, and if we just talk . . . alone, because I don't want any of those he-man cops or agents or whatever taking what I saw the wrong way, I know that you'll listen to me, that you'll understand."

"Of course. But, Casey, please, tell me where you're staying — and call me back to let me know that you arrived safely."

"Yeah, for sure." Casey rattled off an address in Ocala, and when they ended the call, Amy quickly wrote it down. Hunter was looking at her.

"I overheard part of that," he said.

"She said that she wants to meet with me, only me. I'm worried about her. She doesn't believe that anyone in her family would hurt her, but . . . Nothing about this is normal."

"We'll get someone down in Ocala to watch over her, without being seen," Hunter assured her.

Amy nodded.

"Right." She looked at Hunter. "I *have* to meet with her. Our leads keep taking us to dead ends."

"Yes, you have to meet with her."

"Alone."

He turned to grin at her. "Sure. Alone. But I'll be close."

They'd arrived back at the inn. Night had fallen, and the historic house was beautiful next to the moss-draped oaks.

Roger pulled in after them.

"Do you people ever eat?" he asked them. "Okay, I admit, the barbecue thing dimmed my appetite for a while, but . . ."

"We'll order food," Hunter assured him.

"You think we can — out here?" Roger asked.

"Yes, I think that we can."

Food delivery companies had covered just about every possible inch of the country, Amy thought. They could even order a decent meal; they found a restaurant under one of the delivery services that offered everything from a "healthful living" menu to "steaks, fries and grease!"

They opted for steaks, fries and grease that night.

Sitting around the table in the suite, they enjoyed dinner, and a brief respite from the case. Roger Dawson, despite his fierce loyalty to his work, had a wife, three sons and, now, four grandchildren.

Hunter and Amy happily appreciated the pictures Roger showed them.

Then, finally, Roger yawned.

"Tomorrow — another sixteen-hour day. Good night, folks."

Hunter locked the door behind Roger when he left.

"What now?" Amy asked.

"Well, you know, we do keep forgetting that food is necessary for life, for the energy we're needing on this case."

"We just ate."

"But there are other needs . . . that can be just as necessary."

"Did you have something in mind?" she asked him.

"Hell yeah!"

He strode slowly over to her. She came to her feet, ready to meet him, ready to feel the sweep of his arms, and the pressure of his lips, the excitement of his delving kiss. There was something about the way his tongue played in her mouth that was indicative of all else, and she felt him against her as if he were a sweet, searing flame that brought wicked heat but deliciously no harm.

They moved; the table jostled.

She almost fell back; he caught her.

She laughed as he looked into her eyes.

"I had an image in my head of one of those movie scenes where they sweep everything off the table, and make love right there."

"Messy," he said.

"Oh, yeah, far too messy! And the table is hard."

He pulled her up off the table and then literally swept her up into his arms.

"I guess the bed, huh?"

"The bed would be perfect."

He carried her in and laid her down. She came up on her knees as he joined her there on his.

"Guns!" she reminded.

Their weapons were set on each bedside table and they were left looking at one another again, smiling.

"Clothing!" Hunter said.

They started at it, fumbling and laughing as they removed their own and one another's, leaving all a tangle thrown about. Then she was in his arms again and they fell backward onto the cool comfort of the sheets beneath.

Hunter found her lips again, and began methodical, searing wet movement down her body. Sensations tore at her; she cried out softly, rising against him, feeling the fine muscles in his back and shoulders, planting her kisses against him, covering his bronzed length with her fingertips and the teasing brush of her lips and tongue.

Then they were together again. And she didn't think; she just felt. The world rocked. Yes, they needed to live. To love, to know this kind of beauty, to celebrate that life is precious.

After, they lay together, her head on his chest. "Was I . . . ?" she began.

"What?" he asked.

"Um . . . oh, too brazen with you?"

He laughed. "You were nothing but beautiful with me. What brings that up? Our friend Phin?" He was suddenly serious, and he rolled over to look down at her. "Here's the thing, Amy. Do men like him exist — in cults and in the world at large — thinking that they're better than the 'fragile' sex? Totally idiotic? Yeah, sure. But you can't ever let that change anything about you."

"You know that there are even cops out

there who are like that?" She grinned. "John Schultz is a great man, a great partner. But even he admits that he was being macho and didn't want a female partner. Or a young one."

"But he got to know you. And he came around."

She shrugged. "What do you think?"

"I think I questioned your age more than your sex."

She laughed. "Because you're, what — five or six years older than I am?"

"And . . . been around a real big block."

"And now?"

He hesitated, a smile slowly creeping into his lips.

And for a moment, she felt oddly vulnerable — more frightened inside than when she was faced with criminals with guns and knives.

She cared about him so much; she didn't want him leaving her life. She loved working with him, loved the way his mind worked, his subtle smiles, the richness of his voice, the ripple of his muscles, the feel of him.

"Now is easy," he said softly.

"Oh?"

"Now," he said, "I know that you're perfect. Just perfect."

"Totally perfect?"

He laughed.

"For me, yes. For me, totally perfect."

His lips touched hers.

19

Amy took Hunter's car the following morning.

Ryan had called first thing to tell them that they'd been watching Casey Colby but hadn't had a way to stop her when she decided she was leaving town.

It was critical that Amy find out what Casey had to give them. She would go alone, as she had promised. But Hunter would follow with Roger in the van.

She had nearly reached the little diner where she was to meet with Casey when her phone rang.

It was Hunter.

"What's happened?" she asked. Hunter getting in touch so soon meant there must be news.

"Our dear friend Phin Harrison must have been a true believer. He's dead."

"Dead?"

"A pill — poison, we believe. At any rate,

there was no paper trail. Even if we suspect that Morrison hired the attorney, there's no paperwork. Ellison is working on the attorney angle. The man is legitimate, part of a major North Florida firm. And a representative from Morrison's office claims that Morrison wasn't in the state — he's 'traveling' and unavailable for comment. Anyway, Phin Harrison is dead."

Amy sighed. "He was a jerk, but I sure as hell didn't want him dead!"

"Of course not. Anyway, I hope Casey has something to share. We need what she can give us. Ocala police watched her overnight and followed her north. Now she's back in *our* ballpark. Ellison has been advised, though where she's going from here, we don't know yet."

"Hopefully, she'll give us something."

"Go get 'em, tiger."

She grinned and ended the call, pulling into the lot of the little diner. It was a charming one-story building just off the highway, freshly painted and well looked after.

She had looked it up after agreeing to meet here. Family owned. The family obviously cared for it; it made her smile. It was old Florida, and down in her area, there just wasn't much of "old" Florida left.

Maybe it was "old" anywhere, before restaurants were all chains that crept across the country and before you could be in a mall in almost any state that was just like the mall in any other state.

She parked the car.

The owner obviously had a green thumb. The place had myriad flowers growing around it that were well tended. Beautiful orchid plants were on either side of the front door. It was billed as a diner, but it had a hostess stand. An older woman greeted her and Amy told her that she was meeting a friend. The woman led her to a booth where Casey was waiting.

Casey stood and greeted her with a grateful hug.

"Thank you for coming," Casey said.

"I'm happy to help in any way. Have you found Billie, by any chance?" Amy asked her.

"I'm so afraid for her."

Casey slid back into her seat. Amy sat across from her. A young waiter came up. Amy smiled and asked Casey what she would like.

They both opted for pancakes and coffee. When the waiter left, Amy asked, "Casey, what do you know about Maclamara?"

"What's Maclamara?" Casey asked.

"A town, south of Micanopy, north of Ocala."

"I, uh, well, you know how that goes! I've lived in Florida my whole life and I haven't heard of dozens of towns and cities, I guess. I mean, they're incorporating new cities all the time because the population of the state keeps booming."

"So, you never heard of Maclamara before?" Amy asked.

Casey shook her head.

"But your brothers are there."

"They have an apartment in Gainesville, so they must have been just visiting. And they're not bad guys, honest."

Amy frowned. "So, what do you think might cause your brothers to become involved with a cult?"

"Oh, I can't believe that they're really involved with the cult."

"Casey, they are."

Amy fell silent as their food arrived. When the waiter left again, Casey responded passionately. "But they wouldn't hurt anyone. They were raised to believe that life is sacred." She laughed. "Hey, Chase is a vegetarian. I think he worries that the broccoli he eats might have feelings!"

"They're both still at school in Gainesville?"

"Yes, they're registered, doing all their work."

"And they live in Gainesville."

"Yes."

"And they know Ezekiel and Aaron Morrison?"

"Yes, and that's where I wind up scared. Morrison has . . . a lot of money. When he was in Florida, my dad made a point of meeting him, and trying to draw him into our fold. Of course, we met the boys, too. I'm sure I told you that my dad felt a man like Morrison has the resources to do a lot of good. Anyway, that's when my brothers started hanging out with the Morrison boys. And they had boats, they had fast cars, fake IDs when they were young . . . It was a big change. Growing up, we were always looked after, but my dad is a pastor who practices what he preaches. We didn't have a lot of material belongings. And falling in with the Morrison boys, well . . . they had every toy known to man. But even if Morrison's kids might be in a cult and might be dangerous, that's not my brothers."

"What do you know about Aaron and Ezekiel?"

Casey hesitated. "Okay, they're creeps. And here's the thing. I know my brothers love me and that they'd never hurt me.

377

Those boys treat women like tissue paper — used fast and disposed of even more quickly. Zeke started coming on to me one day. I couldn't stand him. Right, I know — I didn't like Hank, either. Dad taught me to respect myself. Zeke tried to basically buy me. I told him he might have all the money in the world, but I wasn't for sale. He went to Jayden and Chase, super angry. And they told him that I was my own person. After that, I didn't see the Morrison boys anymore." She sighed. "I hate to say this, but while my brothers didn't want me treated like tissue paper, they loved the Morrison boys' ability to buy booze, fancy toys — and women."

She looked at Amy earnestly. "If anyone is bad, it's those two! I wanted you to know what kind of people they are."

"Have you seen them down by your home recently?" Amy asked.

"No," Casey admitted, frustrated. "But my brothers haven't been home in a long time, either. Dad was talking about taking a trip up here to see the two of them."

"Hmm. We'll give him a call. Maybe he can get them to talk to us," Amy said.

Casey seemed to look happier. "I tried calling both Jayden and Chase. Neither of them answered my calls. Chase texted me, though. Said he was fine and that I should worry about work. He said I was taking off too much time."

"Are you?"

"I work for an advertising company. I can work from wherever I am. I love my office, but . . . I guess I've been off lately. With all that's been happening."

"Casey, honestly, we're worried about you. You might consider protective custody."

"Me? No, no. I told you — my brothers will not let anything happen to me. And I'm staying at a horse farm. They have some big dogs there. I'll be fine. I might even shake everything off and go spend a day at Disney or Universal! Have a little fun."

"I wish that —"

"I swear to you. I'll be fine," Casey vowed. She stood. "I just wanted to reach out to you. I . . . I'm still praying that you find Billie. That you find her okay. But . . . if anyone is involved, it's those two rich kids!"

Amy stood, too. "Casey —"

Their waiter rushed over with the bill. Amy took it and Casey smiled at her. "I promise I'll keep in touch with you, and I promise I'll be safe!"

She hurried out of the diner.

Amy sighed and went to pay the bill.

Casey hadn't really given her anything

except for the unsurprising fact that a couple of wealthy boys were badly behaved, and the information that Pastor Colby might be on his way north. To see his sons. Casey loved her father and her brothers — could her faith in them be misplaced?

She paid the bill and headed out to the car. She saw that Roger's van was already moving.

Her phone rang, and when she answered, Hunter told her, "We're following Casey. Did she give you anything?"

"She thinks that Zeke and Aaron are involved. Her brothers are angels who will defend her no matter what, and Pastor Colby might be on his way up here. Oh, she says that she'd never even heard of a town called Maclamara."

"All right. We're going to follow her a bit, but I'll get Ellison to assign an officer to watch her before we get too far. We'll meet you back at the inn, see where we are. Oh, Ellison already has a search team at work. They've started with cadaver dogs, searching state and federal land so that no one can intervene."

"Good. You want me to just head to the inn? I'm so frustrated. I should be doing something useful."

"Pieces are falling in. Garza has a team

investigating the detention center where there have been questions about the number of women being held, and where it seems they might have been before disappearing."

"And becoming corpses," Amy said bleakly.

"We'll meet you back at the inn or, if Casey leads us anywhere, be in touch."

"All right."

"Get straight back there. And be careful. I do believe that things are heating up and I don't really trust anyone."

"Okay, I'm heading straight back."

They ended the call. She had the phone pressed to her ear as she headed to her car and was busy digging the car key out of her purse when she heard a rustle behind her.

But she didn't turn fast enough.

She had a brief impression of a young man's face.

Her first thought was that something had been wrong when she paid the tab.

Then she knew that it wasn't that. She knew the young man's face.

Zeke Morrison.

But she made the realization just as something clouted her hard on the head, and the world turned black.

Casey Colby drove along a rutted paved road.

But she didn't turn off when she should have taken the turn for the highway — if she'd been headed back to Ocala.

"Where the hell is she going?" Roger muttered. "Looks like she just might be heading for Maclamara."

"She told Amy that she'd never even heard of Maclamara," Hunter said. "But it sure does seem like she's going that way."

Casey kept driving.

"Son of a bitch," Hunter muttered. "We're worried about protecting her and it looks like she's involved."

"Maybe she's lost," Roger suggested.

"With GPS?" Hunter asked skeptically.

About a mile before the turnaround where they'd parked to stake out the barbecue, Casey pulled off the side of the road.

"Should I stop?" Roger asked.

"No, drive by. We'll stop at the turnaround. See if she's still there, take a walk back and make sure that she's all right."

As they passed, they could see she was looking at her phone.

Roger drove closer to the turnaround and

found a place where he could pull a good distance off the road. Hunter leaped out, aware that Roger was following him and that he would do so at a bit of a distance.

He moved along the road. From the trees, he heard shouting and a dog barking. He drew his Glock and leaned against a massive pine, but then realized that ahead of him a familiar crew was in the woods.

He pulled out his phone to call Roger.

"Hey," he said when his friend answered. "Keep an eye on Casey. I've found one of the forensic teams. A dog seems to have found something. I'm going to check on it, meet back up with you."

"Gotcha," Roger assured him.

Hunter picked his way through the trees, and when he got closer he called out. "Hello! Special Agent Hunter Forrest here, coming through!"

He moved into a shaded grove.

It was a pretty place, the trees moving lightly in the breeze, the scent of the earth rich, the air pleasant, oaks and pines mingling, needles creating a soft carpet on the ground and the sun breaking through to dazzle the place with glints of illumination.

A woman in a county forensic vest walked toward him, extending a hand. "Nellie Rodriguez," she told him. "My team is out here with me. However you figured this, Special Agent, you figured it right."

"What have you found?"

"Come with me — just about fifty yards ahead, there's another clearing like this one."

He followed her, nodding to the two men and the woman who finished out Nellie's team and ducking down to let the two large German shepherds — also part of the team — smell the back of his hand.

"Ajax, Gunther, he's good!" Nellie Rodriguez assured the dogs.

Hunter patted each dog, and stood, and it was then that he saw what the team had been doing.

The clearing had been dug up — just lightly so far, the team having used the dogs for discovery, then used small tools to start to excavate the earth.

There were four sections that they had dug thus far.

Four shallow graves.

One skeleton had been almost cleared. It was all there: skull, rib cage — crushed — arm and leg bones.

Four people.

Four human beings.

"A good call. They've been here awhile, though. We'll get people out from the anthropology department at the university, and they, along with medical examiners, will hopefully let us know just how long all these bodies have been here."

"Anything besides bones?" he asked.

"Not much. Pieces of fabric. Two belt buckles. We haven't gotten very far. But no wallets, no purses, no identification. They might have come from anywhere. From my experience, however, they've been here at least ten years, but they're not historic — there's still too much integrity in the bones."

He'd been right. He didn't feel good about it, but he'd been right. Years ago, when Ethan Morrison had begun his conquest of the tiny town, he'd removed all opposition.

"It's definitely not an old Indian burial ground," he said.

"Definitely not," the woman told him.

One of the dogs — Ajax, he thought — started barking.

They would find more bodies, he imagined. And even though he knew, he found his mind and heart rebelling.

How could this happen? How did intelligent people not see that they were being manipulated?

But it happened; he knew it better than most people.

"Thanks!" he called, lifting a hand to wave to the crew.

"Thank you!" Nellie Rodriguez called to him. "Well, I think. I mean, this is so sad and tragic, but at least we're on our way to allowing these people decent burials."

Hunter wasn't sure how much that mattered.

The greatest cruelty had already been done to them. But he nodded, waved again and moved quickly and carefully back toward the road.

He judged his distance and emerged just a couple hundred feet from where Casey now stood beside her car, leaning against it, Roger at her side.

"I know! I was bad!" Casey called to him.

He joined the two. "Pardon?"

"You people are so good, so wonderful — trying to protect me."

"So, you ride into danger?" Hunter asked.

Casey shook her head, appearing distressed. "No, I didn't know that there was a town here. I mean, I knew there were cities and towns, I just didn't know that there was a town called Maclamara and that my brothers hung around it. When I left Amy, well, I'm sorry. Stupid, I know. But I called Chase when I left the restaurant and he didn't answer. I'd wanted to see him at his apartment, but then I thought, if the little rug rat wasn't answering me, I'd come and find him. And it is on the way back to Ocala, so . . ."

"Casey, I can't order you to do anything," Hunter said.

"I explained that," Roger said.

"But people have died."

Casey flushed. "My brothers aren't killers."

"Even you think that they have friends who could be," Hunter said.

"But they won't let anyone hurt me!"

"If you're seen as a threat, they might not be able to stop the others."

Her bravado seemed to slip a little. "I — I can't, I mean, I can't believe —"

"Casey! You know that we found two murdered women," Hunter said.

She let out a long breath. "Okay, okay. I'll go to Ocala. I won't try to find my brothers. But you need to know that my dad is worried, too. I think he's planning to leave Karyl in charge at the church and come up here."

"Come on, we'll escort you until I reach an officer who will take over for us. Casey, you must understand and accept that you might be in very real danger. If Morrison's sons are in this, they're taking orders from their father. They could see you as a terrible threat — and this group has a particular talent for making people disappear, until they want the bodies to be found," Hunter said.

Tears stung Casey's eyes. She wiped her hand across her face and nodded. "Okay, okay!"

She stood straight and went to open the driver's side door to her vehicle. "Any particular way you want me to drive?"

Roger looked at Hunter, arching a brow.

"This will take us through the center of Maclamara and we can pick up one of the main roads once we're through."

Hunter nodded. "Casey, just keep driving."

"Do I stop for red lights?" she asked with a sigh.

"Yes — the town does have one, I believe," Hunter said, ignoring her nervous sarcasm. "But don't stop otherwise."

She got into her car. Roger and Hunter walked south toward his.

"That was harsh," Roger said.

"She thinks that a family bond can save her. It can't. I had to be harsh."

"What did they find in the woods?" Roger asked. He didn't wait for Hunter to answer. "Bodies?" he said.

"Bones, so far. You talk about your hostile takeover. I know it's Ethan Morrison, good old Brother Darryl's boy. He took everything they learned under Brother William and kicked it up a bunch of notches. I just wonder what the hell else is going on."

"You mean the way that they're playing with Revelation?"

Hunter nodded. They had reached the van; he headed to the passenger's side and hopped in. Roger took the driver's seat and checked the rearview mirror.

Casey was coming. She would drive through the town as she had said.

"How the hell can anyone figure out what they're doing? The New Testament wasn't written in English at the get-go. It was written in something called Koine Greek — that's K-O-I-N-E. Then you have all kinds of languages and versions and the new Bible and the popular Bible . . . It can all mean anything," Roger said.

"I know. And even if we had an answer to the closest version of what was meant, it wouldn't matter, because our killers are using whatever interpretation they choose. But one thing is certain — they are killing, and torturing their victims before they kill them. And they have to be stopped."

"We're close, my friend, we're close."

"Yeah, too close." Hunter gestured out the windscreen. "We're coming up on the biker bar. I'm thinking, by now, the town knows that Phin Harrison is dead."

Traffic signs warned that the speed limit through town was thirty miles an hour.

They had slowed appropriately.

So had Casey.

"We can get her safely through to the next county, but we'll need help keeping an eye on her," Hunter said.

He pulled out his phone and called Ellison. He had to wait a few minutes to get in his request; Ellison was ranting, upset about the bones being found. In his county. But he was also grateful that they had looked, grateful that he had asked for FBI help, for Hunter specifically.

Hunter assured him he was glad to be working where he was most useful, then he was finally able to ask for an escort for Casey, and someone to watch over her, as well.

"I've got it," Ellison told him. "I'll ask the FDLE if I need to, but we cops in connecting counties have a good rapport. I'll have help. We're good. I promise you."

Ahead down the road, Hunter could see the biker bar.

"Hey, do you know anything about the bartender at the biker place in Maclamara?"

Hunter asked him. "I know that several tech divisions have been checking out people for red flags, but that biker bar is where we met Phin, and the bartender was at the barbecue."

He could see, as Roger slowed the van, that there were at least a dozen cars in the parking lot that day.

"Gilbert Bowles," Ellison told him. "Yeah, I checked him out. A few speeding tickets on a motorbike. That's all. Nothing there. He owns the business and works the business. It just hangs on — enough in profits to keep it going."

"Thanks. What about his history? School, married, kids?"

"No college, school right where he is — in the neighboring county. Single, no children."

"Thanks."

"No problem. I'll get right on your request. I'm not far from you. I'm headed to the woods, to look at human remains," Ellison said dolefully.

"Right. Let me know if you have any problems. I don't want to take the time to follow her unless I have to."

"Right, my friend."

They ended the call.

Hunter thought about the man he now

knew to be Gilbert Bowles. He was one really big guy; there weren't that many men who were several inches over his own six-three.

"You were asking about the bartender, the massive guy at the barbecue?" Roger asked.

He dropped his speed more, keeping an eye on the road ahead — and Casey. But she, too, had slowed down.

Curious to see the place, probably.

"Big guy, but that doesn't mean he knows what he's doing," Roger went on. "Then again, fighting a smaller person . . . he could just sit on them and squash them."

Hunter cast him a glare.

"Just saying. Big guys have the weight — if nothing else — to hold on to people. Then again, I saw Amy's move the other day. She knows what she's doing. She's an impressive young woman."

"Yes."

"You think so, too."

"Yes."

"You know, some people have to have people a lot like themselves in their lives."

Hunter groaned aloud, looking over at him. "Yes, I like her. I care about her. Yes, we make a great team."

"On and off the playing field."

"Roger, we're tracking a deadly cult."

"Killers. Yes, and you've done a damned good job of that all your life, kid. Like you make up for something with your folks. Your folks are good people, too."

"Roger, I'm not trying to make up for everything. I love my parents. They were fooled, but then they showed tremendous courage."

"Just remember what I'm saying. You and Amy are a good team, on and off the playing field."

"Right. We're passing the biker bar, Roger. We have to get a handle on this."

"It's a busy day in hell!" Roger said.

The biker bar was hopping that day, so it seemed. There were a lot of cars in the lot for a town this size when it wasn't even noon.

A meeting of the faithful? Hunter wondered.

"Something going on there, right?" Roger said. "Let's see, an early memorial for their friend Phin Harrison?"

"And maybe someone is preaching that he did the right thing, what is expected of all of them, if they love their faith, believe — and want a taste of heaven themselves," Hunter said.

"Maybe once we get Casey out of this

town and on her way, we should stop back in."

"Two of us?"

"I think we'd shake them up. They know who you are, and some of them saw me yesterday. At this point, they'd know that you can have a small federal army down on them in minutes."

"He'll refuse to serve us, I'm sure."

"But do we care?" Roger asked.

"Maybe not a bad idea. I'm going to call Garza, see if there's anything new."

Roger nodded. "Kids in the park. Looks like the happiest little old town in the world, doesn't it?"

They were passing the park. And Roger was right.

There was an area for children with swings and monkey bars and a small carousel. Several young mothers with toddlers were there, watching over their children, chatting with one another. The baseball field was quiet; the picnic tables were empty. There was nothing where the podium had been the day before.

Casey had slowed, as if hoping that she might see one of her brothers in the park.

Then she increased her speed.

At the end of the park, they came to the town's one light; it turned red.

Casey didn't stop; she kept going through the empty intersection.

Roger stopped.

Hunter stared at him.

"Hey! It's a red light," Roger protested.

It changed quickly. Then they were moving again and it only took a minute to catch back up with Casey Colby.

Hunter's phone rang; it was Ellison. A trooper from the highway patrol was going to pick up Casey and follow her to Ocala where a local officer would take over.

They followed her until they saw the trooper waiting on the side of the road. He waved to them, and they let him ease his FHP car onto the road.

Then Roger made a U-turn and they started back.

Hunter swore softly. "I've got to let Amy know what happened. She's expecting to meet up with us at the inn and we're going to be later than I thought."

Roger grinned. "If I know Amy, she's not worried about us. She has her nose in a computer. When she's not physically in the field, she's still in the field."

"Probably. I think she's read every translation of Revelation known to man," Hunter said.

Amy's number rang and rang. Her phone

went to voice mail.

"Amy, it's Hunter. Give me a call. We caught up with Casey. She was heading to Maclamara. We got her through, and we're heading back now."

She would call him right back, Hunter was certain.

But she didn't.

"Why isn't she answering?" he muttered aloud.

"You called ten minutes ago — give it a chance."

But Hunter was dialing again.

And, again, getting her voice mail message.

He called the inn and asked to be put through to the suite. No answer.

Pete Perkins, the owner, had answered the phone. Hunter had no problem asking him if he'd take a look outside and see if his car was out there.

Pete put him on hold and then came back in a minute.

"Sorry, I guess she just isn't back yet. Her car — or your car — isn't out front."

"Thanks, Pete. Please have Amy call me right away if you do see her."

"Will do."

"Thanks."

He dialed information for the number at

the diner. A friendly woman answered at the restaurant. She, too, put him on hold. She returned to the phone to assure him that neither Amy nor his sedan was there.

Finally, Hunter was out of calls to make.

Hunter looked over at Roger and swore explosively.

"What the hell could have happened? She was at the car when we drove away," Roger said. "Don't panic —"

"Roger, they had a poisonous spider bite a woman, and they let ants and other creatures eat her flesh as she lay dying."

"Amy is smart."

"Yes. But they have her, Roger. Somehow —" He broke off and looked at his friend. "Casey," he said.

"What?"

"Is she really a frightened innocent, here to save her brothers? Or was that a setup, a way for them to abduct Amy? Roger, they were trying to get Amy when they held Patty and Martin hostage — they wanted *her*! Damn it, I was a fool. I shouldn't have left her alone for a minute. The lying bastard wants her — a woman who would stand up against him and everything he's managed to create. Roger, we must find her. Now! And I will call out every cop and agent —"

"Slow down. Think, Hunter — use the

brains and the training that your years have given you," Roger said firmly. "Call in an army, and we'll have corpses everywhere — and they'll make sure that Amy is the first to go."

"They have something planned for her. Something . . ." He paused, gritting his teeth.

"Something that buys us time, Hunter. Something that buys us time to find her."

Roger was right and Hunter knew it. He just hated himself at the moment; she was capable, yes, she was a damned good agent, yes.

But they had targeted her.

And he hadn't been watching . . .

He steeled himself to be calm and methodical. He put through a call to Ellison. He needed someone who could bring Casey in, not down in Ocala, but back where they'd interrogated Phin — back in Ellison's realm. "What are we arresting her for?" Ellison asked.

"Highway violation. We watched her run a red light," Hunter said. "Just get her in, where she's watched, where we can talk to her and get the truth."

"The truth?"

"I'm sure that this morning she wasn't trying to help anyone. It was a setup, Ellison. She was setting us all up. She was helping them get Amy. He's wanted to take her down." He took a deep breath and added, "Now the bastard has her. But I'm going to get her back."

20

It seemed forever that Amy lay in a strange
state. She was aware, and not aware. She
was floating in some distant place, and she
couldn't remember where she had been or
how she had gotten where she was.

Then the pain at the side of her head grew
and she was rudely reminded that she had
oh-so-stupidly allowed Zeke Morrison to
come up behind her.

How? How the hell?

*Was Casey in on it all — or had she been
followed herself, duped?*

Well, there was one thing the pain in her
head was doing for her; it allowed her to
know that, at this moment, she was still
alive.

How long she'd stay that way, she wasn't
sure.

She slowly slit one eye open.

And she still had no idea where she was.

It was inside, somewhere. A rustic shack

like the one out in the Everglades down farther south. They were far north in the state — out of the Everglades — but that didn't mean that hunters and weekend campers didn't keep cabins.

She was tied up, hands and feet tied singly to bedposts. But there had to be a way . . .

She pulled on the ropes that held her. They were tight and secure.

She heard a grate and a squeaking sound; someone had just opened a door.

She closed her eyes, waiting. She was sure that she could pass for still being unconscious; it had been one good wallop on her head. She could feel the bump rising where the pain seared her.

A stifled sob sounded, and she realized that someone else was in the room; not the someone who had just entered, but another hostage.

Billie? Wilhelmina? The missing woman some had tried so hard to help?

Had she found her at last, right when she could do nothing for her?

No.

The abduction of a state agent would bring down the wrath of the state of Florida. And, with Hunter attached to the case, the resources of the federal government.

But whoever had her intended to kill her.

That she knew. So, what was the end game? Did they really think that they could get away with it?

Apparently so.

It was a man who had entered the room. She listened to every little movement. He was stooping down, talking to the other hostage in the room.

"Billie, Billie! See, I brought you company so you wouldn't be so alone. How are you feeling? You seem so sad and scared. But you shouldn't be sad or scared. Don't you understand? You're going to be a great sacrifice! And you'll rise so high . . . You'll see. Yes, yes, there will be some pain in the here and now. But after that . . ."

He started laughing.

The man, Amy thought, wasn't religious in the least. He didn't even believe in God, she was certain. He believed in himself — and his great agenda, whatever it might be.

Money or power? Seriously, how could ruling a little place like Maclamara be all that he craved? It couldn't be. Whatever he was doing was supposed to take him farther along his path. And Amy would bet he didn't care if every single resident of the place died if it got him where he wanted to go. Not even the lives of those he should have loved most, his acolytes, like Phin Harrison, meant anything at all. Men like Phin just received their rewards when times were good, and they knew to end it when times were not.

If only Phin had talked! There had to be someone out there who valued their own life more than loyalty to a madman.

There was, surely. But would they come forward in time to save her or Billie?

Someone else came into the shack.

"She's still out?"

"Yep. You hit her hard. You might have killed her."

"I had to hit her hard and fast. She's dangerous."

"She's a woman. What kind of a sissy are you?"

"She'll come to. She's breathing, she has a pulse."

"I want her alive to see how she's going to die."

"She is alive!"

"Well, get ready. They'll know that she's missing now. They'll start tearing everything apart to find her."

"They'll never find her here."

"Let's hope not — for your sake."

The door opened and closed again. The men were gone.

Amy cracked her eyes open again. "Billie?"

403

she asked softly. The sobbing continued. "Billie — Wilhelmina? Is that you?"

"Yes, it's me. And you're . . . well, I know who you are. I saw you come . . . I was so afraid. I thought you were one of them, and now . . . now you're with me. And we're going to die. And he will make it hurt. He'll make it hurt so bad!"

"Billie, how did you get here? You were down south — I know that several people were trying to help you."

"They caught me," Billie said. "I was walking on the road from the diner to the motel and they came with their van and . . . I ran. But they caught me."

Billie had an accent, but her use of English was fine. The young woman had studied hard, Amy was certain, to make her way to the United States.

"They're going to kill us!" Billie sobbed again.

"No, they're not."

"How can you stop them?"

Amy struggled against the ropes binding her. Damn, they were tight.

Hunter would know by now that she hadn't arrived back at the inn. Hopefully, he would figure out that she had most probably been set up. By Casey? Or had Casey been a pawn, followed during her every movement?

Yet, how could anyone know Casey was meeting Amy — unless she had told them?

"How *can* you stop them?" Billie asked, her words partially a whisper, partially a sob, as she repeated her question.

"I don't know, but I will," Amy promised. Yes, Hunter would be searching for her by now. "I have friends out there, coworkers, lawmen who will stop at nothing to find us, Billie. I'm telling you we're going to survive this! Now, tell me — how do they have you tied up? The first thing I have to do is find a way to get out of these ropes."

The word was out.

Between them, Hunter and Roger had called local police in five counties, the FDLE, the Highway Patrol and the FBI.

Special Agent Amy Larson, FDLE, was missing, presumed taken by the same people who had already murdered at least three women.

Hunter had Roger pull the van over. He needed to think. They were near the woods where the forensic team had found the unidentified remains of those killed years before.

"They're not close," he told Roger. "They have spies who watch, I'm certain. That's how Phin nearly got the jump on Amy the other day, except that Amy was too quick for him. They know that the bodies have been found. The woods in this area are dangerous. Besides, they wouldn't bury their dead that close to where they kill."

"Hunter, I don't have any idea — but I will go anywhere, do anything. You tell me," Roger said, waiting. "You know these people, maybe not personally, but you knew Morrison's father — and Morrison himself. Yeah, he was a kid back then. But he's clearly taken a lot for his playbook from Brother William. And he seems to be a creature of habit — he's looked for small communities where there isn't much traffic. He used an old hunter's shed, deep in the Everglades."

"That's it," Hunter said.

"What?"

"A cabin. There's a cabin somewhere. Not here — too close to the old remains, as I said. But there's got to be a shack in the woods."

"Where? Give it some thought, Hunter. Give it careful thought."

He didn't have time for careful thought.

And yet they certainly didn't have the time to go through acre upon acre of rural and forest land in and near Maclamara.

406

He forced himself to pause, close his eyes, breathe, think.

"The biker bar."

"Hunter, I don't think they have her in a public place. They'll know we'd check that out immediately."

"No, not in the bar. And they'll know that we'll be watching the park. But they're going to be near the biker bar. That's where everyone is gathering. I think that this is supposed to be a major public sacrifice — referring to their public, the community, Morrison's followers."

"All right, how far do we drive in?" Roger asked.

"A distance from the parking lot, though they may not know your van. Unless Casey Colby is involved — she would recognize it. I'm going to ask Garza that he makes sure any agents he sends in are aware that they need to stay hidden, not to engage until we find out where Amy is — and get her out before the cult realizes that they're under attack in any way."

Roger looked at him and nodded gravely. "No one questioned you," he said. "She's been missing a little more than an hour, but no one questioned your certainty that she's been taken."

"Amy is . . . an agent," Hunter said. "My

partner. I know that I'd hear from her if she was able to reach me. I know I'm right."

"Yes. And they trust you, Hunter. They trust your instinct in this. That's a damned good thing."

"I have Garza on speed dial. We don't have time to set up communications. We have to find where they're keeping her."

"All right. Remember that they seem to keep their victims awhile before they kill them."

"But the previous victims were women who didn't have anyone looking for them. Amy is different. They know they have a tiger by the tail."

"Fine. We'll get to Maclamara. Stash the car. And look for a needle in a haystack."

Hunter's phone buzzed. He looked down at it and then over at Roger and grinned. "Not quite."

"No?"

"The forensics team used drones to get pictures of the woods — that's how they found the clearings where the bones were buried. They went a step further, taking some infrared images. There are scattered cabins and shacks, which they'd identified on the satellite imagery, but only a few cross-referenced with any heat signatures. And one is about a tenth of a mile behind the biker bar."

Roger nodded approvingly. "You just got that info?"

"Yeah," Hunter said. "Let's do this."

It wasn't easy, Amy thought, trying to save someone who was a pathetic ball of fear when she needed that very person to help her first. She had to save herself in order to save anyone else.

Amy wasn't going to be able to do anything more than loosen the ropes that held her; they'd been tied tight and well.

But she could twist and see that Billie had a single loop around her wrists and that loop was barely secured to a hook against the wall.

Billie's legs weren't bound; she was in a crumpled sitting position, managing that only because of the way her wrists were bound and looped over the hook.

But Amy had determined that she wasn't going to die. She wasn't going to let a chauvinistic, supremacist elitist steal her life. Not happening.

Nor was she going to let him kill Billie.

And so, she had to reason with and calm Billie.

"Listen to me, please, *por favor,* Billie. You must listen to me!"

"I — I'm listening. *Chica,* I am listening."
Amy smiled. Good. Billie sounded a little better. She had a trace of hope in her voice. "They did a horrible job tying you up. They know that they've had you twice now and that you're terrified. You learned your way around the south, but you don't know your way around here. They're not afraid of you. If you stand up, you can slip the rope holding you from that hook. Can you do that? Can you stand up for me?"

"What will happen if they come back?"

"Billie, they plan on killing us — what else can they do?"

Torture was a possibility, but she didn't voice it to Billie.

"I am so weak," Billie said.

"You're not. You're strong. You made it this far. You're still alive and I need you. I need you to help me, so that we can escape."

"Yes."

"Billie, stand up."

Billie was obviously undernourished, exhausted and almost beaten; she struggled first to get to her knees.

"Excellent. Great, Billie, you're doing it!" Amy applauded.

The encouragement helped. Billie struggled again; she probably needed her hands to push up her weight in her weakened state.

410

"You can do it, you can, I know it," Amy said. "Our lives depend on it."

Billie wavered, and then she made it to her feet, falling against the wall, but still standing.

"Just lift your hands. Lift them over the hook."

It seemed to take forever; Amy wondered if Billie would make it or not. Trying to lift her arms made it appear that she had tons of weight on them.

She sobbed softly and tried, and then tried again.

And then succeeded.

This time, she let out a little sob of pleasure and amazement.

"I did it, I did it!" she said.

"I told you. Now, you need to get over to me," Amy said. "But come slowly, carefully. Your strength will come back. Your arms and legs will work better as you move."

Billie did as she was told.

"Look at the ropes that are holding my hands to the poles on this bed," Amy said. "Because they probably plan to move us fast, they've used a slipknot, I'm willing to bet. Can you see a loose end on the rope?"

"*Sí.*"

"Can you pull it?"

Billie nodded and reached above Amy's

411

head for the rope. She let out little grunting sounds as she tried.

"It's so tight!"

"Just keep at it. Think about your strength coming back. Think about freedom — real freedom. About getting out of here and away from these people for good."

Billie let out little sounds as she struggled; Amy was sure the ropes had been tied tight — very tight. With the slipknot, her struggles had just made them tighter.

Suddenly, she felt a release; the ropes binding her right hand had slipped free.

"Billie, yes!" Amy said. "Yes, you've done it!"

Her hand was free. Amy quickly freed her own left wrist, and then the ties that were securing her ankles.

She shook her hands for a minute and stretched, feeling needles and pins. She swung her legs around and slowly, carefully, stood.

"I hear something!" Billie said.

"Quiet, softly, Billie, please!"

Billie went silent.

But she was right; someone was coming through the trees. They'd soon be at the shack.

"We have to get out, now!" Amy whispered.

412

She looked around. They had taken her bag, her phone, her gun — everything.

She needed a weapon.

She saw the hook in the wall that had held Billie.

Billie using the hook for leverage to stand had surely loosened it.

Amy strode over to the hook. It was stuck tightly in the wall. But she needed it; there was a good chance that she would die if one of the cultists caught her and she didn't have anything that resembled a weapon with which to fight.

She stared at the hook, and she reached for it again, jerking and jerking, finding strength she never imagined that she might have.

The hook slipped free from the wall. Holding it tightly, she told Billie, "Follow me, follow me as closely as you can."

"But they know the woods. They'll be out there, they'll find us!" Billie said.

"I'll have friends looking for me by now."

"You're sure?"

She thought about Hunter.

"I am sure," she told Billie. "Yes, absolutely."

She slipped out the front door. It was much brighter outside than it had been in the shack, and she squinted into the sun-

413

light, carefully looking around, listening intently. Her head throbbed.

The sound of someone moving through the brush and trees was coming from their left; they needed to scurry in the opposite direction as quickly as they could.

Amy moved out; Billie remained in the doorway, as if frozen.

Amy grabbed her by the shoulders and pulled her ahead. "Move!" she ordered.

Billie started to pick her way through the trees. Amy followed, but then she paused.

Yes, someone was coming back to the cabin. But she was hearing more. Music, distant in the cool air of the forest.

Music, voices, faded, almost as if they were from another time.

They weren't coming from another time; it sounded almost as if they were coming from a party . . . or a bar.

The biker bar.

She could imagine many of the town's faithful had joined to mourn the death of one of their own — Phin Harrison — and honor the sacrifice he had made for the greater good of the cult.

That meant that, inside the bar, there was a small legion who might come after her and Billie, seeking them out in a forest they knew too well.

She hurried after Billie. "Run," she urged. "Run like hell!"

Hunter and Roger headed into the forested area a quarter mile north of the biker bar. The plan was move deep inland and then circle back toward the road.

They had just started the hike when Hunter felt his phone vibrating. He nodded to Roger and stopped to pick it up. Over the line, Garza told him, "We have agents ready to move in. Also, Special Agent Ryan Anders is almost there. He started the drive up in the early-morning hours. He'll be contacting you."

"He'll be contacting me?" Hunter asked, irritated. Ryan Anders had been assigned to Hunter. His orders to move should have come from Hunter.

"Hunter, you're the best at what you do," Garza said. "You've gotten what we need on this, but the situation seems to be exploding."

Yes, he struck the hornets' nest and the hornets were moving.

At that point, at least, Hunter had believed that anyone back in the south was safe; the action had moved north. The cult wouldn't have taken Amy now if they didn't have something big planned. But there were good people down south who might be in danger for what they knew.

Ryan Anders should have contacted him *before* making any moves.

"I gave him the order to drive up," Garza said.

"I see."

"He's not alone. He's with a local detective, Victor Mulberry."

"Mulberry has no jurisdiction here," Hunter said. "Why —"

"I have agents from the Miami office looking after the civilians in the south. Mulberry is aware that he has no jurisdiction. What he does have is knowledge of the people involved." Garza sighed. "Hunter, this kind of action should have had long, careful meetings — team meetings — with everyone involved. We know that this group we're going up against is heavily armed, but we have no clear evidence of illegal activity by anyone in the town. Our strategy should have been planned out, with the right people in the right places. That proved impossible once they took Amy. We're working in the blind, in a way I despise. You requested backup, and hell yes, it's necessary. I don't want to lose my agents or any civilians — but I don't want a massacre, either! Keep your focus on finding Amy and any other possible hostages. Be careful."

Focus. It was a good reminder. Both he and Amy, in signing up for their jobs, had agreed to put their lives on the line. But "on the line" didn't mean that they shouldn't make every effort to see that they came out of a situation like this alive.

Focus. It was about finding Amy right now.

Too often, when cornered, men like Morrison determined to bring everyone else down with them.

"All right," Hunter said, "have Ryan sweep up a few of our men and get to the biker bar. There's something happening there. I don't believe Amy is in there — it's too public. But there's a gathering going on. No agent should be alone. This is a town where no one can be trusted, and the most innocuous person might well be carrying a weapon. We must be extremely careful. We don't want another Waco on our hands. I think that the leaders are planning a sacrifice, and if we can stop them in the preparation period, we can snap off the head of the snake without anyone extra being hurt."

"It's your call from here on out. I know that you work well with Agent Anders and that he's dedicated. I'm going to order a team to meet up with him south of Maclamara. He'll take a few unknowns with him into the biker bar and keep an eye on events there. Be aware that our agents are combing the woods across the road from you. I have them on the west side — you're on the east. I'll have them cross over before they get closer to town. They'll find Amy if she is there."

"There are no hits on her cell phone?"

"Her phone is off. Last ping was an area off the main road just south of Micanopy."

Of course they had ditched her phone.

"Use everything you've got, Hunter," Garza told him.

"Yup," Hunter said simply.

Roger motioned to him suddenly, a sign that meant he needed to shut up — and listen.

"Out!" Hunter said briefly, pocketing his cell phone. He stilled. He could hear movement through the brush. Someone was near them. Someone moving through the trees and brackens, slowly, carefully.

Furtively.

Roger and Hunter shared a look, then split up, moving to either side of the trail.

And they waited.

Run. Run. Run.

Into the woods, and then . . .

418

Where? They were close to the bar, close to dozens of townspeople who might be ready to search the woods and roads to find them, once an alarm was raised.

Amy motioned to Billie, warning her to silence once they'd gotten into the trees.

She spotted a massive old oak, sprawling in its size and majesty, with great branches that all but created a ladder.

"Can you climb?" she whispered to Billie. Billie nodded.

"All right. Get up there. I'll be back, and if I'm not, hold this position. People will be coming — I know that they'll be coming. The FBI will be out in these woods, so wait until you see law enforcement. I'll be back," she promised. "I need to see what's happening."

Billie looked at her wide-eyed. "You stay here, too. Please. You don't know if there is help coming . . ."

"Oh, I think I do," Amy assured her. She offered Billie a smile. "We're going to make it, but be silent, and don't move from here."

Billie nodded her agreement.

Amy started back, coming close enough to the cabin to see and hear what was going on.

How soon would they notice that she and Billie had escaped . . . and when would her

419

backup arrive? Where was Hunter?

She could hear voices; they belonged to the same two men who had been in the clearing before.

"It's time to start — your brother is ahead, in the clearing?" the deeper voice said.

"Yes, we're good. Aaron is preparing the ceremony table. I still don't understand. How will he make a woman die of disease in a matter of minutes?"

"She won't die of disease. She is the disease," the older man replied. "Why are you so dense, Ezekiel? Yours is not to question, yours is to obey. In time, I can pray, you will have the concept of the power of words, and how they may be perceived. You will lead, but you must learn to listen and obey before you can take it all to the next step."

"I managed our last two sacrifices just fine!"

The deeper voice didn't answer.

Ezekiel spoke up again. "You shouldn't have taken the agent."

"What?"

"You shouldn't have taken the agent. When we had Billie again . . . she should have been enough. For now. They will come after an agent."

"They will never find us."

"They're not stupid."

"Stop questioning me! I am your father, and the Divine Leader!"

Amy all but hugged the tree that was giving her cover, listening. Hunter had known. He had been right.

Morrison had orchestrated everything. He hadn't committed the murders in the south of the state; he'd made quite sure that he'd had an alibi for them.

But he had ordered them.

And now, here, he would officiate for the next sacrifice.

Her.

She felt her teeth grit with determination as the two men came into view — Ethan Morrison in a strange robe with a cowl, Zeke behind him, dressed now in a similar robe.

They headed for the door to the shack.

And then she heard Ethan Morrison shout out with rage.

"They're gone! That stupid bitch! You didn't tie her well enough!"

"She was tied up tight, Dad. She couldn't have gotten out of the ties without help. You're the one who roped that little immigrant. She helped her."

"She couldn't have. She was cowed completely, terrified, just waiting to die! And how dare you — how dare you question me!"

Morrison turned and struck Zeke with a stunning blow; the young man fell back, astounded.

"Find them, get them. And kill her. Kill that high-and-mighty agent bitch the second you see her. The immigrant will work for the ceremony. Kill her — kill the uppity bitch before she can do any more harm!" Morrison ranted.

He started back the way he had come.

"Where are you going?" Zeke called to his father.

"For help! So help me God, that woman is going to die!"

21

Hunter and Roger waited — and watched.

Whoever was coming, they were slow and careful, almost as if they were confused, and not as if they were beating their way through the brush, searching.

Hunter glanced over at Roger. Roger shrugged.

Leaves rustled. They could hear the soft sounds of footsteps coming hesitantly on the forest floor.

Then a man appeared; both Hunter and Roger prepared to take him down, and Hunter streaked out from his hiding place just as the man showed his face.

He went down easily. Hunter straddled him, pinning his arms to the ground, and was then startled as the man's grunts and gasps subsided. With his eyes closed, he begged, "My boys, please, just let me see my sons once again!"

Hunter frowned.

He'd tackled Pastor Jared Colby.

Colby opened his eyes and stared up at Hunter.

"Special Agent Forrest?" he asked.

"What the hell are you doing?" Hunter demanded.

"I'm just trying . . . I don't know what happened. My boys are good boys. I thought . . . I thought that I could help people . . . But I couldn't reach Jayden and Chase, and then Jayden texted to tell me that he didn't want to talk to me, that I was a fake, and he knew a true man of God, and I thought that if I could just see them that I could . . . could make them understand!"

Hunter stood, pulling the man to his feet. Roger was there, quickly frisking Colby down.

"Unarmed," Roger said.

"How did you know to be here, out in the forest?" Hunter asked him.

"Casey called me. She said that she learned that her brothers were in a place called Maclamara. I didn't want to walk right in. I thought that if I could see what was happening, I'd have a better way to reach them."

There were tears in the man's eyes; he appeared to be completely earnest.

But Hunter had seen those who could fake any emotion. He just didn't know. There had been murders committed beneath the man's nose. He had befriended Ethan Morrison. And Casey Colby might well have been the one to set up Amy.

"What the hell do we do?" Roger muttered.

Hunter looked at his old friend, the man who had once saved him.

But this was his call. And he made it. "We can't drag him along."

"Just let me see my boys," Colby said, sagging against the hold Hunter had on him. "I swear to you, they're not bad. They're not murderers!"

"You want me to hold him?" Roger said.

"Get him across to the other side of the road, where the other agents are. See that one of them takes him, keeps him safe — and away from the action here."

"But my sons!" Colby protested. "I will die if that's God's will today, but please let me see my boys before I do!"

"If you're telling the truth and you walk in on what's planned today, they'll kill you before you see your sons," Hunter said flatly.

"I've got him," Roger said.

"Thanks."

Hunter pulled out his phone and reported

the situation to Garza.

Then he nodded to Roger and left the two behind, heading closer to the biker bar and the cabin that stood somewhere in the woods behind it.

Amy watched Zeke. He rubbed his chin, still looking deflated as he stood in front of the cabin.

She was surprised to feel sorry for him.

He'd killed people; she knew now that he had been one of the people to brutally kill two women.

But she had seen just how he was treated himself, how he had probably been groomed since birth to consider himself superior to others — and to believe in his father's words and his father's ways.

He straightened and stared at the ground as if seeking any sign of footprints. He looked into the woods, a mask of weary determination coming over his face.

And then he started in Amy's direction.

She had to lead him away from Billie, and fast; others would soon be out, searching high and low for her and Billie.

Carefully, she turned and sought a trail that would lead to the south and the west, closer to the town of Maclamara itself, but farther from Billie.

She paused and looked back.

Yes, he was following her, and yes, he was carrying a handgun. She wasn't sure of the make and model, but she was sure that he knew how to use it.

She needed more time! Time was something that she didn't have much of.

Keep going, and walk into a possible nest of vipers?

Stop now, take her chance, possibly take one of their number out?

Zeke Morrison was probably good with a gun, but he might not be so accomplished when it came to anything else. He'd been taught that men were superior in power and strength. She'd depend on that.

Finding a position, she flattened herself against an oak along the trail, one all but buried in the dripping moss that made so much of this area beautiful and charming.

She waited and watched.

He came along the trail, pausing every few steps to listen.

She gripped the hook tightly in her hand, ready.

It seemed forever that Zeke Morrison just stood there, listening.

Then he moved again. And he walked by the tree.

Amy took a swing.

■ ■ ■ ■

"Come and see!"

Hunter paused by a sign beneath the heavy branches of a birch. Here, along this trail, the trees rose high and their branches met over the trail, creating a natural archway. The sunlight was dappled along the trail, only breaking through the covering leaves in spots.

The sign led toward the end of the arch.

He hadn't found the cabin, but he had found their place of ceremony. *And when he had opened the second seal, I heard the second beast say, "Come and see!"*

Creeping along silently, he carefully slid closer to observe the preparations.

He saw a group of women gathered with small children; a few older men had brought folding chairs and sat together talking. Older children ran through fallen leaves.

The town's population was about two hundred people; it seemed half of them were already in the forest clearing, where, in the center, there was a bizarre altar. It was formed out of coral rock.

There was a strange insignia etched into the altar. Slashes, with hooked ends. Like those on the faces of the murdered women.

428

The altar was made to look like the devil or a demon. Hunter could only figure that the congregants believed that the killings were to saturate evil with blood, and thus rid them of evil while cleansing a soul that could then rise to heaven.

Most of the people looked as if they were prepared for nothing more than a sunny day, a community outing. Much as they had appeared at the barbecue.

But around the perimeters, he saw that there were armed men.

Colby's boys were among them, and the younger of Morrison's sons, Aaron.

The massive bartender, the man he now knew to be Gilbert Bowles, was with them.

So, who was tending the bar? Hunter wondered.

He counted. At least ten men were carrying different handguns and rifles.

He slipped back into the woods.

Success!

Sad success, but success.

Zeke Morrison was down on the ground, moaning.

And bleeding. Amy had caught him right where the stomach met the rib cage. He wasn't dead, though he was bleeding a lot.

She wasn't a doctor; she didn't know what

kind of damage she might have caused.

Finish him, she thought briefly.

No. She could defend herself, but she couldn't kill a wounded man.

And, in his state, he wasn't getting up again to come after her. He could tell others what she had done, but that didn't matter. They were looking for her as it was, with orders to kill on sight.

She left him where he lay.

In her heart, she knew that Hunter and others were out there. Somewhere.

But which way?

She moved deeper and deeper into the woods, making sure that she was leading anyone who might follow her away from Billie's hiding place, high up on the old oak.

Hunter went back the way he had come. He found a break in the branches and leaves, and looked at the sky, finding the sun. He glanced at his watch and then at the sky again, hoping his sense of direction was good.

As he headed in the direction in which he truly prayed he would find the cabin, he shared a text conversation with Garza, reporting on the position of the people and the altar, and warning him about the firepower they would meet.

He stopped just as he pocketed his phone.

His heart leaped to his throat. There was something, or someone, ahead of him on the path. From his distance, he couldn't be sure, but it sure as hell looked like a human body.

Hunter moved with care, barely breathing.

Praying.

Inching through the woods, he spotted the cabin — two hundred yards or so beyond the bundle of human being that lay in his way.

He heard groans and instinctively knew that it wasn't Amy on the ground.

Even a groan had a timbre to it. The prone figure was male.

He hurried to see that Zeke Morrison, curled in a fetal position, lay on the ground.

Covered in blood.

A metal hook protruded from his body.

Hunter hunkered down; the injured man was in too much pain to pay him any heed. His eyes were closed as he moaned and twitched, clutching his stomach.

Again, Hunter called in. He reported that he'd found Zeke Morrison and the cabin.

The man on the ground managed to speak. "Who . . . You'll die, you'll die . . ."

A sound almost like bitter laughter escaped

him. "No, I'm dying . . . dying. You'll die, too, but . . . I wasn't supposed to die. What is heaven? Why don't I believe in the rewards? I'm in agony. I'm dying, I think. I wish I could feel it, my rewards for all on earth . . . but I don't. Just pain . . ."

Hunter only knew Zeke through pictures and the few times he'd seen the man in a crowd, but Zeke Morrison seemed to know that he was law enforcement.

"She's gone. You won't find her. But they will. The little immigrant girl, they'll get her eventually. But they're looking for the agent — they'll kill her." He laughed again. "She's out of the cabin. My asshole father — the Divine Leader! He blames me . . . and he's the one who barely tied the immigrant to the hook. The hook . . . she got me with the damned hook."

Hunter didn't respond to him. He stood. Garza would have more agents slipping through the woods. They would find Zeke Morrison. EMTs were already on the way.

If his life could be saved, they would save him.

He'd tried to kill Amy, Hunter knew.

And she had taken him down instead.

But how long could she last in the woods with every member of this community on the lookout for her?

With orders to kill.

Amy moved as carefully as she could through the labyrinth of trees and brush, listening, watching.

Armed men were out looking for her. Yes, they would all be men. Ethan Morrison had a place for women, and a woman's place would not include her having a gun, or even being trusted on such a mission as this.

Ethan Morrison had a place for everyone. His sons should have inherited an empire; he had taught them to love money and power and all that it could buy. He had taught them to kill.

What about Jared Colby's sons? Their father was, she believed, if anything, naive. He wanted the best in people. He believed in the best in people. What had happened to his sons?

And his daughter? Was Casey in on all this, or was she just a pawn?

So yes, men with guns were looking for her. But she knew that by now, Hunter would be out here, too.

She just had to stay hidden until she found the right people.

Not really knowing the terrain, she found that she had doubled back. She was not far from the cabin and not far from the biker bar. Close to the tree where she had left Billie.

She decided that it wouldn't hurt to check on Billie, to remind her to stay still, and to hang tight. Help was coming.

At first, she thought that she had the wrong tree.

She was in a forest, after all.

Trees could look a hell of a lot alike.

But she knew this was the tree where she had left Billie. And Billie was no longer there.

She prayed that the right people had found the terrified girl.

But just as that hope went through her mind, Amy heard a voice. It seemed to move through the forest like a gust of wind.

"Amy . . . Amy Larson!"

It wasn't Hunter, she knew that immediately. And it wasn't anyone with the FBI, the FDLE or any other law enforcement agency.

It was a strange husky sound as it came to her. As if the speaker was trying to be quiet on the one hand and heard on the other.

"I have her, Amy. Special Agent Amy Larson. You are so very special, aren't you? But you lost. You don't have Billie. I have her. Ah! If only you were a normal woman! It seems that the Lord cast down kindly upon your face and figure yet offered you no knowledge of humility. But I do believe that you took an oath of office — you're sworn to protect people, aren't you? And I have Billie!"

The whisper seemed to ring through the leaves and become part of the rustle of the forest.

"Come out, Amy, come out. Come and see, come and see!"

Anger overrode fear.

She wanted very much to smack Ethan Morrison in his smug face, and tell him that his interpretation of the Bible was skewed, at best.

And she was furious with herself. Sure, she'd downed Zeke Morrison, but he was just sad, so sad. For a fleeting moment, she wondered about using the man's son against him, shouting out that she had Zeke, what did he think of that?

Nothing, she knew. A man like Morrison might let his son die in his quest to achieve his own agenda.

And did she have Zeke?

She was back at the tree where she'd left Billie, and to have reached that spot, she'd passed the trail where she'd taken Zeke down with the hook.

Carefully, she moved back, following her footsteps, finding that place where she had hidden before, waiting for Zeke.

He wasn't there.

Squatting down, she discovered blood drops on the trees and blood saturating part of the ground.

Zeke was gone.

Morrison had taken Billie; he had her for sure. That was why he could be so mocking in his whisper.

He had to know by now that officers and agents would be searching for her.

Did he care? Did he have an escape plan, and had he set another in motion for all those who had followed him to die, either through a gun battle or suicide?

"Come out, Amy. Come and see!"

She could follow the sound of the whisper. And walk right into someone waiting for her along the way.

But if other agents were in the forest as she suspected, they would be following the sound of the whisper, as well.

She waited, dead still, listening.

"I'm going to start cutting Billie very soon, Amy. Or you can be the very special 'special' agent you're supposed to be and give me your life for hers!"

Amy began to move in the direction from

which she thought the whisper was coming.

Slowly. So slowly. Carefully, looking ahead with every step — and then behind her, as well.

She knew it was coming; she was prepared when a young man stepped out in front of her, grinning, a shotgun aimed at her chest.

It was Jayden Colby.

"You're not going to shoot me," she told him calmly.

"No?" he demanded, but a frown furrowed his brow. "You — you're coming with me. I am going to shoot you if you don't get right in front of me and walk."

"No."

"I will kill you!"

"I don't think so."

"Don't test me!" he said, swearing softly.

"You're not a murderer," she told him.

"Get in front of me — and walk."

He waved the gun in front of her. Amy shrugged and slowly turned her back to him. And then she spun as quickly as she could, slamming the shotgun hard against him.

He fell back; the shotgun fell.

Amy lunged for the gun, grabbing it up as Jayden staggered forward, and she slammed the stock against his skull.

He fell flat on the forest floor without so

much as a whimper.

"Amy!"

She heard her name called again. She picked up the shotgun and started forward.

The whisper was eerie; Hunter didn't have to wonder from what direction it was coming.

He did wonder if the man knew — he had to suspect, at the least — that law enforcement was in the forest.

But he didn't have Amy. If he did, he wouldn't be calling out to her.

He did, apparently, have the missing Billie.

Whispering softly himself, he hit speed dial to reach Garza.

"I'll have men positioned," Garza said wearily. "I fear a blood-bath."

"I will do everything in my power, sir, to see that such a thing doesn't happen. But we need to move into the clearing. Whatever he's planning, it's about to happen. He might not have committed any of the murders thus far, but he plans on killing now. And, I believe, to be as open as he is now, he thinks he has an escape plan."

"Do you think Amy will go after the voice?" Garza asked.

"Yes. She'll try to save Billie," Hunter said. "Even if she knows that he'll kill them both, she'll follow that whisper."

"I figured as much."

"I'm moving back there now," Hunter told him. "Most of the people aren't armed, but he does have that contingent around the trees."

"I've ordered a circular route, a man for a man," Garza told him.

"Try to take them out before all hell breaks loose."

He ended the call and began his careful walk back to the clearing. There would be guards along the way; if they hadn't been there before, they'd be there now.

Morrison really wanted Amy dead.

Ahead, Hunter saw movement. Slight. He stilled. It could have been a possum or raccoon or other denizen of the forest.

It could have been.

But it was not.

An armed man was waiting by the tree, possibly growing bored of being a sentinel. Hunter watched as he shifted his weight back and forth, back and forth. He was armed with an assault rifle.

Hunter slipped off the trail. The going was rough; he couldn't make any noise, and the way was strewn with roots and vegetation.

But neither could he take what was more than a trail; he'd be seen far too easily.

Finally, he was almost within arm's length of the man.

He waited, he watched, for the bored swinging motion the man was making on his feet, to the left, to the right, to the left, to the right . . .

To the left.

Hunter sprang forward, strategically slamming the man hard on the head.

The assault rifle fell just seconds before the man collapsed without a sound.

Collecting the rifle, Hunter moved forward again.

The woods were large and thick — larger and thicker, Amy thought, than what Morrison's population were capable of managing.

She reached the outskirts of the clearing and made a careful observation.

The clearing was almost a perfect circle. If it hadn't been by nature, it had been made so by man.

There were many people in the clearing, and for all appearances, it might have been a grassy square in any town, a park where people came to enjoy their leisure.

Except that walking around the circumference of the circle were heavily armed men.

She tried to get a good count, but they

were moving . . . now and then pausing to look into the trees.

There was a large rectangular altar in the center of the square.

And on it, Billie lay, tied and sobbing.

Morrison, in his bizarre robes, moved behind the table.

"Oh, Amy! Amy, I grow tired of waiting! How can you be so special if you mean for this poor lonely girl to die in your place? I'm so disappointed in you, Amy! She needs you so desperately. And these good people will pray for you — you'll be a sacrifice to the White Horse, you'll honor all that was written. Because it's coming, Amy. My people know that the Apocalypse is coming. They will be ready. You will perish in flames unless you are cleansed!"

She listened to Morrison, weighing her next move.

Then, on the far side of the circle, one of the men looked into the trees, stepped into the shady brush and suddenly disappeared.

Amy waited; he didn't reappear.

Her backup was out there, as she had suspected. The FBI or the FDLE or both. She needed to give them time.

As she watched, another man disappeared.

She remembered that she held Jayden Colby's rifle. The damned thing might not even fire cleanly, and if she went in shooting, so very many would die.

Hunter must be among the men on the outskirts, trying to pick off the guards. It was a good plan; it was the best plan if they were to keep the day from becoming a massacre.

"Amy, God is patient, but now is the time."

Another one of the armed men took a walk onto a trail.

And silently disappeared.

All she had to do was wait.

But even as she willed herself to bide her time, Morrison suddenly raised his arms. He held between his hands a pointed, razor-sharp blade, one that caught the sunlight and cast off a wicked glint.

"It is time. She will wear the horns of Satan and thus enter into death as a great sacrifice!" Morrison shouted.

Children no longer played. Along with their parents, they had fallen to their knees, facing the altar.

He was going to strike; Amy couldn't wait any longer.

She walked out of the trees, making a point of aiming the rifle at Morrison's heart as she strode toward the man and the altar.

"You say you only need one sacrifice?" she

asked. "Then here I am!"

She heard the cocking of guns as they were turned on her.

"Shoot me, go ahead." She kept walking forward, gaining ground on Morrison. "But I promise you, I'll have time to fire. You'll be dead, too."

Morrison stared at her, his face red with fury. She knew he'd realized she'd got close enough to him that she couldn't miss her shot.

He moved his sacrificial weapon down, and for a second, Amy thought that he meant to strike Billie.

But he slit the ropes binding her.

Billie lay still, only her chest moving with her sobs.

"Get up, ugly she-goat!" Morrison said, pushing her from the altar. Billie fell, but then she gained her feet. She looked around.

"Billie, go!" Amy urged.

She ran off into the trees.

"Now, Amy? Shoot me or get over here. Billie can't run that fast. You put the rifle down, or we take her."

"Wait!"

Amy was as startled as Morrison and the whole of his congregation as a new voice sounded from the trees, rich and loud and forceful.

Hunter.

He walked calmly out into the circle.

He didn't appear to be armed.

"Wait. Please wait. We'll find Billie again. Amy is special. Imagine her becoming one of your disciples," he said, coming up to Amy.

His eyes met hers. She saw the plea in them.

Trust me.

"I've been on the fringes. No, in fact, I've been trying to get to you, Divine Leader. I want in. I want to be part of this . . . this greater glory. We can be assets that you can't begin to imagine. Let me do it — I'll get Billie back for you."

Morrison stared at him, stunned.

"You?" He started to shake his head.

Amy dared take her eyes off Morrison for a second, glancing around the clearing. More of the men on the outskirts had disappeared.

"You need me — you need good men. And imagine breaking a woman like Amy, letting her learn what her place is, what it is to learn to honor you!" Hunter said.

Hunter's ploy might not work, but it was buying time.

Then someone else broke into the clearing, shouting.

"No, no, he's FBI! He's out to ruin everything. He's . . . Kill him!" It was Casey Colby.

"Casey!" Morrison shouted angrily. "You're supposed to be at the car!"

"No! No, kill him, kill them!"

But the distraction she caused gave Hunter what he needed; he leaped to the other side of the altar in split seconds, seizing the blade from Morrison and bringing it to his throat.

"No!" Casey screeched, leaping forward, ready to tackle Hunter and claw, kick or do anything to drag him away.

It wasn't happening, Amy thought. Supposedly, sweet innocent Casey wasn't getting away with it.

She threw herself after the girl, grabbing her by the arm and spinning her around. And then she caught her in the jaw with her very best right hook.

Casey went down.

Hunter had swung Morrison around and was speaking to him in an urgent whisper. "Tell them to drop their weapons."

"No, no!" Morrison raged. "They will die! They know the truth —"

Hunter shouted to the crowd. "The truth? This man wants you to die for him. Not for the great glory of God, and not to save your

445

souls. You are pawns to him. I've been here, trust me — you are pawns, and there is no reason that anyone should die."

Guns were aimed at him and Amy. There were still six armed men positioned around the clearing, but the agents hiding in the trees had been taking many of them out, silently, one by one.

"Live! You have the right to live," Hunter said. "What turned you? A great God is a loving God! Live, love your children. Let them live, and have a life!"

One gun went down. And then another. The men exchanged confused glances. Some of the women in the clearing grabbed and held their children, as if they'd only just realized the danger their families might be in.

The last of the guns aimed at them went down.

Someone started crying loudly.

Stepping out from the trees, the rest of the agents moved in. There *was* a small army of law enforcement. Roger Dawson was with them, and Ryan Anders.

And Detective Mulberry. Morrison had clearly ordered his followers to cast suspicion on him. And they had almost fallen for it.

He was a good cop.

Ellison was there, too.

Seeing them all, Amy felt a strange swelling inside. Yes, there were men like Morrison out there.

But there were men and women like these agents and officers and detectives.

And it was good to be among them.

Hunter shoved Morrison to the ground and waited for another agent to come in and cuff him.

Then he turned to Amy.

Shaking now, she threw herself into his arms.

"Billie!" she said. "We have to find Billie!"

"They have her already," he assured her. He turned and watched as agents dragged a cuffed Morrison to his feet.

For a minute, Morrison stared at him. His eyes widened, then narrowed with hatred.

"I know you! You're that stinking little brat, Cameron!"

"I was," Hunter said.

He turned to Amy with a smile. "They've got this — let's get out of here."

She smiled. They'd worked hard, with their hearts, minds and souls.

And now, it was over.

Well, due to the lives they had chosen, it was never over.

But over for now.

And it was time for a break.
She knew that they would spend it together.

EPILOGUE

Fall, present day
Sam

Sam leaned against a tree at the resort in the Bahamas, relaxed, smiling, as he watched his son.

He felt the pleasant bark of the tree against his flesh and thought of how good life had become.

His son stood at the end of the dock, laughing as he and Amy prepared to jump into the water for their dolphin dive. One of the dolphins was entertaining visitors with all kinds of antics, enjoying people even as people enjoyed him.

Hunter Forrest.

It was a good name. And his son was a good man.

Admittedly, he had worried about his son's future now and then. Not as far as his career went; Hunter had made his choice. Life had guided him, and he had determined that he would serve others, first in the military, and then as an FBI agent.

It could have gone so differently.

Of course, Sam didn't know everything. He did know that both Hunter and Amy had received commendations; they had taken down murderers in the middle of cult activity without losing a single life. Not a shot had been fired.

The team had been commended, as well. Their actions, so well played, had taken out a great deal of the firepower, allowing for the positive end result.

There were multiple arrests, and they had Ethan Morrison on multiple charges. The case against him was strong, and horrifying. With any luck, Morrison would rot in prison for the rest of his days.

It would take Pastor Jared Colby a long time to recover, and he would have to test his own faith if he was ever to find forgiveness for his children, and thus for himself.

There were a few who had gone to the hospital.

Both his son and Amy seemed to know how to incapacitate the enemy.

Which brought him back to being grateful. Hunter had spent his first years in a cult that had been every bit as scary as the one he had just broken. It hadn't been about religion; religions — many different religions — had saved many people. It had been a deadly desire for power and money — going how high, they were lucky they would never now know.

Morrison's sons would go to prison or worse — they were facing charges in a death-penalty state and might face federal charges, too.

Sam remembered back — when Ethan Morrison had gone by a different name, too. When he'd been young, but always basking in his father's position with Brother William, always planning on being a leader himself.

Life was funny.

Everything could have been over all too quickly.

Or have gone in a very different direction.

Despite the admirable route Hunter had chosen, Sam had feared for him. He'd taken on a risky job. But that honestly hadn't been Sam's main fear. He'd been afraid that Hunter would never meet the right person for him in life. Someone who was fun, who could laugh and care for others.

And someone who could be just as tough and kick-ass as Hunter was.

Now, watching them, Sam felt that there

451

was a touch of magic between Hunter and Amy.

He knew that magic himself.

Through anger, through fear, through trials and tribulations, through joy, of course — the birth of their son had brought them joy. Watching him grow had always been magic.

And today, Sam loved his wife just as much as he ever had. No matter what life had brought them, Jessie had made it more bearable during the tough times, more wonderful during the good days they'd been so blessed to have.

He watched as he saw that Amy's parents and her brother were heading out to the dock; they weren't going to be part of the swim, but Amy's brother had promised — or threatened — to take the most ridiculous pictures of the two of them that he could.

As he watched, his wife — his love, his life — joined him at the tree.

"Well, Jessie-Connie," he said, addressing her as he did sometimes when others couldn't hear them. "What do you think?"

She laughed, leaning against him as he swept his arms around her.

"Strange vacation!" she said. "They asked us and Amy's family. I mean, this is a beautiful place. So romantic! You'd have

452

thought that . . . well, you know. That they'd want to be here alone."

He laughed softly. "You do know that her family is leaving tonight — we're flying together to Miami, and then we'll head on home from there."

"Right, so —"

"Hunter and Amy aren't coming home tonight. They're here another week."

"They're pretty special, huh?"

Sam looked at the dock again. "They wanted us all to meet. I guess that means they plan on being together for a while."

"It's going to be difficult," his wife said worriedly. "I mean, they're both special agents, but they're based in two different places. Long-distance relationships . . ."

"I have a feeling that they'll figure it out," Sam said.

"Look, there they go!"

He smiled as he looked toward the water. Hunter and Amy were positioned on the side of the dock. As he watched, Amy swam out and, in seconds, a dolphin swam by. She grabbed onto a fin, and the dolphin took her for a sweeping ride around the lagoon.

Hunter was next.

After "dancing" with the dolphins and taking part in other behaviors, the session came to an end with the group stroking the dolphin, getting "kisses" and saying good-bye.

Hunter was out of the water, coming toward them, hand in hand with Amy.

"I can't believe you didn't want to do that," Hunter told his father.

He smiled at his son, feeling a swell of pride again. He'd grown up tall and strong and handsome and, at the moment, looked like any other young man out with the girl he loved. Beautiful Amy, strong and sweet and more: good. Really good. She was someone who hadn't become jaded to the world, but was ready to fight the wrongs within it.

"We just wanted to watch you," Sam said.

"Okay, then, lunch in twenty," Hunter told him.

They met up with Amy's folks and her brother, and the five of them made their way slowly to the charming little thatch-roofed outdoor restaurant where they'd grab lunch before heading to the airport.

Sam was glad that he liked Amy's family so much. Of course, that would have little to do with his son making choices, but still, it was nice.

Soon they were seated and the kids — well, Hunter and Amy — joined them. They laughed and talked, and at times grew serious. Amy said, "Oh!" suddenly, and was happy to tell everyone that Billie — whose name was Wilhelmina Ferrer — was being helped and that she had an advocate and would likely be able to remain in the United States.

"She will be an amazing citizen!" Amy said.

They all agreed.

Lunch went on, and it was so good to be all together as a family.

And again, Sam was grateful.

"They're off!" Hunter said to Amy, joining her on a sun lounger under a big parasol.

The resort they had chosen, making use of online coupons, was spectacular.

The first days after the takedown in the woods had been nonstop busy with depositions and debriefs. But while they did paperwork with their separate agencies, the main work was done. They were able to have a long dinner with those who had worked so closely with them — Roger and Detectives Ellison and Mulberry — and express their appreciation.

Amy and he had both gotten to spend time with John Schultz and Sheila via satellite and express their appreciation there, as well.

Then they found out they had two weeks' leave. Each agency had given them two weeks!

All they had to do was plan it.

The future could be difficult to fathom. Hunter had suggested that he could transfer down to an office in Florida; that was one option. She could leave the FDLE and most certainly pass all requirements to join the FBI. They had to consider their decisions carefully.

They just knew that they had something, and they didn't want to lose it.

She wasn't sure how they'd come about thinking that their families should meet — maybe because they'd grown tired of trying to describe each other to their families.

Amy's parents had just arrived home from one trip and gamely packed up for another. Hunter's had been happy to come.

Her brother had wheeled and dealed for the vacation time.

And it had been great.

And now they were gone, and that was great, too.

"What shall we do first, all on our own?" Hunter asked.

She whispered an answer in his ear.

"I like that idea!" he told her. He grabbed hold of her hand and led her back to their beach cabana.

Draperies covered the window, but the sea air swept in as they made love. It was a place of happiness that Amy had barely dared ever imagine.

"I love you, you know," he said, holding her.

"I know," she said, causing him to grin.

"Yeah?" he asked her.

"I love you, too." She laughed, crawling over him. "What are we going to do?"

"We'll figure it out. Right now, though, let's just . . . enjoy. Play with dolphins. Go windsurfing, diving . . . let's just live."

"I like that idea."

There was a discreet tap on the door.

Hunter frowned. "Who is that?"

She grinned. "Room service. Chocolate-covered strawberries and champagne. Humor me!"

He grinned. She stood and grabbed her robe and hurried to the door. She paused for a minute; they could look out and watch the waves lapping gently at the beach. The sun was just falling.

The air was unbelievably sweet.

The room service man had left the tray bearing her indulgencies on the patio table. She picked it up, smiling — they were wonderfully careful regarding guests' privacy here.

As she picked up the tray, something fell to the wooden patio floor beneath.

She set the tray down, frowning as she stooped to pick it up.

It was a tiny object, but it caused her heart to skip a beat.

It was a child's tiny horse, a plastic toy that belonged to a ranch set.

A red horse.

She looked up and around, but there was no one there. The wind off the ocean suddenly felt cold, and she shivered.

Straightening, she went back into the room. She needed to show Hunter.

She didn't think that they were going to have to decide on the future.

The future was being decided for them, in the form of that tiny red horse.

ABOUT THE AUTHOR

New York Times and *USA Today* bestselling author **Heather Graham** has written more than a hundred novels. She's a winner of the RWA's Lifetime Achievement Award, and the Thriller Writers' Silver Bullet. She is an active member of International Thriller Writers and Mystery Writers of America. For more information, check out her website, TheOriginalHeatherGraham.com, or find Heather on Facebook.